A Poetic Puzzle

A Mystery in 32 Pieces

A Poetic Puzzle

A Mystery in 32 Pieces

Joanne McLaughlin

CELESTIAL ECHO PRESS

ROSLYN, PA, U.S.A.

2025

Cover art and design: Miss Elaneous Arts, LLC
Editing: Gemini Wordsmiths, LLC
Puzzle Image by Clker-Free-Vector-Images from Pixabay

Published by
Celestial Echo Press
An imprint of Gemini Wordsmiths, LLC
P.O. Box 1191
Roslyn, PA 19001
celestialechopress.com

Dedication

For Mary McLaughlin, my paternal grandmother, who died long before I was born. Wondering about you inspired this book.

For Catherine McLaughlin, my late mother. I hear your voice still, certainly every time Cass Jones speaks on these pages.

And for Adrienne Albanese Saddington, the sister-cousin whom I miss and will always cherish. My earliest memories are of you.

Acknowledgments

So many people, so few ways to fully express the deep gratitude I feel.

Lynn M. Ross and Rhonda Dickey offered insights on plot and characters early on, Chris Hepp kindly eyeballed the police stuff for me, and Dianna Sinovic and Susan Snyder helped with later revisions, looking closely at the poetry. I thank all these beta readers for their time and patience and kind words of encouragement.

Amy Junod Placentra continues to work her website magic. Tony Merlo continues to put up with me and my "What if I did this?" moments. Sadie Patkus, my sweet younger granddaughter, afforded me just enough time between her birth and my stint as her full-time babysitter to knock out a first full draft of this novel. Her big sister, Josie Patkus, always makes me smile and asks the best questions.

Of course, I owe much to my publishers/editors, Ann Stolinsky and Ruth Littner, of Celestial Echo Press. Ann and Ruth took an initial look at that four-month-turnaround of a first draft and suggested a road map to this destination. As those GPS voices like to say, "Arrived! Arrived!"

Praise for *A Poetic Puzzle*

"When you share the same name (Mary Irene Jones), employer (college) and profession (poet) as someone else, you can't help ending up with their mail. Or just maybe, clues to a murder. *A Poetic Puzzle* is a romantic romp of a mystery that keeps the smiles coming and the pages turning."
— Kelly Simmons, international suspense author

"When a world-renowned poet disappears, her unpublished works inexplicably arrive at Mimi's door. Is Mimi Jones a suspect, or is she the only one who can solve the puzzle of the missing poet? The unexpected twists and turns of this romantic mystery kept me turning the pages."
— Gail Priest, award-winning author of *Soul Dancing*

"McLaughlin crafts a captivating story filled with intrigue, featuring a missing person, an abandoned pet, and a poetry contest that cozy mystery fans will adore. *A Poetic Puzzle* kept me eagerly turning pages, curious to discover whether the renowned poetess would be found alive or dead."
— Ellen Butler, international bestselling author of *Isabella's Painting*

"Joanne McLaughlin's *A Poetic Puzzle* is a fast-paced, clever mystery filled with delicious twists. The premise is refreshingly original. Mimi is absolutely delightful-- incredibly smart, insightful, and hilarious. She's the perfect package to draw readers in. Within the first couple of pages, readers will be wholly invested in the spunky main character, immediately intrigued by the mystery, and riveted to its pages!"

 — Lisa Regan, USA Today & Wall Street Journal
   Bestselling Author

A Poetic Puzzle by Joanne Mclaughlin drags you by the heart into a subtle mystery. Mary Irene Jones, a stalled poet, adjunct professor, and part-time pet-sitter, receives a surprise delivery from the super-famous poet of the same name—who has disappeared!
She helps the handsome detective assigned to track down the missing poet, turning her life upside down as she examines the effect that literary work has on its creator's life—and the potentially chaotic decisions we make in taking responsibility for our actions. Jump on board and follow the mystery!

 — Carol Gyzander, Bram Stoker Award®-nominated
   suspense author

Wanting peace and never finding

*   always reaching, always striving*

Cycle.

Sitting home, yet always leaving

always seeking, always questing

Cycle.

Always leaving, never lasting

always searching, never ending

building this, yet always yearning

wanting peace and never finding

Cycle.

Always lonely, always tearful

always waiting, always fearful

always watching, never seeing

wanting peace and never finding

always hiding, always seeking

Cycle.

M.I.J.

Chapter One
April 2023

Mary Irene Jones shone like a rare supernova; her brilliant poetry admired from every point on Earth. My own writing light glowed more faintly, detectable only if you knew where in the universe to search. That her name was my name too was pure coincidence — life imitating art, if you considered the kiddie song "John Jacob Jingelheimer Schmidt" art.

As *that* Mary Irene Jones once did, I taught college-level English literature, but only part time. To afford health insurance, I also worked as a part-time pet sitter. Dogs terrified me, though, which seriously cut into my client base. (Blame an overly affectionate Great Dane, aptly named Kissy, who tackled me every time I visited my godparents as a little girl.)

Just to be clear, I had never traveled to Northern Ireland, whence that Mary Irene Jones emigrated in the late 1990s as the Troubles were winding down, more or less. And though she settled in the Philadelphia area and was a longtime professor at the same Catholic liberal arts college in the suburbs where I now worked, we had never overlapped on campus. She stopped teaching several years before I started there, and we didn't move in anything like the same poetry circles.

That Mary Irene Jones was famous, yet extremely private. She declined all interviews while maintaining a grueling schedule of classes, conferences and symposiums for two decades. Unlike her, I would have welcomed any recognition, even a regular instructor's post, as opposed to the patchwork of courses typically offered to me, often with little notice. It was assumed I would be available, and of course I was.

If you believed the campus lore, I might not have gotten my gig at the college at all if it hadn't been for the same-name thing. According to the legend, the human resources folks thought they were rehiring *her* five years ago and pushed through the paperwork without noticing such discrepancies as my age (MIJ was more than twenty-five years older) and my job references (MIJ had not previously taught SAT prep classes, as far as anyone knew). The college administration officially debunked the story, yet it lived on because of new English lit students disappointed to learn who was actually teaching them: *this* Mary Irene Jones, not that one.

Full disclosure: My obscure, yet respected, poetry had been published only under the name M. Irene Jones, the one listed on my driver's license as well as my Master of Fine Arts degree. In my family, we were all Marys, so none of us used the name. My mother, for instance, was M. Catherine "Call me Cass" Jones. My younger sister was M. Patricia "Call me Trish" Jones.

None of this would have made any difference to anyone but the aforementioned ticked-off students if the U.S. Postal Service hadn't delivered a box of previously unpublished Mary Irene Jones manuscripts to my house while I was out pet-sitting two guinea pigs. When I realized what was inside—MIJ hadn't put out anything new in years—I returned the box to my neighborhood post office. Which promptly redelivered it to me three days later.

That, I sort of expected. I didn't expect the police.

Chapter Two

The detective showed up at my house on a Thursday afternoon. Fortunately, I had no classes and no pet clients that day. He showed me his badge and handed me his business card: Michael Quinn, Major Crimes.

Odd, since I was certain I hadn't committed one.

We sat at the dining table in the modest Northwest Philadelphia rowhouse I had inherited from my paternal grandmother and went through a few preliminaries. Quinn asked to see my driver's license, then asked where I worked and what my job involved.

He was really good looking: late thirties, dark hair, blue eyes, no wedding ring.

"Ms. Jones, what is your relationship to Mary Irene Jones?"

"Well, I was named for my father's mother, Mary Irene Gardner Jones, but I suspect that's not who you mean."

"No, Ms. Jones, that's not who I mean. I'm referring to the poet Mary Irene Jones."

"I'm a poet too, you know."

Either he didn't know or didn't care. He scowled—he was cute, yes, but also stiff and cop-like.

"Then I'd have to say I don't have a relationship with *that* Mary Irene Jones, Detective. We've never met, though a number of my co-workers at the college English Department know her."

"Her lawyer found in her home a Postal Service receipt with this address on it. The box that was delivered here—when you opened it, what did it contain?" Quinn pulled a notebook from his pocket.

When you had a name like mine, deliveries got messed up pretty often. Too many Marys, too many Joneses. I'd gotten into the habit of taking photos of shipping orders, or the actual contents of a package if there wasn't an alternative to opening it. On my phone, I scrolled to the pictures I had taken of the MIJ box.

"Swipe left. There are about ten photos."

Quinn scrutinized them, checking them against what looked like an official form folded inside his notebook. "Postal Service says there should be eight binders inside, says that's what the sender insured and valued at $150. There are only seven binders in these pictures."

"I photographed everything that was in the box, then I repacked and retaped it, and returned it to the post office. See the before-and-after photos? It wasn't damaged when I got it, and it didn't look as if anyone had tried to open it. Maybe the postal clerk got it wrong, or the sender miscounted."

"Maybe." Quinn sounded unconvinced. "But it seems Mary Irene Jones herself is unaccounted for now. Her lawyer says that her bank account has been emptied, her car is gone, and she isn't answering her phone, behavior he claims is wildly uncharacteristic of his client. He referred me to the president of your college, a longtime personal friend of Mary Irene Jones. She told me Professor Jones missed a scheduled meeting with her two weeks ago and has not responded to phone or text messages since."

Quinn studied me — to gauge my reaction, I guessed — then consulted his notebook again.

"A neighbor contacted animal control because Professor Jones's dog has been barking constantly for two days. I understand you also work as a pet sitter —"

"Not for dogs, I don't." I handed him a business card that read, *Mimi Jones, Cats and Critters. If it doesn't bark, your pet is my pet.*

He looked at me like I was crazy. "Who doesn't like dogs? What do you mean by critters?"

I pulled one of my brochures out of a kitchen drawer and proceeded to recite, "Cats, hamsters, guinea pigs, rabbits, mice, fish, snakes, iguanas —"

"Where were you on the afternoon of April 11th?"

"What? Are you accusing me of something?" He couldn't be serious. One minute we're talking about a dog, and the next he goes all tough cop on me?

"Just answer the question, Ms. Jones."

I checked a planning app on my phone to reconstruct that day. "Taught a creative-writing workshop from 9:30 a.m. to noon. Grabbed lunch at the college cafeteria. Met with a student in the English Department conference room at 2 p.m. I left the campus about 2:45 and got home at 3:15. When I returned from some guinea pig clients just around the corner, the box you were just referring to was sitting on my porch. I barely got it back to the post office on Germantown Avenue before closing time at 4:30. When the box was delivered here again three days later, I took it back to the post office and insisted they slap a 'refused' label on it."

There would be security department video of me on campus, and my doorbell camera would show my comings and goings here. Not that I would lie about my whereabouts, regardless. And I certainly hadn't emptied out anyone's bank account but my own recently.

Quinn nodded, gestured to his business card on the table. "You think of anything else, you call me, Ms. Jones."

"Call me Mimi. It'll be less confusing."

"Mimi," he repeated, and walked to the door.

Chapter Three

My department head summoned me to her office the next day. I had four rabbits to tend to—Easter season acquisitions someone needed to be responsible for, and for which I charged a premium rate to new clients. So I darted around after my morning class, fed, watered, and tidied up after Bunny, Big Bunny, Wabbit, and Fred (their actual names), then hustled back to campus for the mid-afternoon meeting with Dr. Bernstein.

Traffic was terrible. I was late. Sharon was not happy. Neither was I when I saw the box.

"This arrived at the college president's office, after you twice refused to accept delivery of it at your house, according to what Sister Marlene's secretary told my secretary. Also, there's this separate envelope addressed to you in care of the college president. It's in Mary Irene's handwriting."

The penmanship certainly looked like the handwriting on several precious MIJ manuscript pages displayed proudly in the hall outside the English Department offices along with a rare photo of the woman herself, our hero and inspiration. The brief note to me read:

Mimi,

We don't know each other, though naturally I am aware of your work. I regret any inconvenience leaving these papers with you may cause. I trust you will safeguard my manuscripts as you would your own.

Mary Irene Jones

I showed my boss the note. "Why did you refuse the box?" she asked. "Did you know what was inside?"

Sharon Bernstein had succeeded the English Department head who somehow lured Mary Irene Jones to this country and this college, thus she felt a certain ownership of the legacy. Sharon was less attached to my presence here, as she frequently noted when the future of my teaching career came up every semester.

"Yes, I opened the box immediately, but how was I supposed to know it hadn't been delivered to the wrong Mary Irene Jones? This note purporting to be from MIJ was never sent to my home. A police officer did show up, however."

Sharon's eyes widened. Detective Michael Quinn had gone to the very top of the college food chain and the very bottom, but he clearly had not been in touch with her. Nor, evidently, had her own boss.

"When was the last time you heard from Mary Irene?" I asked. "Or that anyone at the college did?"

Interest in MIJ, always intense here, peaked around the annual Mary Irene Jones Poetry Festival, a major spring fundraiser at which a $15,000 prize was offered to a promising young female poet each year. I had been that young poet ten years ago, my "promise" often a topic in those employment conversations with Dr. Bernstein.

Sharon shoved her reading glasses up and over her bangs. "About three weeks ago, when we wrapped up judging this year's festival entries. Sometimes, Mary Irene wants to get on a conference call and debate why this submission should win and not that one, and she fights to get her own way. Sometimes, like this year, she sends a reply email to me and the rest of the judges with her rankings and not much else. Why do you ask?"

I didn't think I was supposed to keep Detective Quinn's information secret.

"Nobody knows where she is. The police detective who visited me says her bank account was cleaned out and her car is gone, but her dog was left behind."

Sharon jumped out of her chair. "Yeats? That dog was a gift from this school. Mary Irene would never leave him behind. Who's caring for him now?"

From the bag at my feet I retrieved Quinn's card, punched his number into my phone, and handed it to her.

We met Quinn at MIJ's house, a detached dwelling on a block near a wooded area in Upper Roxborough, maybe a twenty-minute drive from my place. A dog that had to be Yeats paced the length of an enclosed porch, barking with each step closer we took.

"Neighbor next door said she didn't have a key, so she picked the lock to this porch. She's been feeding the dog from those bags of kibble over there and letting him out to do his business," Quinn said, sliding open the door.

"Sounds like breaking and entering," I said, biting the insides of my cheeks to keep a straight face. "Is she under arrest?"

Sharon and Quinn pinned me with identical glares. "Just joking, sorry."

A doghouse sat at one end of the porch; it had a cushioned bed inside. Yeats, a diminutive thing whose breed I couldn't have identified, was probably warm enough but certainly lonely. He came bounding my way, of course.

"Someone grab him, please," I begged, as Yeats stood on his hind legs and ran his paws over my knees.

"Right," Quinn said, "you don't like dogs." He whistled for Yeats to come to him. Sharon found a leash draped over an Adirondack chair whose paint had seen better days and tossed it to the detective. Once leashed, Yeats proceeded to wrap himself around my ankles, as if trying to ensure that at least one human wouldn't escape today.

Quinn tugged on the leash, and Yeats unwound himself from my lower extremities. With the dog in tow, he headed from the porch around to the front of the house, followed by Sharon and me, though I stayed as far away from the pup as I could get.

"A patrol officer did a wellness check here, but no one responded," Quinn said. "At the insistence of her attorney, a Mr. Lisle, who gave us access, we will be searching the property because nobody has seen or heard from Mary Irene Jones for more than ninety-six hours now, her car and her cash are gone, and the dog was left behind. Professor Jones adored that dog, according to her lawyer and the neighbor."

"Do you suspect foul play?" Sharon sounded more fluttery than usual, but I detected her public relations wheels turning, calculating whether misfortune would be good or bad for the college.

"We're here out of an abundance of caution, Dr. Bernstein. To that end, I'm hoping you and Ms. Jones might be able to assist me and the forensics team that's due to arrive any minute."

He handed each of us a pair of thin gloves. Sharon gave me an eager "I've never been in MIJ's house" look. I certainly never had. What kind of help could we offer?

"Sometimes," Quinn said in answer to my unasked question, "what looks random to an outsider might seem significant to someone who knew the missing person, or to someone who has unexpectedly become the recipient of a bequest from that person." He stared at me. "I understand the box of manuscripts has found its way back to you, Ms. Jones. Maybe you'll see something that relates."

A uniformed officer appeared. Quinn handed him the leash and instructed the young cop to walk Yeats around the block a few times. Yeats trotted away willingly.

Inside, MIJ's house was quaint and cluttered. Her decorating style sort of matched my own, with books in bookcases and stacked on tabletops. A chipped but sturdy-looking white teapot sat amid chipped white cups and saucers on a kitchen shelf. Some framed photos were lined up on the fireplace mantel; one that looked fairly recent showed a weathered barn, a pen filled with sheep, and a young couple with a baby. MIJ lore said she was pregnant when she left Belfast in the late 1990s, but she never spoke of, nor wrote about, family. If one of these adults was her son or daughter, maybe Quinn and Company would have a lead to follow. I cleared my throat and pointed to the picture.

Sharon rushed over. "The hidden offspring grown up? No one knows what became of Mary Irene's child."

Quinn directed a crime scene tech over to the fireplace, to photograph the snapshot and dust all the pictures and their frames for fingerprints. He smiled at me, seeming to approve of my suggestion.

"Mimi, he likes you," Sharon whispered.

"He thinks I'm a suspect because I live in MIJ's literary shadow."

"Nonsense. Eliminating her would only make her more popular and gain you even less notice. Totally counterproductive," Sharon argued. "And anyway, she's your idol—admit it—and it's why I still torment you about winning the poetry competition that honors her. You'd sooner genuflect before Mary Irene Jones than do her harm."

So naturally, she'd want *me* to have her papers? Like that made sense?

We poked around the house as the forensics folks dusted and catalogued. I was drawn to two vintage typewriters, one a really old Smith-Corona manual with at least a dozen mismatched replacement keys, the other an IBM Selectric office model. They reminded me of my mother. Cass worked for the federal government for decades, as a secretary at the beginning. She could type like the wind, and during summer vacations she'd let me bang away on the portable Olivetti that was once my grandmother's. I wrote my first poem on that thing when I was in middle school—I had to retype it twice because I kept ripping the paper when I yanked it from the roller.

From my briefcase-sized purse, I pulled the note MIJ had sent me via the college president's office. It was handwritten on very thin paper, the kind people used in typewriters back when several sheets of carbon paper might also have to be tucked into the carriage as an original was composed.

"Hey, Detective," I called out as I returned to the living room. "Have your people looked at those old typewriters?"

He eyeballed the note in my hand and asked me to drop it into a plastic zip bag. "Could be evidence. Why should we check the typewriters?"

"This is not the kind of paper you can buy in just any store nowadays. Printer and copy paper are thicker. If Mary Irene Jones handwrote this note to me on old-fashioned typing paper, maybe she routinely used the typewriters, too. Isn't it possible someone might know that about her?"

Insistent barking near the front door quickly shifted Quinn's attention away from me. Yeats wanted in, which was not going to be conducive to a thorough search of the house.

"Mimi Jones, pet sitter, any chance you'd make an exception to your 'no dogs' rule and take care of Yeats for a few days? Secure crime scene, chain of custody, and all that. Seems Mary Irene Jones trusted you with her important possessions. Our buddy here would be another."

Secure crime scene, I understood. Chain of custody of the dog? I was no expert on police protocol, but that sounded like a stretch.

"Two birds, one stone, Detective? Keep me under surveillance and Yeats in good hands at the same time?"

He didn't deny it, just waited as I pondered the situation. Whose eyes got to me more, Quinn's intense blues or those deep brown puppy eyes, I couldn't have told you, but I also suspected I had little room to bargain just then.

"He's not much bigger than a cat," Quinn said. "I'm sure the neighbor will rescue you in a crisis; I'll get you her phone number. And if something else comes up, you'll keep me informed. Once my team is done processing the scene, I'll talk to Professor Jones's lawyer about the fact that I'm passing a house key on to you."

Quinn opened the door just enough for a wet nose to sneak past. Yeats nuzzled my hand. I jumped back and shrieked.

Behind me, my department head giggled. Quinn smirked triumphantly.

Damn it.

Chapter Four

After morning stops to feed the four rabbits and two guinea pigs, plus a pharmaceutically supported visit to tend to Yeats—who may also have been a bit frightened of me, given my Screaming Mimi routine the day before—I drove to the college. I persuaded the English Department secretary to give me the key to the conference room, where Sharon had stashed the box of manuscripts pending some assessment of their status. Evidence? My property? The college's?

I spread the contents of one black leather binder across the conference table. I hoped something would leap out, since at that point there was no way to know whether crime or fear or eccentricity was behind MIJ's absence and her apparent determination that her papers come to me.

The binder was labeled "1981." Mary Irene would have been twenty that year, notable for hunger strikes protesting the British government's treatment of Irish Republican prisoners in Northern Ireland. Inside were pages typed on that same kind of thin paper, perhaps fifteen drafts of a single poem that began, more often than not, this way:

> *Nourish souls starved for justice*
> *forcing water on dead men?*
> *Too late.*
> *Respect stripped away one indignity at a time*
> *rots like flesh hanging from the bone*
> *until the body collapses.*
> *Strong be the spirit that survives in its place.*
> *Fear that.*

Nothing like the Mary Irene Jones revered for her nature imagery, and for themes of finding greatness in the small that seemed born of Emily Dickinson and St. Therese of Lisieux. Not in this first binder at least. If I was going to understand what was going on in her head, in her life as she'd written these verses, I was going to have to study *her* more closely, and not just these new manuscripts. I returned the file to the box, locked the conference room and returned the key, and walked across campus to the library, whose collective works by and about MIJ numbered more than I could read in a year. It was hard to know yet what to make of her disappearance or the likely duration of my custodial duties, so what the heck.

The day was unseasonably chilly, a strong breeze knocking back whatever heat a weak sun tried to deliver, but the quad was crowded with students making the best of this poor excuse for a spring afternoon. Someone's music app was cranked to the max on an Americana tune so ubiquitous I knew all the words. Lots of distractions, which was just the way I liked it when a trip to the library stacks was in order.

In addition to my fear of dogs, I was claustrophobic, so I avoided libraries. Tall walls, crowded shelves, and narrow aisles stressed me. But poet plus English professor equaled way too many library hours, since some of the best volumes were not widely available at the touch of an e-reader. One MIJ master work that weighed about thirty pounds resided up on the third floor. I knew just where to find it, and also that it was checked out fewer than a handful of times each semester. In, out, done, that was my plan.

When you're in a part of a library where people seldom venture, you easily spot the unexpected fellow visitor. This one was big, exceptionally hard to miss. I had taken the stairs up and hadn't seen him, so he no doubt had taken the elevator. Could this guy, who looked more like a linebacker than your serious student of late twentieth-century poetry, be following me? Or was my claustrophobia also making me paranoid?

I wandered down a few aisles, while simultaneously trying to remember my meditation app's exhortations to breathe slowly and thus avoid hyperventilating. The big man seemed to stop when I stopped, move when I moved. When I couldn't bear it another minute, I blasted around the corner toward my Jones biography destination. I crashed right into his chest and whiplashed off it.

"Ouch!" I shrieked.

"I think I'm lost," the man said. "They said he was up here."

We were the only ones up here. "Who's 'he?'" I asked, rubbing my neck.

"Begins with an H. Wrote a book about a guy who went fishing a lot. I was supposed to read it in high school, but I ditched class a few weeks."

Fish, high school. "You mean Ernest Hemingway? *The Old Man and the Sea*?"

"Yeah, show me where it is."

Not until I got my book and a good enough lead toward the exit. I found the MIJ doorstop bio I'd come for and pointed toward the stairs. "Wrong floor. Twentieth-century American literature is down one."

"Show me," he hissed. It wasn't a request.

I backed up slowly, keeping my eyes on him. I didn't see a weapon, but those hands looked as if they'd be effective. "Follow me," I encouraged.

He did, too close, which only ramped up my discomfort.

When I got to the stairs, I pulled the fire alarm and took off, fortunately with enough of a head start that I made it down to the checkout in time to see dozens of students filing in front of him, blocking his path toward me. He pointed a middle finger directly at me and pushed through the crowd. I swiped my faculty ID card, scanned the book's code, and dashed out of the building.

Clutching book and purse against my chest with one arm, I fished around my coat pocket for my keys and ran to my car. I hit the gas and roared out of the parking lot. At the first traffic light, I found Quinn's number in my phone and called him.

"Ms. Jones, my second favorite poet."

Not funny on a good day, which this wasn't.

"Some goon followed me up to the Mary Irene Jones section in the college library. Would have followed me out too, if I hadn't pulled the fire alarm."

Silence on the other end of the line spoke loudly.

"You don't believe me?" I snarled. "Fine, you take care of the damn dog. I have better things to do, like figure out what's in those manuscripts Mary Irene Jones wanted me to have so badly."

A car door slammed. A seatbelt alert rang. An engine started. "I believe you. I'll be at your house when you get there."

Please make him be there, I prayed.

As I pulled over to the curb, I started to shake, then cry. Quinn knocked on my car window. I unlocked the door, and he escorted me inside the house. He set a glass of water in front of me and waited until the tears subsided.

"Where were you in the library?"

My voice emerged very small, as if the strange man had forced it into hiding. "Up on the top floor, where the MIJ reference materials are. Everything is concentrated in that one space, though it's not easy to find. We've applied for a grant to set up a formal research center, something more accessible to the public, to do better by Mary Irene. If we get to keep the early manuscripts, there will be a lot of interest in studying them."

Quinn squinted at me, as if I, too, were a specimen for study. To stop my babbling, I sipped at the water, which was warm and over-chlorinated but oddly comforting.

"Would this individual have been able to find the reference area on his own? Is it possible he was searching for a rare book there and hoping you'd lead him to it?"

"Rare? Hardly. Some of the books are still in print, and the ones that aren't you can buy secondhand and cheap."

Which meant that, more likely, the big man was there for me.

Quinn seemed to understand what I was telling him. What it meant for his investigation was another thing altogether. "I could use coffee," he said. "You?"

I needed something way stronger, but I'd lay money he suspected that. "There's some on the counter, if you don't mind it reheated. Mugs and sugar are right above the coffeemaker; milk's in the fridge."

After a gulp of my hours-old caffeinated offering, Quinn settled into a chair across from me. "Start at the beginning. Everything you did today, everywhere you went. If that guy followed you into the campus library, it's a good bet he followed you all day."

"Not what I wanted to hear."

My day had been boring—rabbits and guinea pigs are easy enough to feed and clean up after—and maybe I was in a gentle drug-induced, Yeats-fearing haze. But I was certain I would have noticed a car tailing me through residential streets, and I told Quinn so.

"Then we're back to asking why Mary Irene Jones sent a total stranger her unpublished manuscripts, in addition to why anyone might care that she did."

I had an answer, at least a partial one. "I won the MIJ Festival prize ten years ago, so I'm not exactly a total stranger."

My coffee table started life as a trunk; I bought it at a flea market in upstate New York when I was in college. Inside was a lot of Mimi, the Poet, stuff: a copy of every magazine or anthology that had ever published my work, including my high school literary journal, as well as the citation that went with that now-decade-old MIJ Poetry Prize.

I located the award program that included the five winning pieces I had submitted to the competition's judges, and handed it to Quinn. "A stanza a day keeps the stalker away."

Maybe Quinn was used to terror-induced lunacy? For the first time since we'd met, he laughed. "If this poetry thing doesn't work out for you, Mimi Jones, maybe you could do standup."

He paged through the program, spending time with each of my poems. "I'm no expert," he finally said, "but I think the poetry thing *is* working. Tell me about this contest you won."

How to describe, without sounding like a complete loser,

hitting my literary peak at the fair age of twenty-four? How I had a shiny new Master of Fine Arts degree in my pocket and how a move to New York City with my husband lay just ahead? My now ex-husband.

"The year Mary Irene Jones joined the college's faculty, she endowed an annual $15,000 prize, a national competition that would be based there and judged by her and three other poetry luminaries. To qualify, you had to submit five original poems that fit the contest criteria for that particular year. When I entered, those included a standard sonnet, a Shakespearean sonnet, and three selections in the form of the writer's choice. My poetry is largely unmetered, about free will versus destiny, agency versus fate, more political but also more personal than MIJ's work. I didn't know what to expect, but she was very generous with her critique and her praise, as were the other judges."

"Sounds like a big deal. Poetry isn't my thing," Quinn said, not even faking that he was impressed. Candor I appreciated.

"For me, back then, yes, it was a very big deal. I leveraged the award by applying for a poet-in-residence and doctoral program at NYU the same year my husband was chosen for a playwright's fellowship. I got in, and Daniel and I were quite the literary golden children for a few years, until he met Giacomo. It was love at first sight; they are absolutely the perfect couple. When Daniel and I split five years ago, I moved back to Philly, to this house that Grandma Mary Irene left her namesake."

Too much information, said too quickly. Much more than one police detective needed to know about the blips in my life to date. I needed to breathe.

"Let's get out of here," Quinn suggested. "Fresh air, sunshine, they make the brain process better."

What was there to process? The fact that I'd likely given him more possible motives for my abducting Mary Irene? *Frustrated in life and love, struggling poet loses her grip, decides to make headlines by taking out her idol.* Did I strike him as a criminal mastermind?

"Yeats needs a walk about now, doesn't he?" Quinn looked at his watch.

"He can go a little longer." I wasn't ready to face the dog again.

"Now is better." Quinn wasn't suggesting this time.

From the mail-strewn table in my foyer, I reclaimed the key to MIJ's house. We took Quinn's car, the police radio chattering through the silence between us.

Yeats scampered around the yard while I checked his food and water bowls and snagged a few plastic bags from a stash on the screened porch.

"What are those woods? Part of the nature center?" Quinn pointed to the trees on the other side of MIJ's property.

"Probably. There's an entrance to one of the trails a few blocks from here. I've walked it a few times."

Once Yeats was leashed, he was not about to wait for some wimpy pet sitter, not when he had one of Philadelphia's finest willing to sniff around with him. The day had gotten a little warmer, a little less breezy. I was hungry, having fed several beings that day but not myself. My stomach growled impolitely. I hoped the boys—or the human one, at least—didn't notice.

Petals large and small, from the cherry and magnolia trees on either side of the path, created a sort of pink—rather than yellow brick—road for us. I cast myself in the role of the Cowardly Lion, gasping each time Yeats stopped to sniff a fallen cherry blossom at my feet, as if I had no concept of canine behavior whatsoever. I hoped Emerald City would rise from the end of this route fairly quickly, so I could escape both my companions and go home. There really was no place like it for me right now, when all I wanted to do was open a tub of hummus and a bag of tortilla chips and settle in with a glass of wine and a Hallmark Channel movie.

"You're divorced. Me too," Quinn said, stopping so suddenly that I walked right into his back. He twisted around and pulled me to his side. I stepped away quickly.

"Anyway, we grew up together, went to the prom together in high school. Everybody assumed we'd get married, so we got married. Didn't make it a good idea. She lives in Texas now. Her husband works for an oil company; she's a nurse. They have a couple kids, seem happy, based on the pictures she sends in her Christmas cards. I'm glad for her. Being a cop's wife wasn't easy."

Being a poet's husband was, except maybe financially, but that wasn't our issue.

"Daniel and I met as freshmen at Syracuse, the first week of classes. We were in love from Day One but didn't want to limit each other. It felt like it was too soon. So he dated other women and men, I dated other men and women, but we always made each other better, so we got married between our junior and senior years. And we were really happy, until he met the man of his dreams. Giacomo is wonderful, and Daniel is still a good friend. He calls me every few weeks. I get a lot of things about him that Giacomo doesn't, you know? We have history."

I sank onto a bench, which Yeats saw as an invitation to jump up next to me. I didn't care. It had been a frightening day just made stupidly awkward, and if a dog's snuggle was the best I could do comfort-wise, I'd take it.

Quinn squeezed into the space on the other side of Yeats and wrapped a restraining arm around him. "Everybody describes Mary Irene Jones as reclusive, but her neighbors tell me they know her. Dr. Bernstein and many of the faculty members have had longstanding professional relationships with her. Is it possible she's just on vacation, or that something urgent came up with the son or daughter she's supposed to have? Until we get some of the financial forensics back and the surveillance video from the post office visits, I'm out of leads to pursue. Unless—"

"—Unless she turns up somewhere, living or dead." Stating the obvious was always one of my talents.

"Precisely," Quinn said. He stood and tugged on the leash, urging Yeats down to the path, and we headed back toward MIJ's house.

They played fetch with a chewed-up ball as I added more kibble to a bowl to hold Yeats through to the morning, then we said goodbye and I locked the dog in the enclosed porch. The return drive to my house was no more chat-filled than our earlier twenty-minute trip had been, but this time there was clearly something on Quinn's mind.

"Did you bring any of the manuscript binders home with you?"

"No, everything is still at the college. I looked through just one today, skimming mostly. As far as I could tell, it contained only multiple versions of a single poem, a good example of how Mary Irene refined as she worked."

He pulled over to the curb in front of my house. "Tomorrow is another day, for both of us. Sometimes, you just have to step away from the puzzle."

Quinn moved around to the passenger side and opened the door for me. As he held my hand to help me out, he rubbed his thumb across my knuckles, which felt simultaneously unsettling and consoling.

"Call me if you need me, Mimi Jones. Like today. Don't hesitate."

"I'll remember, Detective."

He smiled. "My name is Mike. Remember that, too."

Chapter Five

My four rabbit-parent clients had gotten the hang of things and transferred over the remainder of the cash they owed me. That was that, bunny-wise. After I made my rounds Saturday to feed and water the remaining critters in my care—two cats, two gerbils, and Yeats, though I'd hoped (in vain) Quinn would let me off that hook—I ordered an extra-large pizza. I had food enough to burrow in and binge-watch a show set in medieval Europe I had been itching to see, yet I found it hard to focus. Not even the witchery playing out on my TV could settle my jangly nerves. Eventually, exhaustion won over anxiety, and I dozed off in the living room.

When I woke Sunday morning, Barrett, my yellow tabby, was tucked in next to my head, his blond paw anchoring my blonde hair to the couch pillow.

"You'll protect me, won't you, baby boy? You won't let them get to me, right?"

Barrett purred into my ear, oblivious to my increasingly weird world.

My mother's fourth voicemail before 7 o'clock Monday morning suggested a cat's help alone was not going to be enough. When Cass showed up at my door an hour later, I was positive.

"What is the matter with you, you don't return my calls anymore? I could have been dying, Mimi."

"In which case, you could have dialed 911 or alerted your other daughter."

"You don't have a husband and kids to take care of like Trish does. Where's your remote? Mary Irene Jones is on the news."

Sure she was.

"Mom, I have to teach a 9:30 class. I need to get into the shower."

"Hush, look."

A bulletin crawled under video of a blue hatchback being pulled out of some water; it identified the car as belonging to noted local poet Mary Irene Jones. A disembodied voice said the police officer standing behind a thicket of microphones had just acknowledged that Jones had not been seen for several days, and that her attorney was about to speak to the press about her disappearance.

Cass turned up the volume.

I knew much of the story already, except for the part about the car, which viewers learned had just been found in shallow tidal waters near a seashore resort in southern Delaware. The state police officer at the mic introduced Detective Michael Quinn of the Philadelphia Police Department, lead investigator on the Jones case, who proceeded to do that thing where cops thank all the collaborating police agencies before they give what little information they intend to put out there. Quinn's spiel was cut short by Mary Irene's attorney, Jordan K. Lisle, who spelled his last name for the reporters and who was clearly responsible for convening the press. The cops certainly didn't look happy to be there.

"My client, a poet of international renown, has been missing for days. Somebody dumped her car here after ransacking it," Lisle said.

"We don't know that the car has been ransacked or that anything has been taken. It has not yet been examined," Quinn interjected.

A reporter from Philadelphia's all-news radio station identified herself and asked whether there was any evidence Mary Irene Jones had been in the car at the time it landed in the tide pool. Quinn deferred to the Delaware State Police officer, who said there was no such evidence at this time.

"Any indication the driver lost control of the car?" another reporter asked as his TV station's helicopter hovered over the scene. "You know, skid marks, signs of high-speed impact with any of the scrub trees or those very tall reeds? Any footprints or other signs indicating how the driver left the scene or how many people might have been out here?"

"We'll be bringing an accident assessment team in shortly," Quinn and the Delaware State Police officer said in unison.

"Mr. Lisle, sources close to the suburban Philadelphia college where Mary Irene Jones once taught tell us that a box containing some of her manuscripts was delivered to the home of another poet, M. Irene Jones, in the city, then ultimately taken to the campus." The video feed shifted to a reporter from the Philly NPR affiliate, zeroing in for a split second on the station call letters on his mic. "What can you tell us about those?"

"I'll take that question." Quinn edged the lawyer away from the microphones, to Lisle's obvious dismay. "Philadelphia police are working with the other Ms. Jones as well as college administrators to determine what, if any, significance the delivery of those manuscripts might have. Thank you, that's all we have for you right now."

The TV feed returned to the anchor in Philadelphia. Mom muted him. "Well?" she asked. "Is Mary Irene Jones dead?"

I poured some dry cat food into Barrett's dish and ran the water to fill his bowl. "If she is, nobody told me."

Cass followed me into the bathroom. I could give her my full attention and be late, or half-ignore her and try to get ready for work. She would stop before walking into the shower with me, of that I was pretty sure.

"Mimi, she sent you a box of her manuscripts. Why would she do that?"

"You heard MIJ's lawyer and the police. You know what I know, Mom."

She growled, not something Cass did even when she was so aggravated she could spit, notably when I first told her Daniel and I were divorcing. (Unlike Daniel's family, who, I'd always suspected, rejoiced.)

"You have read dozens of poems that woman has written. You know more about her life than you do about your own, so don't tell me you have no idea why she'd entrust something of value like that to you. There has to be something going on. Somebody at the college obviously leaked the story to the press."

"Believe me, don't believe me, Mom, I don't know why she sent me the manuscripts. I intend to read every one of them to find out, though. Let me go do my job so the school doesn't fire me before I can accomplish that."

Cass put her hands up in mock surrender. "They need you. Press them for a full-time position. Speak up for yourself, Mimi."

I could hear what she wasn't saying: Speak up for yourself *for a change*, Mimi.

I texted Mary Irene's neighbor to say I wouldn't be available to take care of Yeats until the afternoon. Then I slammed the bathroom door shut on my mother.

My "Poetry as Protest" class was a popular free elective, three credits for examining song lyrics. Think everything from outcry over racial injustice to antiwar messaging to labor union advocacy, Billie Holiday and hip-hop to Bob Dylan and Pete Seeger, and more. Social commentary meets entertainment, with accompanying audio and sometimes video. Since the start of this decade, outrage over police killings and the prevailing culture wars had produced a torrent of new material.

Monday's class was supposed to focus on Gil Scott-Heron, but his classic "The Revolution Will Not Be Televised" went straight out the window after what my twenty students had streamed on their phones that morning.

"Ms. Jones, you're a poetry superhero right now. You have a secret identity as a verse detective."

"A what?" My face must have revealed complete confusion.

"You know, someone with the ability to discern crime clues via poetry. Tell us about the ones Mary Irene Jones gave you."

Not a lot to tell yet.

"I haven't had much time with the manuscripts. I've only quickly looked through one binder and its multiple drafts of the same poem."

"Then you gotta post that poem! The world has to see it."

"Not gonna happen, sorry."

Groans rose. Time for a lesson on copyright.

"As the police mentioned at the press conference you all obviously watched, we don't know why those manuscripts were sent to me. I do know there was absolutely nothing included with them that said, `Mimi Jones, you go right ahead and post my poetry online for everyone to see.' Without that, I have no permission to publish her unpublished work. As far as I know, someone else may very well have the exclusive rights to do so. Just because I have possession of the manuscripts, that doesn't mean I'm free to do anything I want with them. Plus, they may be evidence. Nothing is clear just yet."

Much muttering ensued, about how it wasn't all about the legal crap, it was about access for the masses.

"Yes, you're right, access to MIJ's poems is a wonderful thing. She's a brilliant writer, which is why this college has put a special spotlight on her work for years. But let's imagine a different scenario. Let's say Chevrolet uses 'Little Red Corvette' in a commercial without asking Prince's estate or whoever holds the rights to the song for permission ahead of time."

That message, everybody in my class got. Who hummed the song, who sang it, who took selfies as they did and posted them.

"See, you're making the connection Chevrolet might want. But what if it's not the connection everybody who has a stake in the song wants? Maybe I own the rights and I don't believe they should be associated with a giant corporation. Get my song out of your commercial, folks. Sometimes, copyright issues are more complex than I pay you and then you let me do something."

Just when I thought I'd made my point and we might get to Gil Scott-Heron's revolution, as opposed to Prince and the Revolution, someone shouted from the back of the classroom.

"Or maybe you're just choosing to make it more complicated. You call yourself M. Irene Jones and Mimi Jones, but isn't your actual legal name Mary Irene Jones? It's not like you stole her name or her poems, right?"

"That's right. No one is disputing either of those things."

"So, if you post that poem, doesn't she get the credit all the same? Who's going to think it's you, not her, doing it? No offense, Ms. Jones, but has anybody ever heard of you? Is anybody going to think, 'Wow, the real Mary Irene Jones isn't on this social media platform?' Seems to me you're the safest person of all to put her unpublished work out into the universe."

Someone whistled. Other kids clapped.

"But what if it were *your* work?" I countered.

The applause abruptly stopped. At the classroom door stood my department head. Sharon moved toward me. "She's in trouble now!" a few of my students chanted, as the rest ad-libbed their way through the other verses of "Little Red Corvette."

"Sorry to interrupt this lively discussion," Sharon announced, "but I need to steal Ms. Jones away. You all have final projects to work on for this class. I expect you to devote this time to them."

"Dr. Bernstein, what's the latest?" someone shouted. "Don't make us wait for the noon newscast."

She stared that student into silence as I gathered a few CDs and a VHS tape of a Scott-Heron performance. Then we walked out, leaving the class to wonder what was going on.

I had a few questions too. Was I being rescued or ambushed?

Chapter Six

The seven manuscript binders sat in a stack on Sharon's desk. Quinn nodded in my direction. Jordan Lisle offered me his hand and his business card. His law office's address was just over the Montgomery County line, close to MIJ's house rather than in some tony Center City Philadelphia tower. That struck me as something she would prefer.

"You're probably curious why we went public this morning about the disappearance of Mary Irene Jones," Lisle said. "The *other* Mary Irene Jones, that is. I regret we didn't give you advance word, Ms. Jones, or the college."

Sharon had already given him hell about that, unless I was reading the room wrong, and she looked poised to fight another round. "*You* probably leaked that business about the manuscripts to the local media, Mr. Lisle. 'Sources close to the college' indeed."

A laugh slipped out of me. Quinn, however, was definitely doing a slow burn.

"You blindsided Ms. Jones, you bet she's curious." His fingers drummed the desktop. "Hell, I'm curious, Mr. Lisle, since you haven't given me or the police in Delaware anything further that might help this investigation."

"Attorney-client privilege demands—"

"*MIS-ter* Lisle," Quinn enunciated, his voice harsher. "You asked for and a judge approved a search of your client's home based on the fact that you and she routinely communicated directly twice a week, and that you had not heard from her or been able to contact her. My department found neither Mary Irene Jones herself in the house nor anything that pointed to a reason to suspect that her absence up to that point was involuntary. In light of today's discovery of her car and at the risk of more wasted time and potential danger to your client, if there's anything you haven't told us, you need to speak *now*."

The clock on the campus quad tolled. I had cats and gerbils to tend to before my next class, but they would have to wait. "Take it from the top please, Mr. Lisle," I urged. "I feel as if I've walked into the middle of the story."

The key points went like this:

Lisle had been MIJ's lawyer for years. Negotiated some green card business for her when she first came to the U.S. Handled all her publishing contracts and whatever other legal matters needed attention. Mary Irene called him twice a week, every week, on his personal cell, leaving a voicemail if he didn't pick up. She refused to text, saying anyone could do that and claim to be her. She and Lisle had a code word she used in every phone conversation or voicemail. Lisle refused to tell us what it was.

"She'd work that word into some innocuous comment or other after saying, 'Hi, this is Mary Irene Jones,' and telling me the date and time and that she was checking in. That was the extent of her calls unless she needed me to tackle something."

Lisle said he hadn't heard from MIJ at all last week, on either of their two usual days—he refused to say what those were, too. And that, combined with no response to his calls to her, prompted him to involve the police. When, after the search at Mary Irene's house, Sharon mentioned to him delivery of the box of manuscripts to me in care of the college, it was the first time he had heard about it, Lisle said. Something had to be wrong.

"Mary Irene was always very wary, as if she expected something to happen and wanted me to be alert for it when it did," Lisle said. "I know that sounds crazy, but she was quite sane and quite serious about it."

We all looked to Sharon for confirmation. "Mercurial. That's how I'd describe Mary Irene. But she was predictably unpredictable. This sounds like her."

Quinn's drumming on the desktop accelerated, in syncopation with his questions. "Had she been threatened? Blackmailed? Subjected to bodily harm?"

"I'm not sure," Lisle admitted. "It's no secret that Mary Irene never discusses why she left Northern Ireland when she did, just as things were settling down over there. She was supposedly pregnant, and there's always been speculation that she had an affair with a politician whose star was rising quickly then. There also was talk about a certain very married British rock musician, you probably heard those rumors—there were betting pools in the U.K. for months about it, I understand. But she never asked me to do any legal work involving a child, one who would be an adult by now. If the child was given up for adoption or placed into someone's guardianship, it was handled by another lawyer. If she got an abortion, over there or in this country, she never said."

Over the years, many Mary Irene Jones biographies had been written, and, as I recalled, none of the authors was able to establish definitively whether she was pregnant when she landed at JFK Airport in New York in fall 1998 for an international poetry conference at the United Nations. Only group photos were taken at the conference. Though some of her contemporaries maintained that she was fatigued and complained of nausea, they also noted MIJ brushed those off as the effects of jet lag. A newspaper article written a few months later, when she was shortlisted for a major European literature prize, included the last photo taken of her in Northern Ireland, shot by a friend in Belfast. Often reproduced, that photo shows MIJ's face rounder than it had looked in previous pictures. Her passport photo was two years old when she immigrated to the United States, so that proved nothing, her biographers noted.

"What about her car?" I asked, since its discovery appeared to be the most recent odd occurrence. "Anything in there, or anything significant about where it was found? Unless the video on this morning's news was totally misleading, it was sitting in a kiddie pool's worth of water, so it's not like someone was trying to drown her."

"The state police in Delaware are still going over it," Quinn said, "but the gas tank was just about empty, and so far the most common fingerprints check out as belonging to Mary Irene Jones, her longtime mechanic, and the board chairman, I think, of this college." Again, Quinn looked to Sharon for confirmation.

She nodded. "He's the last living member of the board of

trustees who voted to approve MIJ's hiring in 1999, and she sometimes drove him to campus and then back to the continuing care community where he lives. It's close to her house."

"Delaware law enforcement began sweeping the area even before the reporters Mr. Lisle summoned had left, in the hope that evidence had not been disturbed," Quinn said, his tone sharp enough to cut a metaphorical swath from the lawyer's hide. "No skid marks or any other sign thus far—say, fresh damage to the car's bumpers—that suggested the driver lost control or was forced off the main road. One set of footprints led from the hatchback's driver's side through the reeds back to the road, from a size eight woman's boot. Gardening boots, according to the manufacturer's imprint on the sole. The footprints continued for a little more than a mile along the road, then stopped. It's possible she hitched a ride, or that she managed to contact someone to come get her."

Lisle popped up from his chair like a jack-in-the-box. "Or maybe someone lured her there then abducted her from the roadside. That's not beyond the realm of possibility, Detective Quinn."

"We're checking traffic cameras on nearby highways and bridges to see if we can track her car's movements beforehand," Quinn said. "It's possible we might spot another vehicle whose movements are too similar to be coincidence."

Were we afraid of that?

"But there's nothing so far that screams blackmail, or a revenge-seeking jilted lover who fathered her possible child, or some unknown creditor she was trying to keep away from her unpublished manuscripts?" I asked.

Worst-case scenarios all, surely.

My three companions' reactions silently replied, "No. At least, not yet."

The binders on the desk before us might yield answers, but not without a lot of careful examination—by me, by Sharon, by police forensics types.

The clock on the quad now tolled the half-hour. Still awaiting me were cats, then gerbils, then English lit students, then Yeats. I hoped MIJ's neighbor would be home when I got to that last stop.

Mary Irene Jones had managed to leave me in charge of her manuscripts and her pet, as if she had designed distracting tasks specifically for me. I hoped this was the end of them—you know, as opposed to the twelve labors Hercules was assigned by a mythic king.

Just as well I had devised my own plan.

Chapter Seven

"Yeats was distraught, poor puppy. I couldn't just leave him here, waiting for her. What's a little breaking and entering?"

Jen Dill, lock-picking canine savior, kept a grip on the dog's collar so Yeats wouldn't tackle me, he was so happy to see people—even me.

"Mary Irene loves this guy. There's no way she wouldn't arrange for someone to take care of him if she had to be away," Jen assured me. "I don't have a key, but my little boy is in preschool a few days a week now, and I told her I was always willing to help with Yeats in a pinch. Maybe she put extra food on the screened porch for that reason? Thank goodness it hasn't been really cold overnight."

I dangled the key I was given by MIJ's lawyer via the Philadelphia Police Department. I would have been happy to hand it over the first day to Neighbor Jen, but that still wasn't my call, as she no doubt knew.

"When you showed up here with that detective, I was sure you were a relative sent by Mary Irene to take care of Yeats, because of your name."

"Strictly coincidence. My grandmother also had the same name." I stepped onto the porch and unlocked the back door to the house. Jen tossed the dog one of his toys and walked in after me. What was a little unsanctioned nosing around?

Everything was as we had left it, Quinn, his crime scene team, Sharon, and me. Just the breakables I'd noticed before, the teapot and the framed pictures, were good enough reasons not to let Yeats stay inside on his own; he might work his way out of a crate. But he couldn't stay on the porch indefinitely either.

"Since we don't know when Mary Irene is coming back, would you be willing to have Yeats stay over at your house? We can leave a note for her saying that's he's next door. I'm just not a dog person, Jen, and I don't want her to find he's destroyed the place in her absence. Could be she'll be back any time now."

Maybe nothing dire had happened to MIJ. You might leave your dog alone if you thought you were coming back soon.

"I can take Yeats, no problem," Jen said. "Like I told the police, I have no idea when Mary Irene left. I didn't see her car pull away, and now they found it in that water."

That was something else again. "A tidal pool. Not deep, but still, it didn't look like someplace you'd just leave your car."

I wondered what else MIJ had left behind, whether willingly or under duress. Inside her refrigerator was the better part of a quart of milk, plus a half-empty box of mini croissants and part of a cantaloupe that was going moldy. The freezer was packed with low-calorie dinners and a box of yogurt pops. Didn't look as if she planned to be away long, assuming she *had* planned to be away.

A hall closet door was ajar, and I could see a large green roller suitcase propped up in the back. Maybe she had packed an overnight bag instead and took it with her from the car when she left it in Delaware?

Tucked next to the suitcase was a box marked, "Paper." I pulled it forward to find a couple reams of standard printer paper and a bundle of legal pads. None of the very thin typing paper MIJ had used to write her note to me and the work I'd seen in the first binder of her manuscripts. I slid the box back where I found it.

Jen leaned over my shoulder. "I was going to ask if that box was empty. Guess not," she said, her arms full of doggy toys and treats, plus a couple of blankets. "We need to carry a few of his things over to my house if Yeats is going to stay with me. I'm okay with watching him indefinitely, if it's okay with the police. They cruise this block every hour or so. They wouldn't have to record my comings and goings anymore, or yours, I guess."

I fetched the dog bed, piled cans of dog food and a bag of kibble on top of it, and walked it over to Jen's house, leaving it on *her* porch. "I'm going to get rid of a hunk of cantaloupe in the fridge before it goes bad, bring in the mail, and close up over at Mary Irene's. If you can slip that note for her about Yeats through the screened porch door at some point, I think we'll be covered. I'll let the cops know that you have him, and that the porch door will be locked in the meantime."

On cue, Yeats barked a few times, chasing something across the yard. He would be much happier with Jen than with me.

The mail was all junk, no bills; maybe MIJ paid hers online. I left the stack of envelopes and circulars on the kitchen counter. I found a grocery bag to stash the rotting melon and knotted it for disposal, then locked the door behind me. That got me thinking, though. I might never get back into the house again, and surely there might be things in plain sight that seemed insignificant now but might help as I went through the rest of the manuscripts. Like the framed photos and the old typewriters, or the books on her bookshelves and the stuff on her desk. So I went back inside and retraced my steps from that first day with the crime scene team, quickly taking cellphone pictures of random and not-so-random items lying around, even the junk mail I'd just deposited in the kitchen. I opened her pantry cupboard and clicked off more shots there, too.

At my car, I opened the bag with the cantaloupe and texted Quinn a picture of it with this message: "This was going bad in Mary Irene's fridge. I'm going to toss it when I get to work unless you tell me not to. FYI: Yeats is living with Jen Dill, the neighbor next door. She has his food, toys, etc. Let me know when you want to collect the house key."

I didn't wait for a reply, or an objection to my decision about the dog. Instead, I drove to the college for the third time that day.

The campus glowed rosy as dusk approached, pink and red-orange hues complementing the sedate gray of the old structures and the white of the just-blooming azaleas and dogwoods. I gloried in this time of day, though I was typically hurrying from a classroom to my car rather than strolling as I did now, from the parking lot to the building housing the English Department. I could see a light on in Sharon's office as I crossed the quad, and the janitorial crew silhouetted through the window shades. I stuck my head in the door leading from the main hall, waving wildly for someone to turn off the vacuum cleaner.

"I left something up in the conference room. Can you let me in for two seconds?" I showed them my faculty security badge, and a woman with a ring of keys walked up the stairs ahead of me and waited by the door. From the box in which they had been delivered, I took the binder with the "1981" poem and a second binder marked "1999." I gave the cleaner a thumbs-up and headed home to take a crack at the poetry portion of the big mystery.

And to feed Barrett, of course.

Revisiting "1981" and the Irish Republican Army hunger strikers, I went through every page of that first manuscript binder, to ensure I hadn't missed something and to confirm my original impression that the top page was, indeed, the finished version of the poem. Every time MIJ revised, she added new material, fleshing it out eventually to eleven sections touching on the deaths of Bobby Sands and the others that followed. The completed work felt immediate, yet not—some retrospective awareness seemed to imbue it at the same time, which made no sense at all. Clearly, I had spent way too much time scrutinizing the piece. I was overthinking it.

A text message startled me out of my musing. "Det Q," my phone informed me.

"Just wanted to thank you for the cantaloupe pic, and for disposing of it," Quinn wrote. "We, of course, inventoried the contents of Mary Irene's refrigerator last week and took a melon sample as evidence."

I giggled, as I did when I was overtired and overstressed.

"In case you were wondering"—he must have guessed I would be—"we didn't find poison, or at least none of the ten or so most common ones we test for. And I suppose this new solution for Yeats is a better one. Your gerbil and guinea pig clients take priority."

No more guinea pigs, just gerbils and cats for now. "Maybe a tortoise next week. We're trading emails," I replied.

"An emailing tortoise certainly deserves your full attention," he responded. Maybe Detective Michael Quinn could also get silly at the end of a long day.

"I'll stop by the college for the house key tomorrow," he added a few seconds later.

"No classes tomorrow. I'll be on campus the day after."

Quinn didn't need to know that I intended to be at home tomorrow, neck-deep into Binder Number Two, hoping for insights into MIJ's creative process and anything else its contents might yield.

The "1999" binder followed the pattern the first had established: one poem, revised over and over, with the version in the first position presumably the one that satisfied MIJ. That prevailing version began:

> *Apart, individual.*
> *Lyrics stranded without melody*
> *until we aren't.*
> *Until a note resonates, a chord strikes…*
> *the smallest sound, the shortest beat.*
> *Until is born, little wonder, a symphony.*

She extended the metaphor to other examples of disparate elements coming together in service to a new whole, an entirely original entity. Animate, yet not previously existing except in concept. The idea, newly incarnated.

Thematically, this piece was more like the poems that made Mary Irene Jones a cultural phenomenon in Europe in her twenties and a worldwide legend before she turned thirty. But something was off. The writing was wonderful, so it wasn't that. More like MIJ had altered light somehow, refracting it through a different prism.

It was disorienting. Nothing about this poem, in its many iterations before me, felt familiar, not that I was among the acknowledged authorities on Mary Irene's writing. Despite my mother's opinion, I had never fully immersed myself in the MIJ canon. I didn't dare. If my work was going to be judged derivative, it must never be derivative of *hers*—no way was I going to be known as a Mary Irene Jones wannabe. But I also couldn't stay away from her. Given what we had in common, I was more than a casual consumer of her poetry.

What I did recognize between these "1999" efforts and the work in the "1981" binder was the same editing process. MIJ reduced, whittling away lofty or redundant imagery until a poem was smooth, spare, stark. From one draft to the next, it was as if she searched for the single word that best conveyed her intent and discarded the rest, distilling impurities of language.

More difficult to discern from the few words that remained, especially in the "1999" piece, was what MIJ wanted of her readers—if anything. Take the words at face value? Follow wherever the metaphors might lead? Was it me, or her? Was there something I was just not seeing, or was she being purposefully inscrutable?

In the conference room a day earlier, I had resisted the urge to locate a guide to all this, even a chronological one. I opted instead to select whichever binder came to hand, as someone stumbling upon the poems by accident might. Now, after reading these, I was tempted to go back and search all the binders. Which poems lay between Mary Irene Jones, newly blossomed poetic voice, and Mary Irene Jones, mystic interpreter? Something told me that wasn't a good idea, though, that there was nothing to be gained from trying to approach the poems left in my care logically. That I should embrace them as I might children, tending them lovingly but equally, idiosyncrasies and all.

My head ached, and my eyes felt dry. I needed a break, and it was past time for feeding a couple of furry afternoon clients. I repositioned the many "1999" drafts in the binder, to protect the fragile papers from Barrett's claws and paw prints, and drove five blocks to Echo and Whisper's house.

The cats were waiting for me just behind the door, purring, yet also judging me for my tardiness. Good thing they couldn't fill out the survey the agency that referred me would send their pet parents. "We like this sitter, she plays with us," I imagined them reporting, "but we have to be patient kitties with this one. She operates on Mimi Time."

I filled food and water dishes and put out a good supply of the dairy-flavored treats they enjoyed, then I sat on the floor and let them climb up for stroking and scratching.

"It's okay, your mom and dad will be home tonight. They only went to a college reunion at Stanford for a few days of reminiscing and drinking. You know, 'You tell me what you've been up to for the last ten years, and I'll raise you a new angel investment and a stock split.'" The cats seemed satisfied with that explanation and settled along my legs, one on each side. I did a short daily meditation with my phone app, hugged the girls for a moment, and locked up.

I no sooner got home when the boss called. I didn't bother getting out of my car.

Chapter Eight

"Where are you? All hell is breaking loose."

"I don't have classes today. I was feeding cats, not checking texts and email."

"Damn, that's right." Sharon indulged in a few other choice words as well. "Can you get over here? It's too complicated to go into on the phone."

I dragged over my jacket and jeans the emergency lint roller I kept in my car. Thirty-five minutes later, I was in the same conference room as the box of binders, along with Detective Quinn, MIJ's lawyer, and the college's vice president for finance, the man who signed my paychecks.

A fourth man rushed in as Sharon was pulling down the projection screen. "Dr. Bernstein, I'm here as legal counsel for the college," he said.

That couldn't be good.

Across the conference table I slid Quinn the key to MIJ's house. "Where have you been?" he whispered.

"No classes, remember?" I smiled innocently. How I spent my days was none of his business.

"Can somebody bring me up to speed here, something about a new issue concerning Mary Irene Jones?" the college's attorney asked.

On the screen, the VP for finance flashed a spreadsheet for all of us to study. "As Mr. Lisle and Detective Quinn have just learned after a forensic financial investigation of Mary Irene Jones—the absent Mary Irene Jones, that is—it appears that money recently removed from two of her bank accounts was deposited into the college fund that underwrites the annual poetry festival in her name. The withdrawals match exactly, amount and date, with the deposits into our account. The balance of a third account in her name apparently was taken in cash, in increments of nine thousand dollars each over the last fifteen weeks.

"You can also see from the spreadsheet the deposits that were regularly made to the poetry festival's account by Mary Irene Jones," the VP said. "Over the last twenty years, give or take, those poetry fund deposits have apparently followed, within a day or two, transfers of funds into one or more of her own accounts."

What were we supposed to make of these details? As if we had rehearsed the move, we all turned toward Quinn.

"The FBI is investigating whether Mary Irene Jones could have been laundering money through the poetry festival account," he said. "Not huge sums, but the bureau wants to rule out the possibility that she might be part of a larger network. The bureau also is looking into whether she had still other bank accounts she was moving money through. Everything is preliminary at this point. When a missing-person case involves bank accounts, federal investigators routinely work with local police departments, and just as often they find nothing worth pursuing. In this particular situation, because Mary Irene Jones is an international celebrity, the possibility that she has been kidnapped also has to be considered. Mr. Lisle is still trying to contact her, of course, but with no success thus far. My understanding is the college president has been trying as well, again unsuccessfully. The hope is that Mary Irene Jones will return soon and clarify the situation."

Lisle and the college's attorney exchanged a "We need to talk" look.

"We're keeping this information quiet, I hope. This college has a lot riding on Mary Irene Jones and her reputation," Sharon said, blunt as always.

"I'm not privy to everything the FBI has or how it plans to handle news, if any, about it," Quinn said.

The poetry festival was only a few weeks away. Sharon shot visual daggers at Quinn. "And what about the unpublished manuscripts, which Mary Irene Jones entrusted to Mimi and the college? Are we allowed to talk about them? Look at them?"

"Out of my jurisdiction, Dr. Bernstein, but I can tell you those manuscripts do need to stay in this room, locked up at all times. They're evidence, potentially even more important now."

"I have two binders at home that I'm studying," I said. "I'll return them before my class tomorrow morning."

"Tonight would be preferable," Quinn countered. "We need to maintain a transparent chain of custody."

I had seen enough of him by then to know when Quinn was annoyed. I could get annoyed, too, and I'd be damned if I was driving back home and back to the college again so he could cross T's and dot I's for his bosses and the Feds.

"How does it get more transparent than 'I have two binders at home and will bring them back tomorrow?' Do you expect someone to break into my house—?"

The words froze on my tongue. Suddenly, a break-in seemed like a terrifying possibility, given what had happened in the library. Which Quinn understood.

"I'll have a patrol car stationed outside your home immediately," he said, texting someone. "But those binders need to be back here first thing tomorrow."

"Can law enforcement insist on restricting access to them?" Sharon stared down MIJ's lawyer and any opinions he might voice about that. "Fending off questions about the manuscripts has already become difficult. With the poetry festival approaching, it will be even more so if we haven't been able to examine the binders' contents—especially if Mary Irene hasn't turned up by then."

Lisle seemed determined to have the last word. "As Dr. Bernstein has just reminded us, those manuscripts are the legal possession of Ms. Jones here, in care of this college, until such time as a change in Mary Irene's circumstances or a judge dictates otherwise."

Working on the manuscripts at home would be a lot more comfortable, but making sure I had access to them, period, was the priority. "I'd like a key to this room so I don't have to chase down Dr. Bernstein's secretary or the cleaning staff again. There are security cameras on all the doors in this building, Detective, so you know I wouldn't dream of taking any other binders off campus."

Quinn arched a "Better not try it" eyebrow at me. Okay, maybe I'd dream about it, but I wouldn't actually do it.

A yellowed copy of John Fowles's 1960s novel *The Magus* lay open on my lap at page 175. I was less than a third of the way through the book, the tale of a stranger stepping into an ever-stranger world, but my mind instead kept wandering the labyrinth into which Mary Irene Jones had led me. Money laundering on top of possible foul play on top of a box of anomalous poetry? How did those things mesh?

Barrett jumped down, jostling the book off my lap and onto the rug. "You made me lose my place. Like I can remember anything I just read anyway." I caught him and scratched behind his ears, cupping his little cat face with my hands and kissing him on his terracotta-colored nose. "Tell me, my perceptive friend, what do you know about money laundering?"

How the heck did the FBI track it, and what type of profile did Mary Irene Jones fit? Her house was modest enough. Based on what I'd seen in my two visits inside, nothing she owned looked like a priceless antique or a rare book. Was she a bitcoin investor hiding cash illicitly? For whom, and why?

The doorbell rang and Barrett bolted, sending the Fowles book skidding behind the coffee table. The bell camera recorded Quinn's profile. I quickly scraped my hair into what I hoped was a respectable ponytail using a rubber band I yanked off a pile of junk mail in my foyer.

As greetings went, mine leaned more toward exasperated than cordial. "Now what? Another revelation?"

"Have you seen the car that I asked to patrol the neighborhood?"

Based on the evidence before me, Quinn had just come from the gym: His hair was damp, curling up a little, and sweat rings discolored his T-shirt. He smelled, well, *manly*—which reminded me how much I missed that scent.

"Mimi? Patrol car?"

"I haven't seen one, no. But I haven't exactly been looking."

He muttered a four-letter word and texted someone, who responded right away. "A guy called out sick. They can't get anyone here until shift change at eleven."

It was 9 o'clock. "If you're staying, you'd better come in. I need to close this door."

Quinn assessed my bare feet and the half-scraped-off remains of a hot pink pedicure my four-year-old niece had administered about a month ago. "Can't have frozen toes," he said, and stepped inside. I retrieved my book, folded the shawl my grandmother had knitted, and resumed my place on the sofa.

"You're obviously off duty. You just decided to swing by here and look for a strategically placed officer?"

He lowered himself into the worn wing chair I'd inherited with the house—I regretted not having ordered a slipcover by now—and swiveled his neck to work out a kink. "You were pretty shook up after that incident in the college library. Call my showing up here inappropriate or unprofessional, whatever you like. I just wanted to be sure you were okay."

Quinn smiled, and all sorts of inappropriate and unprofessional tingles tingled inside me. "I need to check windows around the house, to get familiar with the sightlines," he said. "I should pass any vulnerabilities along to the patrol officer who arrives."

Vulnerabilities? "Should I turn on the outside lights? I wasn't sure if they would help or foil an intruder."

He looked back toward the foyer. "Are those the switches near the front door? I'll get them."

I nodded, warning myself to chill as the very hot detective did his job.

"Is your bedroom directly above us?" he called from the threshold. "Do me a favor, go upstairs, turn on a lamp, and stand there. I want to see what there is to see from the street."

Could I chase out of my traitorous brain the image of him watching me? I switched on a reproduction Tiffany lamp sitting atop the bedside table farthest from the window, hoping for a soft silhouette. Not that there was much danger of my looking alluring in yoga pants and an old NYU sweatshirt, no matter how dim the illumination. Barrett butted against my shins, purring like a tiny motor. I picked him up, grateful for the company while Quinn gauged whatever he hoped to gauge. I scratched the back of the cat's neck, staring into the semi-darkness rather than dwelling on the object of that moment's very inconvenient fantasy.

"Got what I needed," Quinn said from the hall behind me.

Startled, Barrett leaped out of my arms, dragging his claws over my skin, drawing blood.

"Jesus, that hurt!"

Quinn spun me around to face him, lifted my right forearm to his lips, and kissed the nasty scratch. "Booboo's all better now," he declared, and smiled.

I rushed downstairs to the kitchen, where I washed my arm with the antibacterial soap I kept in a glass dispenser on the counter. My eyes darted to the microwave's clock — 9:25 — which meant more than ninety minutes to go until a patrol car arrived.

"Hungry?" I asked the man behind me. How, I wondered, did I manage to say exactly the wrong thing all the time?

"You bet." How was it, I wondered, that he managed to say exactly the thing that would drive me crazier?

"Cold pizza? It's from a couple hours ago, not, like, last week." I pulled the box from my fridge and opened it for his perusal. "White with broccoli, artichoke hearts, and green pepper."

"Looks good. Any beer?"

I pulled a cookie sheet lined with aluminum foil out of the oven and selected a preheat temperature. "I'm a wine person. White's open, but I can open red." And, of course, the thought of red wine reminded me of Quinn's kiss on my scratched arm. Totally innocent, right? He probably had little kids in his life—I did that sort of thing all the time with my sister's pair.

I opened the oven door, slipped two slices onto the cookie sheet, then rummaged through my designated drawer full of random utensils, rattling them as I searched for the corkscrew. "White's fine." He moved in beside me and opened the refrigerator, finding the bottle of Sauvignon blanc on the door and passing it to me. "I'm not here to make trouble."

And yet, there he was, making trouble.

I handed him a filled wineglass. "Drinking alone isn't any fun," Quinn said, sipping from it then pushing it along the counter back toward me. What the heck, we'd already exchanged germs, so I took a quick sip, then sidestepped him to get a plate for the pizza, damning whoever had conceived of the galley kitchen. While I fiddled with a placemat and napkin, I heard the tinkling of more stemware behind me as he found a second glass.

"Sit," I ordered. "It'll be five more minutes for lukewarm, ten for crispy."

"Let's go for crispy, so you can sit with me now." He gestured to the chair next to him. "You don't have to play waitstaff, you know. I'm the one who barged in on you."

"To check on me."

"To make sure you were safe."

"Me and the MIJ manuscript binders I," and here I made air quotes, "'spirited away' from the college. What is it that makes the Feds think she's been laundering money?"

Quinn studied his wine through the glass. "When bank accounts empty out and people go missing, we look into all kinds of scenarios. I can't tell you much more than I already have."

I checked the pizza. Warm enough for somebody who claimed he didn't want to be waited on. I put the slices on a plate and returned to my wineglass.

"You haven't told me much of anything, Detective. Mary Irene Jones may be a big name on the poetry circuit, but she certainly didn't earn much when she worked at the college, and she probably only gets a stipend, sometimes room and board, . when she travels to university symposiums and writers' conferences. I'd guess that's why she does so many of them every year."

"You know this how?"

I pointed to myself. "I also apply to speak at these gatherings. We're not talking fast cash here. Depending on who's hosting the event, who's sponsoring, and who's on the program, a few pay well. Others don't pay much, my college's Mary Irene Jones Festival included. All of which you can verify online. Poetry can be eloquent and egalitarian, but don't look for grace when poets dish among themselves on social media about who undeservedly got the bigger honorarium."

Quinn ate without comment.

"I didn't see anything especially ostentatious in MIJ's house. If she's laundering money, what is she getting out of it?"

He shrugged. "Future freedom maybe? How much is it worth to live your life without interference?"

The wine bottle was almost empty. I topped off both our glasses. "So she's laundering money to hold off blackmailers?"

He gnawed on a crust and studied me. I felt much too warm and checked the oven to be sure I'd turned it off. The clock on the microwave said 10:10.

"I'm still not well versed on Mary Irene Jones, what her private life might entail, what her vulnerabilities might be, except for the mystery child you and Lisle and Dr. Bernstein talked about. The FBI will go through her tax returns, check where and how often she travels, that's pretty standard, and they'll see where that takes them."

Quinn pointed a finger at the zigzag Barrett had scratched into my forearm. "I can try to keep *you* safe, even if I can't control what the Feds do. I like you, Mimi Jones, and the fact that I make you so uncomfortable makes me think you might like me a little too."

He pushed his plate away. "Thanks for the pizza. If you need a cop, I'll be out in my car until eleven."

For the next forty-five minutes, that was all I could think about.

Chapter Nine

We were ten days out from MIJ Fest, and Sharon was in full panic mode. That was early, even for her.

If the college's English faculty was inclined to honesty on the topic, its members would vote May the most hated month of the school year, and not just because we were giving and grading finals and enduring the students' teacher evaluations. Playing the poetry festival supporting roles Sharon inevitably assigned us aggravated everybody. Expletives abounded in our group text chain.

Because I was an adjunct, Sharon typically relegated me to the fringes, giving me such tasks on the big day as signing in advance-ticket holders and accommodating those who arrived unregistered by collecting the cost of admission. Thus, I had no part in the planning process, none of the onerous duties my colleagues despaired of, nor even the slightest contact with the festival's founder.

Just as well, the full-timers would tell me when I lamented the fact that no one at the college had thought to introduce us. When it came to the festival prize, they said, the great Mary Irene Jones was a total control freak more often than not, very particular about who won and occasionally overruling the consensus choice, as well as being fussy about how the award was to be announced. She was particular most of all about pre-recording the keynote speech. MIJ never delivered it in person—she was giving the college money for the prize, she argued, and no one was paying her to mingle. Counter-arguments that attendance suffered as a result apparently fell on deaf ears.

And thus every spring, her nagging made Sharon insane because MIJ did little to organize and produce the festival itself. That job fell to Sharon, who consequently delegated negotiation of the printing and catering contracts and other party-planning minutiae while she mediated disagreements between Mary Irene and the other award judges, selected panelists for the day's various workshops from the lists the faculty had already assembled and vetted, and took care of whatever ego-stroking was necessary to ensure that a critical mass of those notables showed up in person and on time. Sharon steered the always unsteady ship of poetry and didn't care much how the decks were swabbed, just that they were. It was only after each year's festival that my colleagues and I were grateful.

This year, however, Sharon was not the calm, if demanding, captain we were accustomed to. She seemed convinced the poetry festival, already buffeted by the high winds and choppy waters of Hurricane Mary Irene, would crash onto the rocks. The still-MIA MIJ had not left even a written draft of her keynote address hailing the award winner, extolling the college, and affirming poetry as a provocateur for civility in a society where civil discourse no longer seemed possible.

So when I was summoned to a hastily convened festival committee meeting, I thought it was odd, but not more odd than every other MIJ-related development of the past few weeks. "We need a Plan B," emphasized the email sent to committee members and cc'd to me. "We can't sit around and wait for Mary Irene to send a postcard from Moscow or Burkina Faso, or, heaven forbid, for her body to be found somewhere. The show must go on!"

I carried my coffee over to Sharon's office — MIJ's manuscripts meant restricted access to the larger conference room — and squeezed into the crowd gathered there. I did not realize I was about to be lashed to the mast.

Turned out, I was Plan B, a summary of which had been circulated to everyone in the group but me. The presence of the college president should have been my first clue that debate would be limited, and opposition futile.

Sister Marlene St. Vincent de Paul Flaherty had risen through the ranks of the religious order that founded the school. In the fine tradition of nuns who taught generations of Catholic children, she took no guff from anyone, let alone pipsqueaks like me. Over my very loud protests, the festival committee voted unanimously—officially, this time—that I would deliver the festival's keynote address.

"With all due respect, you don't think the poetry world would consider substituting me for *the* Mary Irene Jones insulting to her and offensive to them?"

"If we did, Mimi, would we be having this conversation?" Sister Marlene speared me with a "Don't use that tone with me, young lady" glare.

"This is not some desperate attempt to cover up the fact that Mary Irene is unavailable," she asserted. "This is an opportunity to honor her and offer the hope that she is safe and will be back among us soon."

How anyone, presumably Sharon, had mesmerized the college president into thinking this would work, I didn't understand, and I made the mistake of saying so, thus volleying the idea back to the pro-Mimi forces.

"For one thing, you are a past winner of the Mary Irene Jones Poetry Award, not to mention a member of the English Department faculty," Sister Marlene said.

"I'm an adjunct," I clarified, earning another glare.

"That can be rectified, I'm sure, with swift intervention by Dr. Bernstein," she said, redirecting her glare at Sharon. "To continue, not only are you a respected poet and member of this faculty, but Mary Irene Jones also entrusted some never-published manuscripts to you, and you are, unless I have been misinformed, currently studying them. Those facts alone, Mimi, would have made you worthy of standing in as the face of this year's festival."

That implied the existence of other *facts*. As if she had anticipated my doubts, Sharon passed out copies of my "Poetry as Protest" syllabus.

"I don't want to presume that Sister Marlene and the several college trustees on this committee have had time to digest the material I emailed over the last few days, so I'd like to summarize it here. But when you get the opportunity, do look at the video links. Mimi's rapport with her students is remarkable. Her approach to the class is notable for the way it illustrates that poetry is breathing art, changeable art that addresses in the moment such issues as racial and environmental justice and economic equity. We're not just throwing a raw understudy out there to represent this college and Mary Irene Jones. Mimi is the real deal, and this is the perfect time to show how new voices are embracing a time-honored tradition and making it their own."

I began to object again. "Oh, ye of little faith," Sister Marlene interrupted. Discussion over.

"We will, of course, be streaming the keynote live for those who can't attend the poetry festival in person, and posting video on the website almost immediately thereafter," Sharon said, ignoring the tech department manager rubbing his temples over by the window.

Ticket sales were up this year, the committee treasurer noted for the record, and he submitted a report showing sponsorships had increased also—a local restaurateur and two luxury car dealerships had signed on. This festival needed to be a big, splashy poetry good time.

The prep work would be staggering. I took deep breaths, to slow my racing heart. I would need to ensure that I wasn't missing the latest new poetry voices protesting via music, as well as discover where I could find audio and video of those voices, including interviews about how they had succeeded in making themselves heard.

Was it too late to see whether Bob Dylan was available and willing to travel to the Philly suburbs? Could a hastily arranged bake sale raise enough for the honorarium if he were? And where on God's green Earth was MIJ when we needed her?

Straight from the meeting, I walked into my "Poetry as Protest" class and tossed the day's lesson plan. Told the kids to step up to the whiteboard, write down the titles of their favorite musical examples of contemporary protest, artist and album, and find snippets on their phones to share. By the time the ninety minutes were up and the students had debated the merits of their choices versus those of their peers, I had a dozen worthwhile leads to check out for my MIJ Fest presentation, including links to music and/or video, with more welcome. Everybody would be getting a slight bump in grade, I promised them. Win-win.

Was that cheating? Nah. No way I could have known all the possibilities out there without their help. I would give the students all the credit due them in my presentation, just as soon as I figured out what the hell else I would say.

Because it had been decreed on high: I was the Mary Irene Jones we had, even if I wasn't the one any of us wanted.

Chapter Ten

A third manuscript — labeled "Now" — contained fragments, nothing instantly identifiable as a full poem, at least as I defined it given MIJ's previous work, or for that matter anything I'd seen in the first two binders.

When was "Now," as she saw it? Excellent question, and one I couldn't answer based on the dozen pages I'd leafed through. Some of the fragments felt contemporary, as if the writer were musing on age, maturing, loneliness. But they were ambiguous as well. A 23-year-old Mary Irene Jones might just as easily have written them as the woman now in her sixties.

Afternoon sunshine streamed through the clerestory windows along one wall of the English Department conference room, and I wanted to flee the campus and all things MIJ, anything to get relief from the new burden the festival committee had dumped on me — keynote speech as quid pro quo for a full-time faculty spot. Maybe if I juggled and nailed a perfect walk on the high wire, I'd end up on a tenure track — circus metaphors rode through my head like a clown on a unicycle. If my phone rang, I didn't hear it, or maybe I was just too scattered. The voicemail notification, I saw.

"Uh, hello, Mimi? This is Jen Dill, Mary Irene's neighbor. I totally forgot about my son's pediatrician appointment at three today. He's due for some booster shots. I'll have to reschedule if I don't leave now. Could you come and take care of Yeats this afternoon? I put him on her screened porch — I picked the lock again. Text me if you can make it, no need to call me back. Thanks."

Yeats was my new (that is, my only) doggy best friend, and just the excuse I needed at the moment. If I shut down my laptop and quickly locked away the manuscripts, I could be at MIJ's house in Upper Roxborough by 3:15. I texted Jen a thumbs-up, packed my gear, and sprinted down the steps and across campus to my car.

Goofy guy that he was, Yeats greeted me like a long-lost pal, pawing my shins the second I opened the porch door. The leg-climbing, I still didn't love, but I had gotten used to it. I also had been around him enough to know that he'd settle down after a few polite pats on the head. Once we'd been sufficiently friendly, I checked to see whether there was kibble in his dish. One of those little coolers, a new addition to the porch, held bottles of cold water. I added some to his drink bowl, and after a few messy slurps, Yeats was ready to go.

During my earlier, thankfully short, stint as his caregiver, I had established a couple of routes through the neighborhood to walk Yeats. Each seemed to satisfy him and prevent me from breaking out in nervous hives. I opted for the one with more concrete and asphalt than shrubs and trees, to avoid the inevitable woodland smells and sights that prove fascinating to dogs. Yeats did his business, I cleaned up after him, and we were efficiently on our way. My plan was to let him run around MIJ's yard for another twenty minutes or so, ignore the Frisbee he'd likely drop at my feet, and check email until it felt like I had done my duty.

I deposited the bag with his offerings into the trash can outside the porch and liberated Yeats to explore the grass. As I hung up his leash, I noticed a folded piece of paper anchored down with a rock near where MIJ had kept the dog food.

I'm keeping Yeats at my house, per your friend Mimi's suggestion.
We miss you.
J.

Who was *we*, I wondered, unless that was just Jen speaking for Yeats too? I put the note—which I had asked Jen to leave, after all—back under the rock and sat on the garden bench. Yeats, on cue, dropped a gnawed-on blue disk to await a throw-and-fetch opportunity. I tossed it to the edge of the yard, but Yeats wasn't the one who caught it.

"This is private property, miss. What are you doing here?" Yeats nuzzled the police officer's hand. The cop got the message and threw the Frisbee.

"I came to take care of the dog for the neighbor, Jen Dill. You're watching the house in case Mary Irene Jones returns? You must be new, we haven't met."

He scowled at me with his worst Officer Friendly demeanor. "Can I see some identification, miss?"

I pointed to my purse, sitting on the other side of the screened enclosure. Never taking his eyes off me, he opened the porch door and handed me the bag. "Open it so I can see inside please." I did. Evidently, he didn't see anything objectionable, like a weapon. "Your ID, please?" he requested again. I extracted my wallet and located my driver's license, which I knew would only complicate the situation.

"This says M. Irene Jones."

"That's my name." I couldn't help but smirk.

"You're not her," he replied. He had, of course, seen the photo MIJ's lawyer had circulated to every law enforcement and media operation in metropolitan Philly and South Jersey and on down through Delaware to the Maryland border.

"Are you related to her?"

"No, more like a colleague. We just happen to have the same name. In fact, I've been helping out with the investigation."

That, he wasn't buying, and before I could say anything more, the police officer walked to his car, my license in hand, presumably to radio in the presence of an intruder. Yeats and I followed—I figured I didn't dare do otherwise. The dog whimpered dismay at this interruption in his play time. I sat on the grass, and Yeats put his head on my lap. I tried to push him away. He whined pitifully.

"This is no fun, I get it. But I'm kind of stuck here." I relented and reluctantly let Yeats nuzzle my hand. "Let's just say I owe you a good workout next time." Not that there would be a next time—his missing owner or her neighbor were going to have to work that one out themselves.

When Officer Suspicious gestured us back to the screened porch, a hopeful Yeats retrieved the Frisbee and bounded over to him. The cop tossed it, then held a cellphone out to me.

"What are you doing there, Mimi?"

"Having a fabulous day, how about you, Detective Quinn? Please tell me the Philadelphia Police Department is so busy that you're recalling your minion to more important duties."

"Answer the question, Mimi."

"I did answer it, when your friend here asked ten minutes ago. Mary Irene's neighbor, Jen Dill, called me to say she had to take her son to the doctor and asked if I could take care of Yeats. I have now done that, so if I'm free to go—"

I didn't wait for his response and returned the phone to my temporary police handler. He got an earful from Quinn, who was rather irritated, unless I missed my guess. I could hear shouting on the other end of the line, something like, "No, she has *not* stolen the victim's identity. We aren't even sure if Mary Irene Jones *is* a victim," though I couldn't make out everything that was being said.

After several minutes of intradepartmental discourse, the officer motioned me out of the yard and returned my driver's license. "I'll finish up here with the dog, Ms. Jones." Yeats looked at me sadly.

"Bye, Yeats." I blew him a kiss. "Time for you to go back to doggy jail for a little while. Don't miss me too much." They stood on the sidewalk and watched me pull away. I imagined sad brown puppy eyes as Yeats watched yet another familiar person leave him.

About a block away, the words I'd just said, "Don't miss me too much," made me hit the brake. I parked along a grassy shoulder, put my emergency flashers on, and scrolled through the photos on my phone. I searched back to that first day at MIJ's house, when Quinn invited me and Sharon to look around for anything that might look like a clue to Mary Irene's disappearance. No, that wasn't right, I took the picture later, the day I handed the care of Yeats off to Jen Dill.

"There you are." My picture of the photo framed and sitting on MIJ's fireplace mantel. The young couple with a baby, posed in front of a barn. I expanded it as much as my fingers would allow, to bring the faces into focus.

The woman was definitely Jen. The identity of the man and the location of that barn sent me racing back to the college again. It was starting to feel as if I lived on campus. If I set up a tent on the quad, would anyone have been shocked?

Unfortunately for me, this last trip of the day would take me back to the hated library stacks, where who knew what variety of Yeti-sized creep might await. With a recently acquired can of pepper spray in my pocket, I ducked in, then hurried to locate and check out *Mary Irene Jones and Northern Ireland*, a coffee table book that had virtually nothing to do with the poetry MIJ wrote. What it did have, in an effort to capitalize on her fame, were gorgeous photos of her birthplace and the town where she grew up, as well as abundant scenes of agricultural life in that part of Ulster.

Lots of barns—images big enough to compare to an enlarged cellphone photo, I hoped. And maybe one that fit a fragment of poetry I'd read that morning in MIJ's manuscripts, from the binder called "Now."

> *Silence frightens,*
> *or rather, the prospect of it*
> *when the workday is without conversation,*
> *without consultation,*
> *without convergence of our labour in the produce we grow,*
> *when the evening brings paused plows, stilled voices.*
> *Listen, but for what?*

What indeed? The sounds unheard in this book's random photographs? A wordless travelogue of the poet's soul?

Mary Irene Jones had told the world little about her early life. We couldn't know what we didn't know, we could only follow where others' speculations took us, and that had led precisely nowhere thus far. Who was to say the barn in the picture of Jen Dill and her family wasn't significant?

I emailed the photo of the framed picture to myself. When I got home, I opened the image on my laptop, enlarged it as much as I could, and looked for a match in the *MIJ and Northern Ireland* book. A few of the barns could have been a match based on paint color, but the photo of Jen, her baby, and, presumably, her husband, didn't offer much architectural context. It was hard to know what the other sides of the barn looked like, or to get a better feel for its setting. What type of animals lived inside the barn, just sheep? Which crops grew around it? What country was it even in?

After too many hours of staring at rustic scenes, I gave up, went to bed, and snuggled against Barrett. But not before I planned a few stops for the next morning.

My presence at her door at 6:15 a.m. surprised my mother, though it shouldn't have—I texted her twice and left a voice message. She was usually up with the birds. Yet Cass appeared at the door in her bathrobe, violating Protocol Number One of the M. Catherine Jones Etiquette Handbook: Always present your best face to the public.

"Mom, are you all right?"

"No, I feel like crap. What time is it?" Cass squinted into the thin morning sunlight. "What do you want, Mimi?"

I eased her backward into the foyer and turned her toward the kitchen. "Flu? Hangover? What can I get you, coffee or ibuprofen?" She pointed to the vintage cookie jar where she kept her vitamins, etc. "Allergy pill please. Sinus headache kept me up most of the night. Should have stumbled down here to get one then."

We're pretty susceptible to medication, my mother, my sister, and I, some inherited trait or another. In a few minutes,

Cass was almost back to normal, but I didn't want to push it—I needed her brain fully functioning. I brewed her some strong coffee, the way she liked it, and toasted a bagel for her and served it up browned and crunchy and ready for the cream cheese and blackberry preserves I set before her. Then I excused myself and found in my late father's desk photo albums of his boyhood home in rural central Pennsylvania. Barns abounded in those pictures, at least in my recollection they did.

Cass followed me. "You came here to look at your dad's albums?" she asked around a bite of bagel, thus violating another of her etiquette dictums, the rule about not talking with one's mouth full or otherwise behaving as if one had been raised by wolves.

"I'm trying to figure out if this barn is somewhere nearby." I opened my laptop and showed her the enhanced photo of Jen Dill and her family. "Or it might be in Northern Ireland. You and Dad spent a lot of time at the farm when you were first married and again when Poppa got sick. What do you think?"

Cass had reading glasses in a pocket of her robe; she kept pairs everywhere. "It's a bank barn for sure. Is it in Pennsylvania? Could be, or else someplace like Maryland. Your grandfather loved the one on his property, built by his English ancestors on his mother's side. So if the barn in this picture isn't in the United States, I suppose it could be British."

I paged through three of the albums and pulled out a few snapshots of the barn at Poppa's farm. "And where do you think you're taking those? Mimi, don't."

"I'll bring them back, I promise, Mom. I just need to borrow them for a day or so." I stepped around her and back into the kitchen. I poured a few sips of coffee, drank them down, and grabbed my purse. "Gotta dash. Feel better."

No way I was waiting around for her lecture about keeping family memories intact for the next generation. My niece was four years old, my nephew, two—time was on my side where they were concerned. But possibly not when it came to Jen Dill. I didn't know what her situation was. She said her son went to preschool a few days a week. Did she work outside the home? Work remotely from home?

I made it from Mom's condo over the city line to Jen's house in Upper Roxborough in twenty-eight minutes on roads already sluggish with morning rush-hour traffic. Two cars were parked outside, though getting Jen alone seemed like my best move. I took a space closer to MIJ's house, hoping I'd missed the police patrol's latest cruise-by. After about ten minutes, a dark-haired man I recognized as the guy from the barn photo came out of Jen's house, got into the smaller of the two cars, and drove off. I walked to the door and rang her bell.

"Mimi, hi, what's up? Wait, is there news about Mary Irene?"

"Sorry, no, not that I know of. I didn't mean to worry you. Do you have a second to talk? It's not urgent if you need to take the little guy to preschool."

She checked her watch. "Come on in, we have a few minutes before we have to get going. Liam is eating breakfast now. It's a cereal and vanilla yogurt morning, beware the sticky surfaces everywhere."

The house was a twin of MIJ's. Jen led me past a hall table bearing the identical photo of her, a baby, and the man who had just departed, and into the kitchen, where she introduced me to her son. Liam looked to be about two years old now, same as my nephew. I waved, he laughed. I noticed the spoon in his left hand and positioned myself as far from his throwing arm as possible.

"Everything go okay with Yeats yesterday?" I asked. "I had to leave in a bit of a hurry — the police officer responsible for patrolling the block wasn't happy to see an unauthorized person, me that is, on Mary Irene's property."

"You're joking, right?"

"Nope. He took one look at my driver's license, freaked out when he saw the name on it, and called it in. From what I could overhear of the conversation, Detective Quinn disabused him of the notion that I had stolen Mary Irene's identity and that Yeats and I were criminal associates."

Jen laughed, which elicited giggles from Liam, yogurt all over his chin and along part of his left cheek. She pulled a fistful of baby wipes out of a strategically located container, tidied up her son, and disengaged the straps on his booster seat.

"Anyway, I thought you'd like to know that the police are watching Mary Irene's house very closely. Waiting for her to return or for somebody else to show up, who knows? But I'll get out of your hair. Sorry to delay you and Liam."

"No worries, I really appreciate that you came to the rescue yesterday." Jen hoisted Liam onto her hip and preceded me into the hall. Where I stopped, naturally.

"Hey, that's the same picture Mary Irene has on her mantel, isn't it? Great old barn, looks like the one at my grandfather's farm near Harrisburg. Were you guys on vacation?"

Jen set Liam down and picked up the photo. "I'd forgotten I gave a copy of this to her. We were in the Lake District in England. My husband has family there."

"Such a beautiful part of the U.K. Is your husband English?"

"No, just has relatives living there." Jen grabbed her keys, her purse, and a small backpack with dinosaurs on it. "Time to hit the trail, buddy. Ready for school?"

"Yessssss," Liam assured us.

I wanted to learn more, but that was my cue to say adios. "I have to get to school too. Have a great day, guys."

I pulled away just as a patrol car turned onto the block.

Chapter Eleven

Small colleges and small towns had a lot in common: News traveled fast.

Within minutes of the committee's announcement that I would deliver the keynote address at the upcoming Mary Irene Jones Poetry Festival, the decision was being applauded, or questioned, or mocked, all over social media. Since then, students who didn't know me from Sylvia Plath had been staring or whispering as they passed me on campus. The ones whose grades I controlled congratulated me or figured out some way to similarly high-five me.

I had already sketched out the speech, spending less time on smooth composition and more than was wise on consumption of caffeine, alcohol, and the dark chocolate rabbits I'd bought half-price at the after-Easter sales. After reading the keynote-in-progress in front of a mirror at home and timing it, I decided it needed to simmer for a while.

I reviewed the rest of my to-do list as I sat with my laptop on a bench at the wooded far edge of the college grounds. That list included the thing I had spent a lot of time talking about lately and little time doing — writing poetry. Exposing myself to even this tiny bit of nature, quietly considering it, would, I rationalized, do wonders for my creative output overall and one very important speech in particular.

Quiet was tougher to achieve than I expected, however, what with people going out of their way to stop by and chat. Still others gawked. I'd written only this so far:

There once was a poet from Philly
Whose assignment had proved quite a dilly
Her ideas were trash
She might write better smashed
Incoherent is better than silly.

"Not your best work, but not bad for a shitty first draft. I'd be interested in seeing where the revision takes you."

Crap. Sister Marlene was reading over my shoulder and quoting Anne Lamott's wisdom about writing, to boot.

I shifted on the bench and offered her a space to sit.

She sat. Double crap.

"I'm interrupting you, my apologies, Mimi." She pulled sunglasses from her jacket pocket. "It's such a lovely day. Reminds me of the spring I spent in England the year before I took my final vows, when I wondered whether I *should* take them. I was quite distracted, as I suspect you are right now."

That, I was. "Happens to me especially when I'm ambivalent about the thing I prefer to tell myself I most want to do. The biggest obstacle to a poem by me is, at the moment, me."

To my surprise, she pulled a cigarette from another pocket. "I won't light this, though I really want to. Just holding it helps me remember what I enjoyed about smoking. Helps me face down the temptation, or so I prefer to tell myself."

She lifted the cigarette to her lips and caressed it there for the briefest moment. "When we relinquish something, we don't always realize how hard it will be to do without it. How hard it will be once we become the person who has given it up."

Regret, viewed not so much as being about loss as about how loss changes us. Poetry fodder, for sure. Sister Marlene put the cigarette away and turned on the bench to look at me more directly.

"Sharon Bernstein thinks very highly of you. I know you don't believe that, probably even less so now that I've all but ordered her to put you on full time. But it's not just a quid pro quo for the keynote address. It will be your job to lose."

What was she trying to say? "Publish or perish, that's even more important for the creative-writing faculty. I get it, Sister."

She kicked off the blue clogs she wore and wiggled her toes in the grass in front of her. "I was in my twenties when I met Mary Irene Jones that summer before I took my vows. We became fast friends—we loved poetry, of course, and we talked about our favorites endlessly. We even talked about creating a writing competition someday to encourage young women poets like ourselves. Mary Irene joked that we would be the perfect judges, since we were the two sides of a penny: She was the clangorous, chaotic one; I was the contemplative, controlled one."

"Opposites, in other words?"

Sister Marlene stared at toenails painted a vivid teal. "Opposites, and not. She was at a crossroads then like I was, having set out on a certain path but questioning it. I feared I would rue a decision to forgo marriage and children. Mary Irene feared the pressures of success, though in her case fear of *continuing* success might have been more accurate. We were two women about the same age who happened upon each other by chance in England as we both were having crises of confidence."

Confidence was not something Sister Marlene seemed to lack. I couldn't speak to Mary Irene's issues with it, just my own.

"Do you think I'm having a crisis, Sister? I know Sharon has her reservations about me. Why don't I finish my dissertation and get my doctorate, that's one of her favorite topics."

"And why don't you?"

Because I no longer felt as if I had anything new to say? Probably not something I should acknowledge to the college president and onetime head of the English Department, but how often was I genuinely honest about the fact that I no longer saw my dissertation as proof of concept, and the writing of it worthwhile?

"When I inherited the house I now live in from my grandmother—another Mary Irene Jones, God help us—I thought I'd explore further through my poems and associated research the ways in which personal agency derives from personal location. The whole 'Who we are is where we are' thing. My grandmother's house was a place where I played as a child, where I found comfort when my father, her son, died just before my twelfth birthday. The place I fled to when my marriage ended and I had no freaking idea what I was going to do with the rest of my life."

Sister Marlene smiled knowingly. "Except the poems didn't come."

"Not exactly. The *right* poems didn't come. The ones I could pound into anything that didn't sound incoherent or silly, I offered to anthologies, which deemed them worthy and published them. So words weren't the problem—it was finding the words that expressed who I had been at that house, who I was now, and who I hoped to become. After a while, I simply stopped searching for them."

An alarm buzzed on her smart watch. "I have a meeting in ten minutes. They'll just have to wait for me to start. I have no intention of sprinting to the administration building."

Sister Marlene rose stiffly. She lifted her arms over her head and twisted at her waist. "I love spring, but the seasonal temperature variations don't love me. That's one thing I took away from my time in England all those years ago, the spring I first met Mary Irene. The other lessons we both learned, I think: that the only expectations you'll never truly meet are the ones you set for yourself; that only if you strive as hard as you can to achieve them will you ever come close; and that if you don't strive at all, total failure is inevitable."

She reached out and patted my hand, as my grandmother used to when I was a child and my mother seldom did.

"Sister, are you worried about Mary Irene? I'd hate not knowing where my friend might be."

She thought a minute. "Worried, yet also not. Mary Irene has always gone her own way, though where that might be leading her today, I couldn't say. Even after all the years she's spent in this country, I have never felt as close to her as I did that spring in England. The Lake District must have cast a spell."

I had been under that spell. Daniel and I went to the Lakes on our honeymoon. We visited the great Romantic poet William Wordsworth's house in Grasmere. Who we were when we were there had mattered.

But it didn't anymore. Daniel and I had dissolved a long time ago, and so had the future with him that I'd envisioned. If pressed, I could barely articulate a vision of my present. It was mortifying to realize how stuck I still was, my writing being a glaring symptom of what ailed my life.

Maybe MIJ kept that photo of Jen Dill and her family on the mantel for a reason—as a reminder of the time she had spent in the Lake District reconciling her past with what she hoped lay ahead.

Because my protest poetry students had contributed mightily to the keynote, I decided to run through my speech with them, to be sure of pronunciations, to ensure that the music and video clips were the timeliest possible—basically, to see whether I would be making a fool out of myself in any way except the obvious one, in which I attempted to take on MIJ's much-honored role as the voice of the festival.

The class critiqued, and I tweaked wording as we went along, editing the text on the projection screen for everyone to see. After ninety minutes we were satisfied, and I uploaded everything—speech, clips, and some old BBC footage of Mary Irene at a One Ireland protest in London several decades ago—so the college multimedia crew could get to work. I copied it all onto a memory stick for Sharon as well.

Whether Sharon would have even a minute to look at it was doubtful. We were five days from show time. It had been four weeks since Mary Irene Jones dropped off the radar.

That new poem I was hoping for, maybe even publish somewhere in advance of the special occasion that was MIJ Fest, refused to write itself. Cerebral congestion might not be a medical thing, but it was afflicting me, with no cure in sight. I contemplated a cross-country drive, to force me to pay attention to anything but the void that existed in my skull. A couple days here, a couple days there; I'd never been to the Grand Canyon or Vegas. Daydreams about Elvis impersonators and high-stakes blackjack games ought to help knock images of Mimi Jones, impostor and literary fraud, out of my consciousness. But, no, that would have been easy. Also, I would miss the poetry festival and likely damage my career, such as it was, for many years to come.

The better option was to scoop into my bag twenty blue books, each representing a final class project. My students' assignment: original lyrics to protest songs of their own, no fewer than six verses plus a repeating chorus, with accompanying explanations about the inspiration for their lyrics and why and how their work had been influenced by noteworthy songwriters or poets, either contemporary or from the past. The final counted for sixty percent of the grade. In semesters past, there had been a few excellent examples of protest lyrics. I gave credit for the idea behind the verses and the effort to make the vision come alive. Actual musical execution was, of course, more than I could ask of students not enrolled in a music program.

I expected to spend the rest of the day reading the lyrics aloud, hearing them rather than only seeing them on the page. I refused to let my students submit their final projects on the college's online platform for assignments, arguing that poetry — especially protest poetry—needed to be not only visceral but sensual in all ways, including tactile. I staked out a picnic table along the perimeter of the quad, armed with two bottles of water and a pack of gum, to keep me from getting hoarse.

From that vantage, I could see a township police car, a campus police car, and a black sedan parked in the loading area behind the building housing the English Department. A meeting about security for MIJ Fest was on Sharon's calendar, according to the online planning document she circulated with the committee, of which I was now a member. I had declined the official invitation to this gathering, citing the need for grading speed.

A text foiled my plan. "My office, now!!" Sharon commanded. "We'll wait, so we don't have to repeat ourselves. Everybody needs to be on board with this strategy, especially you, since you'll be front and center as the keynote speaker."

Minutes later, I was crowded with the rest of the committee around the table in Sharon's office, where the township police chief and the head of campus security simultaneously urged calm and extreme vigilance. Not to diminish their expertise in emergency management, but their slide presentation seemed on the same kindergarten level as the annual Fire Prevention Month visits we got in elementary school: Know where the exits are, drop to the floor, and crawl toward them if you smell smoke or see fire. The chiefs did not add the more nuanced active-shooter protocols we heard repeatedly the first week of every semester. I could only hope that was intentional, that they did not honestly believe someone might take a shot at me or anyone else during the festival. I channeled my grandmother— Mary Irene the First, as I'd come to think of her—and said a quick prayer to Our Lady of Perpetual Help, her go-to when intercession was needed.

"Do we have a good plan?" Sharon asked. "Have we covered all the bases?"

The township police chief deferred to his on-campus counterpart, who dodged the question. "Dr. Bernstein, the only true way to gauge whether a plan is effective is to have everyone on site emerge unscathed from a crisis situation," he said. "There are so many variables with the kind of crowd the festival might attract this year. We are increasing the number of uniformed and plainclothes security personnel, and bags will be checked at the entrance."

"Checked how? Eyes only? Metal detectors? Or do you also anticipate explosives, thus necessitating body searches and bomb-sniffing dogs?" A nervous Sharon was a snippy Sharon. She had been pacing the carpet behind my chair throughout their PowerPoint.

"That hardly seems necessary in the absence of any known threats against Mary Irene Jones herself or the college in general. But we intend to control what we can control," the township police chief said. "We must anticipate, but there's no crystal ball. We can't see into the future."

Sharon sank into a chair and put her head in her hands. "I foresee a disaster. Who knows how Mary Irene's fans are reacting to the news of Mimi as keynote speaker?"

I slid the memory stick with my speech and the audio/visual material across the tabletop toward her. "Thanks for the vote of confidence. I have finals to grade."

Enraged, I marched out. I had had it up to here with being afraid, and with being dictated to. And I was certainly not about to let Sharon Bernstein insult me in front of these people, Sister Marlene's earlier words about a full-time faculty position notwithstanding. If MIJ Fest flopped, there was always next year—the college would survive. Sharon would be screwed more if twenty students didn't get their grades on time, and twenty sets of parents shelling out tens of thousands of dollars each year to send their darlings to this school decided not to do so hereafter. She could chew on that.

My usual picnic table was occupied, so I hoofed it to a bench in front of the bell tower, pulled out a red pen and a blue book, and resumed grading a protest lyric about the latest U.S. involvement in foreign wars. The writer was wise not to try to rhyme phrases about surveillance drones and refugees, though the unrhymed phrases he did write were not exactly smooth. I made a few suggestions in the margins.

"Don't you have an office?"

I didn't have to look up to know who had interrupted me. "I'm an adjunct; I have a mail slot. Also, a verdant campus on which to do my work *al fresco*."

Quinn put his right foot up on the bench and leaned over until our heads were about level. "You're an odd bug, Mimi Jones."

"And you're out of your police department's jurisdiction, Mike Quinn, unless you were supposed to be part of the big MIJ Fest security confab I just exited."

He chewed a wad of gum furiously. "I'm here to inform the college president that Philly P.D. is putting its investigation on the back burner. The FBI's financial unit says there's no evidence of suspicious money transfers to or from Mary Irene Jones, so we're back to not knowing whether a crime has even been committed. No sign she booked plane tickets, rental cars, cruise accommodations, or anything else suggesting she left town on her own, but there's also no sign she didn't. No recent Jane Does in any U.S. database that match the fingerprints we took from her house and car. No ransom demands have been made. No charges at all on her credit cards in almost five weeks now, but we know she pulled cash out of that one bank account. She may or may not have her phone—whatever she used all these years isn't registered with any of the major carriers and either doesn't have a tracking feature or it's been disabled."

A dull ache settled over my eye, the one closest to Quinn's face. "It's been four full weeks. Her lawyer hasn't heard from her?"

"No, and Jordan Lisle is under orders to report to me if he does. Officially, she's still missing, but with every day that goes by, my gut tells me something different—"

"—That something else is going on."

Quinn saluted, stepped away from the bench, and headed for Sister Marlene's office, having killed what was left of my focus on the budding protest poets.

All my pet parents had returned from wherever it was that prompted them to hire me as a sitter. Not even a hamster to take care of. So I packed up my paperwork and made for my car, throwing my bag onto the passenger seat just as the skies opened and dumped sheets of rain over our quiet academic corner of the Philadelphia suburbs.

I knocked off five blue books before the headache got so bad I had to rest my eyes. Not that the pain had anything to do with eyestrain necessarily, it might have been the change in atmospheric pressure. More likely, it was brain strain and stress.

What was MIJ up to? Where was she?

The woman was mystifying, everyone at the college agreed. She never showed up in person to the poetry festival she created, instead doing that damn video every year so—she claimed—she could go out and make the cash that underwrote the damn award. She tolerated corporate and foundation sponsorships, but only for promoting and staging the festival. The prize bore her name, and she would come up with the money. She made demands like a monarch. Yet people who knew her liked Mary Irene, even as they complained that she was picky and could be downright bitchy at times.

The year I won the Mary Irene Jones Poetry Award, her comments about my work were enlightening, uplifting, flattering, and utterly wonderful. I memorized every word, quoting them endlessly to poor Daniel. She had urged me to get in touch via the college if I had any questions about what she had written, and wished me the best of luck in my career. And then, a month ago, she left her own unpublished work in my care.

For what seemed like the millionth time, I wondered if it was it an act of faith in me. But for the first time, I speculated: Was it just a ploy to divert attention from her?

My doorbell rang, and I instantly knew who it was—my partner in crime, or possibly no crime at all. He had a six pack of craft beer in one hand and a pizza box in the other.

"What kind of pizza?"

"I asked myself, 'What would Mary Irene eat?' I decided on pesto chicken."

Good answer, though any pizza without anchovies would have been a winner. I bowed and waved an off-duty Mike Quinn through my door once again. As before, he'd been to the gym. This time, he was freshly showered, though he hadn't shaved. I, at least, had shoes on.

"I owe you dinner, Mimi. Plus, the Mary Irene Jones case is inactive now—no more police guardians officially, they ended as abruptly as they began. So I figured you could use comfort food. I also figured the element of surprise would work in my favor. Was I right?"

The fragrance of basil and garlic rising from the pizza was certainly working for him. Okay, so was the post-gym vibe.

"Is this your usual protocol with onetime, albeit for a short time, persons of interest, Detective?"

He smiled a smile that made me feel gorgeous, even in rolled-up jeans and my ex-husband's old Chase Utley Phillies jersey. "I'm making it up as I go along here. Kind of creative so far, don't you think?"

After depositing the pizza on my coffee table, he walked straight to the kitchen and checked the fridge door for wine. Finding white, he spun around to the cabinet where I kept the glasses, found one, and poured me some. He twisted the top off one of the beers and joined me on the couch. Under the lid of the pizza box, balanced on one of those little plastic things that look like tables for a fairy tea party, were paper plates and napkins. Barrett poked his head into the room. Quinn crumbled some chicken onto a napkin for him.

"You just won over my cat. An easy victory."

"Depends on the endgame, of course."

The California Sauvignon blanc was as smooth as Quinn. I savored the taste, my jangled nerves unknotted, and I sank into whatever was happening. Two glasses and two slices in, I still had fifteen finals to grade and a speech to rehearse, but I really didn't care. None of which I mentioned to Quinn, who fetched his third beer from my refrigerator, resumed his position at my side, and stretched as if he'd never felt so relaxed.

Maybe we were mellow because we hadn't said much to each other in almost half an hour. Maybe it was because of the alcohol. All I knew was that when he leaned in and kissed me, it was what I wanted, and I kissed him back.

Michael Quinn was one hell of a kisser. I imagined other fine talents he might demonstrate if one thing led to another. Instead, his phone buzzed and vibrated off my coffee table, and he knocked over a lamp as he twisted to reach for it.

"What?" Quinn barked, presumably at some poor junior officer who had been told to call him even though he was off duty. "Jesus. Tell them I'll meet them at the scene."

He tucked his shirt into his jeans. At the kitchen sink, he splashed water on his face, then swished some in his mouth and spit. I righted the lamp and waited for information.

"There was a break-in at Mary Irene's house. Patrol just called it in."

"I'm going too."

Quinn leaned over the back of the couch, smooched me full on the lips, and sighed. "Like I could stop you."

No, he couldn't. No way.

Chapter Twelve

Squad cars lined the block. Neighbors clustered on the sidewalk to watch the action. Police radio chatter filled the air, growing louder as I got closer but no easier to understand. It was like an episode of one of those crime shows in permanent rotation on cable television.

My detective friend leaned against his car, watching as a pair of uniformed cops exited the house, holstering their weapons. A plainclothes guy, another detective I supposed, followed them out and walked straight to Quinn, notebook in hand.

For an interested bystander like me, the best view of the scene was from one house over, where Jen Dill had stationed herself midway between her front door and the curb. I parked my car and joined her there. "All the commotion didn't wake Liam, I hope."

Jen held a baby monitor. I could see her little boy turning from his tummy onto his back, kicking a stuffed monkey aside as he rolled.

"Surprisingly, it didn't, though that may not last long," she said, sounding as if she'd like to join Liam in dreamland. "I'm glad we haven't switched him into a big boy's bed yet. If he tries to climb out of the crib, I should be able to see him in time to make a dash for his room."

"My nephew is about Liam's age. He's a master of the crib escape, no doubt with help from his big sister. Some fear of missing out is going on there, for sure—if Deirdre's on the loose, Duncan wants out."

A police van pulled up onto Mary Irene's lawn, disgorging crime scene techs wearing uniform jackets I recognized from my first visit to this street. "Any idea what happened tonight?"

"Not really." Jen fussed with the diamond-encrusted gold band on her left hand. "Yeats started barking like crazy about an hour ago, but that's not unusual. He spends a lot of time looking out the side window toward Mary Irene's house, as if he expects her to show up any minute. I was folding laundry and didn't pay any attention, just shook the bag of doggy treats. After he ate a couple of those, he quieted down and stayed that way, despite arrival of the police."

She didn't question my presence in the neighborhood, for which I was grateful. I didn't know how I would have explained that.

I could see Quinn on his phone, nodding every so often at what was being said on the other end but saying little. The only word of his that I could make out was "inventory," which made sense. They would no doubt have to compare the list of what had been in the house that first day with what was there now. Sounded like a very long night. Many of the neighbors had already lost interest and gone inside. Was it worth it for me to stay? Quinn probably wouldn't have time to talk to me, and it might prove awkward if someone he worked with put two and two together and figured out how I knew to be here.

Just then, Jen tossed the evening's second curveball my way.

"I guess we'll be taking Yeats with us when we move to South Carolina. A corporate relocation team is coming to pack us up—it's the only good thing about being transferred—and Liam and I will be on the road early Saturday morning."

What? Was that even possible? Yeats wasn't her dog, he was Mary Irene's. Once again, I felt as if I had walked into the middle of the story.

"You never mentioned you were moving, Jen. If I had known, I wouldn't have asked you to care for Yeats full time."

"No problem, I didn't give it a second thought. Yeats is such a sweetheart," she said. "I'm driving down, so *that* will be interesting, alone in a car for two days with Liam plus the dog plus a load of plants and boxes. But this way, my husband and I don't have to transport my car separately. And once we're all living in one spot again, everything we own will be there too. We probably can't afford to buy a house anytime soon, but someday I'll own a place like this one. And I'll miss Philly."

Sounded as if the plan called for Jen's husband to drive down ahead of them. She was one brave woman—but also sort of presumptuous, not that I wanted the dog.

"Have you talked to anyone about taking Yeats with you, like Mr. Lisle, Mary Irene's lawyer?"

"I would never leave without letting someone know I'd taken Yeats. What if Mary Irene comes back?"

Yes, that was the big question. Saturday's poetry festival raised the stakes higher every day.

"Uh-oh, Liam's awake. Gotta go." Jen hustled inside, abandoning me on the sidewalk. Quinn heard her door shut and looked over.

My phone vibrated with a text. "Head home. This will take a while," he wrote. "I'll be in touch."

I texted him a thumbs-up. Then I snapped a picture of Jen's license plate. Like letting Mike Quinn kiss me silly earlier, it seemed like a good idea.

Not even three more protest poetry finals could put me to sleep, I was so amped. I told myself I wasn't waiting up to hear from Quinn. "I'll be in touch" wasn't commonly accepted code for "I'll call you as soon as I can." But since I couldn't slow my brain down, waiting up was exactly what I was doing.

Eventually, though, fatigue vanquished the urge to grade papers. I woke up on the sofa, a blue book on my chest and Barrett on my stomach, with no idea how long I had been zonked out. I found my phone wedged between my hip and the couch cushion. My lock screen informed me that it was the Wednesday before the Saturday of the Mary Irene Jones Poetry Festival; my only class did not start for another six hours. Praise the Lord.

Barrett licked my hand, then bit me, commonly accepted code for "Get your butt moving and feed me." I dragged myself into the kitchen, poured some dry food into his dish, and prayed coffee would miraculously appear.

And then it did.

Per his latest routine before showing up at my house, Quinn had recently showered, or maybe he'd just stuck his head under the faucet, my powers of perception were not especially keen. But he came bearing French Roast and croissants, thus guaranteeing him entry. I unlocked the front door and ran to the bathroom, to at least brush my teeth and comb my hair before facing the man I had been kissing mere hours ago, before a certain missing poet cosmically intervened.

"Looking good," he teased on my return, handing me a cup and depositing a fistful of sweeteners and creamers on the coffee table. "Weren't you expecting me? I'm crushed."

I gave him a dirty look and took a sip of black coffee. I needed my caffeine uncut just then.

"After last night? I'm not sure what to expect anymore."

"Hmm," he said, moving in for a not-so-tame kiss. "Damn, that's good, but we need to talk shop."

That sounded ominous. I helped myself to a croissant, flaky crumbs falling to the rug for a grateful Barrett to sample. Damn, that was good, too, extra credit to Quinn for his breakfast selection.

"Can't talk with my mouth full," I mumbled between bites. "You go first."

He winked and shifted to the wing chair, sliding his cup and croissant over. "Safer here. More professional."

I nibbled and nodded.

"Ms. Jones, I want more than anything in the world right now for your namesake to turn up some way, somehow, so we can close this case. Every time I think the department is finished with it, something hits the fan, last night being yet another sterling example. World's worst timing."

With even that small reminder of what had been interrupted, I felt incredibly warm all over. "Did you guys figure out what went on at Mary Irene's house? How did the intruder get in?"

"Talk about one weird mess. I didn't leave that house until after four a.m., and I still can't make any of what happened there add up." Quinn took a long pull of his coffee. "First off, the patrol guys didn't get word that we were back-burnering the case, so the middle shift cruised by and saw lights on in the house, on the first floor. God forbid Mary Irene should have any kind of alarm, let alone a silent alarm or a camera on the place, so the officer called it in, and the desk called me. Before the guy in the cruiser could confirm whether there was anyone inside the house, the lights were off again. We knew it couldn't be as simple as an animal setting off a motion detector, because Mary Irene doesn't have those inside or out. So even before I arrived, the patrol officer was ordered to look for signs of forced entry. First thing you have to do, right? But entry hadn't been forced, so either our intruder had a key, or the front door was unlocked. We've checked those doors once a shift for the last four weeks. Every time but this one, they were locked."

I had needed the key to get inside the day I handed care of Yeats off to Jen. When I left, I double-checked to be sure the door was locked. And the patrol cop who pounced when I turned up there unannounced to walk Yeats probably had checked the door at some point.

"So last night, we combed the entire property again," Quinn said, "and I went through every line of the inventory we took during our initial search. Only thing missing as far as we can tell is the white tea set that was in the kitchen. No manufacturer's mark on it, according to the inventory, nothing that indicates it can be fenced for much cash."

I closed my eyes and remembered what I had found in this house when my grandmother left it to me: lots of things with no value other than sentimental. Would somebody have strolled into Mary Irene's house just to take a tea set, the same way someone might have walked in here and taken the blanket my grandmother crocheted?

I moved into the kitchen to brew more coffee. "What are you thinking, Mimi?" Quinn called from the couch. "I can hear the mental gears grinding."

I made him wait until the carafe was full. "Does Mary Irene have a will?" I finally asked, removing the takeout cup from Quinn's hand and filling it with the fresh stuff.

He blew a kiss, waved away the steam rising from his cup, and sipped. "She does, according to Lawyer Lisle, who said it dictates that a permanent self-sustaining fund be established at the college to endow the poetry award. Current market value of her house is conservatively about $450,000, Lisle said, and that's without the contents."

That tea set was worth something to someone. "Was there anything inside the tea pot, did the inventory list say? A key maybe, or money?"

Quinn put up a "One moment please" finger and typed into his phone. "About a half-dozen British coins, the inventory says, all from the late 1970s and in ascending denomination. You know, like a person might have a full set of penny, nickel, dime, quarter, half-dollar, dollar."

The coins would have some value in this country depending on the exchange rate between the British pound and the dollar, whether they dated to before MIJ's arrival in the United States or after. "But would someone want the coins alone? The tea set, if it has any value, might be worth more because Mary Irene owned it."

"Correct, Ms. Jones, so round and round and round we go. But get this: The stolen tea set wasn't even the best part of my late-night adventure. I got a text from Jordan Lisle about three a.m. apologizing for leading us down a blind alley. Said Mary Irene Jones never implied that she was wary of any danger, that he may have misinterpreted her desire to maintain regular contact with him. What does *that* mean?"

Quinn put his elbows on his knees and his head in his hands. "I shouldn't be telling you any of this, but geez, at least you understand how it feels. Mary Irene Jones dumped on you the only thing that may have any value at all — those manuscripts."

Was entrusting them to me an insurance policy? Was MIJ trying to keep Jordan Lisle's hands off her unpublished work, so he'd see no financial gain from the manuscripts, not even legal fees for representing her estate?

Quinn's thoughts were racing down the same track. "Does Lisle now top a suspect list of exactly one in her disappearance? I guess I'll spend a lot of today trying to figure that out."

"While you're at it, ask Lisle about the dog. Jen Dill told me last night that she's moving to South Carolina, and that she and her husband plan to take Yeats with them. I told her to get in touch with Mary Irene's lawyer."

I fluttered my eyelashes at him, knowing that I had added one more thing to a long to-do list. "Please, Mike. Yeats deserves a good home with someone who loves him."

"As long as you're not that person, right?"

I walked behind his chair and massaged his shoulders. He sighed as I pressed my knuckle into a knot of stress. "I understand you probably wish you'd never been assigned this case. Hang around me, Detective, and you'll never be rid of Mary Irene Jones problems."

He twisted, wound a hand around my wrist, and tugged me down onto his lap. "You're the genuine MIJ," he said, then nibbled his way along my throat.

"Ah, but you've read only my winning Mary Irene Jones Award entries. Maybe the rest of my poetry is garbage."

"I've seen enough to know what I like."

I debated whether he was being sweet or shrewd. A couple more morning kisses, Quinn was out of the door, and I was no longer sure I cared.

It was a hole from which I might never emerge. Six protest poetry finals left to grade, plus the last class itself, plus rehearsing the poetry festival keynote, plus a meeting with the A-V team to go over the cues. And Quinn, breathtaking man that he was, had me so flustered I couldn't think straight. I found myself staring at the photos on my phone of the tea set now missing from MIJ's house and of Jen Dill and her husband and little Liam.

I switched over to my laptop, to the enlarged version of the latter picture. I ran Jen's name through a search engine, and a handful of Jennifer Dills appeared with links to a popular business social media site. That seemed the most likely place someone might post about a change of job or a job-related relocation.

Our Jen, Jennifer Noreen Dill, had graduated two years earlier from an Ivy League school in New England, so she was roughly twenty-four years old. Did two internships while in college, moved to Philadelphia for a marketing job with a biotech company, left that job after six months, and currently characterized herself as a freelance marketing contractor. Liam's birth probably contributed to that decision. Her husband's career seemed the likely reason they would be moving.

I sent Jen a request to connect — it was the best way to see who her contacts were — and she responded right away with a "Hi, Mimi!" and a waving-hand emoji. I dug in immediately, guessing she was probably doing the same on her end. Listed among her connections was Conor Tilden, whose head shot showed a cute guy about Jen's age who looked just like the man in the photo she had given MIJ.

Conor Tilden had gone to the same Ivy League school as Jen for undergrad. He was a systems engineer and worked for a multinational consulting firm. Apparently got his master's degree last year in Philly. His profile offered those few facts and nothing more.

Jen and Conor were an attractive young couple with an adorable toddler and were probably relocating to advance professionally. Not unlike Daniel and I once were, without the small child, though we had talked about maybe having one or two.

Don't go down that reminiscence rabbit hole, I warned myself. Keep your eye on the ball.

I glanced at the short list of Conor's business-website contacts for something that jumped out. Couldn't say what I was looking for, but figured I'd know it when I saw it. Except I didn't.

Jen answered my phone call on the second ring. "Mimi, hi, I'm on my way to pick up Liam, so I only have a few minutes."

"I was wondering whether you talked to Mary Irene's lawyer about taking her dog with you to South Carolina. If it's not happening after all, I can talk to my pet-sitting agency about arranging for someone to foster Yeats."

Car horns blared in the background. "Sorry, traffic is a beast this afternoon, and now I'm stuck behind a trash-collection crew. I left Mr. Lisle a voicemail a few minutes ago and got a text back saying that, as far as he was concerned, we could take Yeats with us because there was no one else to care for him."

As a lawyer, Jordan Lisle would know about property rights and how they pertained to pet ownership. Still, it seemed odd that on this particular day, Mary Irene's attorney would agree to her dog being moved a half-dozen states away by her soon-to-be ex-neighbor. That, combined with the text Quinn had received from Lisle early this morning, left the reek of plausible deniability. I imagined Quinn in Lisle's office when Jen called, trying to pry even the smallest bit of useful information out of the man.

"I have to go, I'm finally here at Liam's preschool," Jen said, then hung up.

I punched in Lisle's number, and I too got his voicemail rather than a secretary or an answering service. Not willing to let that stop me, I drove the twenty-five minutes or so to Lafayette Hill, to a faux-Colonial structure I might not have noticed had my car's GPS not nagged me to turn left into the parking lot. On the stairs to Lisle's second-floor office, I heard shouting.

Quinn's shouting.

"You were at the house about six this morning, Lisle. The officer patrolling the neighborhood saw you open the front door with a key. His report says you were inside about thirty minutes. You want to explain why?"

"Mary Irene Jones is my client. My business with her is none of yours."

"So you were at the house on official business this morning, after an intruder entered the premises last night? Was that business related to your earlier text informing me that you never meant to imply that Mary Irene Jones was in danger when you called a press conference about her car being found in the tidal pool in Delaware?"

"I was checking on the house, of course. To reiterate, Detective, details about whatever I do for Mary Irene and why are protected under attorney-client privilege." Lisle slowly backed into the hall outside his office.

Quinn looked over Lisle's shoulder and saw me about three steps from the top. "I should charge you with obstructing a criminal investigation—the one *you* demanded be opened when Mary Irene Jones went missing."

"That's ridiculous," Lisle protested. "Mary Irene gave me access to her house, which I then extended to the police."

Lisle turned and saw me, then hurriedly typed something into his phone.

"Ah, here's the other Mary Irene Jones, the not-so-famous one. Posturing to impress your new girlfriend, Quinn, is that what you're doing here? You think I don't know you were at her house last night, and again earlier today, involved in some very interesting activity anyone could see from the street? Surely you don't think you're the only one keeping a close watch on this cheap knock-off of the great poet? I have a few minutes of video I bet the TV news will be all over."

Lisle pushed past me and ran down the stairs, shouting, "Get out of my way, Mimi Jones, I'm a busy man."

My shoe caught on the rug, and I tripped up the top step into the hall. Quinn lifted me by the shoulders and out of his way. "Go home," he commanded, his voice low but furious. "Let me do my damn job."

"But—"

"For God's sake, Mimi, not now."

I heard Quinn slam his car door and tear out of the parking lot.

Chapter Thirteen

I couldn't escape the video. It had been shot through my living room window—you could even hear my lamp hitting the floor before everything went dark.

Quinn kissing me, me kissing him. His arms pulling me closer, my hands in his back pockets. Pretty tame stuff if you were looking for titillation. Network TV offered racier fare. But if you wanted to wag an ethical finger and suggest impropriety—and, of course, Jordan Lisle did—this did the trick. Stories about us aired on the local television newscasts and were picked up nationally because of our connection to a certain missing person of some prominence.

Philly area stations showed only a bit of the kiss, plus Lisle's assertion that Quinn and I had conspired to enhance our careers at the expense of his missing client, the acclaimed poet Mary Irene Jones, and his professional reputation. But news websites and social media offered up the longer makeout scene along with Lisle's remarks. My phone did not stop ringing. Given the abundance of unknown callers, it seemed possible that someone had found and shared my personal cell number. My own social media accounts, set for a public audience to draw attention to my poetry, lit up with nasty comments, though also mixed in there were requests for interviews.

My email contained much screeching, illustrated by bold-faced capital letters and exclamation points in multiple entries from Sharon Bernstein and my mother. Both seemed intent not only on angry phone calls but also on written documentation of their deep disappointment with me. I took some comfort in the atta-girl text Daniel sent from New York City to cheer me up amid the multimedia humiliation. "Cute cop," he wrote. "You always could pick the good-looking ones, me included. I'm here if you need to talk."

Did I need to talk? Yes, about so many things. I wasn't sure which of the disastrous potential consequences of the video upset me more—the likelihood that my job was in jeopardy, or that Quinn's was. Despite her raging at me, Sharon was smart enough to know that this mess was great publicity for the poetry festival. Odds were better than even she would argue that the festival could survive a little scandal surrounding me as well as the maybe-not-missing Mary Irene Jones, so I figured I was safe through the end of the week at least. But Lisle's next best move was striking out against Quinn and calling for his dismissal from the force. I dreaded hearing that the hammer had fallen, and that Quinn was on suspension pending an investigation into his conduct.

How unfair would that be? Did I question where I stood with Mike Quinn at the moment? You bet. But I didn't doubt that he wanted to find out what happened to MIJ and whether she was safe. One minute, her disappearance was a police matter; the next, it wasn't. It was hard to know where the line was, let alone whether we had crossed it and ever would again.

I barricaded myself in my house, where I had driven directly after the confrontation at Lisle's office. Curtains and blinds were fully closed at every window in the front and back. Poor Barrett learned the hard way to stay off the windowsill—the press hum that rose as the video circulated grew louder every time he peeked outside, frightening the poor little guy. Stress eating commenced for both of us. I opened a can of tuna to share with him, giving myself an extra dollop of mayonnaise and sweet pickle relish on my sandwich.

To avoid further burying my woes in the tub of cheese curls that beckoned from my pantry, I plowed through the remaining protest poetry finals I had to grade. If push came to shove, I would post the results online and mail the blue books back to my students when I could step outdoors again.

One of the local news operations sent an alert that Quinn had been placed on desk duty while the police union and the department sorted out whether he had compromised the investigation of Mary Irene's disappearance by entering into a romantic relationship with me.

Around 8:30 p.m., my phone rang yet again. Caller ID showed the college's main number.

"Sharon?" Had her cellphone finally died from overuse?

"Not this time," Sister Marlene said.

This couldn't be good.

"I don't know what to say."

"We nuns have that superpower, you know, the ability to strike people speechless. So just listen. I'm sending a car around, marked with the college's seal. Martin Hernandez from Security will come to your door; he'll be there in thirty minutes. Pack an overnight bag and grab whatever work you need to finish by the end of the semester. Also, bring what you need to finish prepping for the festival. You're staying with me tonight. We'll worry about tomorrow, tomorrow."

"My cat—"

"Call a pet sitter. I'm sure you know some good ones."

I did at that, and one already had a key to my house. The call cut off, leaving me to ponder what other superpowers the college president would manifest.

One half-hour later to the minute, Martin pulled up in a black Town Car. He elbowed us through about a dozen people aiming tape recorders, cameras, and microphones, and off we went.

On the seat lay a note addressed to me.

Mimi,

I'll be attending an emergency meeting of the board of trustees this evening. Take the back bedroom. See you at breakfast, 7 a.m.

S. M. V. de P. F.

A plate of crackers and cheese and a bottle of Italian spring water awaited me in the bedroom, on a slim writing desk. I texted my pet sitter friend the details as I knew them and sent a quick payment for her services through tomorrow. Then I settled in with my laptop, the very last of my students' finals, and a not-inconsiderable number of misgivings about the trustees meeting Sister Marlene was attending.

Had I slept much, I could have said the luscious aroma of baking woke me, but I settled for a mere "Thank you" when she set a mug of coffee and a raisin scone in front of me.

"Grades finished and filed?" she asked, without so much as a "Good morning."

I added milk and sweetener to my coffee. "Yes, all twenty completed. I also brought whatever material might be needed for a tech dress rehearsal for the poetry festival."

"Eat, you'll need your strength. This will be a busy day, I'm afraid." She poured herself a cup of coffee and took the counter stool next to mine. "More than a few arms were twisted last night to keep you on through Saturday's festival. Don't thank me for that, thank Sharon. She has the rhetorical skills of the best politician. She missed her calling."

Sister Marlene held up a finger before I could open my mouth.

"You're on a thirty-day probation, however. If the festival is the success Sharon now assures us it will be, we will evaluate your status and proceed accordingly. You will not mention the assertions being made against you and Detective Quinn except to say that Poetry Festival Week is always exciting, lest you risk a full stop to your career at the college. Am I understood?"

I nodded meekly, afraid to speak until I was given permission.

Coffee cup in hand, she pushed away from the counter to stand in front of a set of French doors. Her small deck, with its patio umbrella and dinette set, must have beckoned because she walked outside, then turned as if she expected me to follow. I brought my mug and scone along and sat at the table. She did not, instead circling it and me.

"Mary Irene portrays herself as serene, untouched by her fame and the world around her. In reality, she sometimes can't cope with them or much of anything else. I'm her closest friend, one of the few she has left. She spins stories in which she is the major character, and leaves the rest of us to sort out the havoc she wreaks. Bringing her to this college was the most foolhardy professional risk I've ever taken. I didn't see any other way to break her out of an endless loop of self-doubt and self-destruction. Eventually, she agreed it was for the best, but making things easy isn't her way. Never will be."

Once again, Sister Marlene had rendered me speechless. She filled in the blanks without my asking, as if she needed to tell someone, anyone.

"By the nineties, Mary Irene was an international superstar. Though she would swear she hated being in the spotlight, she couldn't seem to avoid it. She spent money impulsively, slept with the most unavailable men, pledged herself to causes and people that even she knew wanted to exploit her. Then, when the consequences of those actions became apparent, indecision tormented her, and she escaped into alcohol or pills until she worked her way out of her mess. But the pregnancy pushed her to the edge. I got a phone call from a police station in Helsinki—she was in tears, half hoping that she'd had a miscarriage and half praying that she hadn't. I talked a police officer into putting her into a cab that took her to a shelter run by my religious order a few towns over. Mary Irene knew I had that connection, knew that if she called me from Helsinki, I couldn't possibly refuse to help her. And she was right.

"As I was flying to Finland, my contacts there got her settled down and persuaded a doctor to come to the shelter to examine her—Mary Irene was bleeding, but she refused to be taken to a hospital. The doctor recommended a week's bed rest, at the very least. That gave me time to arrange a position for her at the college, as poet in residence. We sent announcements to the press and emphasized her new role in fundraising mailings.

Everything was in place on the appointed date one month later except for the woman herself.

"I was fired as English Department chair, then rehired by the board of trustees when I threatened legal action on the grounds that I was not responsible for Mary Irene's failure to abide by the contract she had signed. A slim majority on the board claimed to believe me when I said Mary Irene would begin the residency within a year. She showed up eleven and a half months later."

Questions queued up in my mind, waiting to be asked, but I couldn't get the words out. What happened? Did MIJ lose the baby? Did she have it? If so, what became of it?

Sister Marlene ended her circuit of the deck at the chair across from me, almost vibrating with frustration. "I can't tell you what happened during that time, because she's never given me a consistent story I could trust fully as the truth."

My mouth must have dropped to a point where she anticipated a different line of questioning.

"And, no, I don't know where she is. But I know Mary Irene—she can be both impulsive and compulsive. There must be something in those manuscripts she entrusted to you, Mimi, and I need you to find what it is. We're going to get through this festival, and you're going to spend whatever time you might have left as an employee of this college redeeming yourself. Now finish your breakfast, check on the arrangements you made for your cat, and pull yourself together. Martin will pick you up in thirty minutes and take you to where you need to be."

A nun hadn't barked orders at me like that since the eighth grade. "Yes, Sister," I replied, because she gave me no alternative.

Before I left the deck to get ready, I checked my phone. A voicemail from my fellow pet sitter brought assurances that Barrett had survived the night without me, as well as an update that a few TV vans were still parked on the street in front of my house, awaiting my return.

A text from Jen Dill included a selfie of her wedged into the back seat of her car between Liam and Yeats. "Just checking to see what kind of room the boys will have when we head south. Woof!" she wrote.

What neither a text nor a voice message offered was word from Quinn. I had no doubt that he was done with MIJ professionally and me personally.

Martin navigated past news vans stationed at the college's main entrance and dropped me off at the loading dock behind the building where my first class awaited me. My "Poetry as Protest" students eyed me with what seemed like new respect.

"Anything *exciting* going on, Ms. Jones?" one teased as I distributed their graded blue books.

"Nope. Life continues to be boring," I said. "Just the usual end-of-semester loose ends. Your final grades will be available online tomorrow morning, and I expect to see all of you at Poetry Fest on Saturday. I will be mentioning your contributions to the keynote address. Come and be recognized."

"Getting recognized yourself these days, aren't you?" the student persisted.

"Kenny, I've learned that people recognizing your face complicates things a bit more than when they only know your name. That's all I'm saying on the subject. Call it my own protest."

That, of course, led to many questions about my detective friend, and did we know each other before Mary Irene disappeared or only since she dropped off the planet, and where was MIJ anyway. I summoned my inner Sister Marlene and gave them a stern look that actually worked, though I suspect it was their way of showing their support and letting me win this one round at least.

Martin arrived at the classroom door as the last student was assuring me she couldn't wait for the festival. We made our way to the auditorium for the A-V check, and afterward he drove me to the nearest shopping mall to pick up some makeup as well as an outfit and some shoes to wear for the keynote. Hidden under my baseball cap and escorted by a burly companion, I had no trouble wandering around to find the wardrobe I needed for my Saturday appearance as Mary Irene Jones 2.0.

A lot was riding on this. I hoped it was a role I was born to play.

Chapter Fourteen

"You don't need me — or some video that's gone viral — to tell you that poetry is exciting and alive. How can it not be? It's about us and the world we inhabit — flawed individuals and wretched injustices, selfless acts of kindness and personal sacrifice, Earth in its glory and its desecration.

"Poetry embraces the extraordinary and the ordinary, the epic and the everyday. As Mary Irene Jones, the founder of this festival, would no doubt tell you, poetry is both of the moment and an enduring record of it. As a vehicle for outrage especially, it outlasts the era in which it is written to inspire later generations.

"Every one of us gathered here today knows the words to a poem that calls us to action — to stand up, speak out, right wrongs. We experience this poetry all the time, and most often it's when we're not holding books filled with stirring verses.

"Take a few minutes and listen..."

My audience shifted forward in their seats as the opening notes played. Some smiled and nodded. I saw a few couples holding hands.

"You recognize those songs, don't you? 'Blowin' in the Wind' and 'Strange Fruit.' Marvin Gaye's classic, 'What's Going On.' Jazz great Gil Scott-Heron's declaration that the revolution will not be televised. Examples of protest poetry, every one of them.

"As long as popular music has been recorded, its lyrics have pumped up the volume of protest. Let's immerse ourselves for a little while in this tradition, through the words of well-known practitioners. Pete Seeger is here, of course, and Bob Dylan, but so are Pops Staples and Laura Nyro and Curtis Mayfield, Janelle Monae and Teyana Taylor and some very new writers giving voice to the issues of these times.

"If this presentation were to be comprehensive, it would take weeks. Alas, we have only about an hour left.

"I warn you, you may leave this auditorium much angrier than you were when you walked in. That's the whole idea — "

Poetry festivals, especially academic ones, didn't draw big numbers. Single-day events such as ours certainly didn't. Last year, attendance at MIJ Fest was about five hundred people, with only about half participating in person on campus.

But as the various video clips played on the screens flanking me, with performers representing rap and folk music, Jim Crow-era blues and Vietnam-era rock, I looked out into a standing-room-only crowd. Teenagers and senior citizens and all ages in between raised fists, yelled, and sang along with "If I Had a Hammer" and "War (What Is It Good For?)" and more recent examples of protest lyrics I wasn't aware of just two weeks earlier. It felt good to be connecting with other artists' poetry and connecting poetry to the larger world, even if that wasn't the reason why some people had bought their tickets. Sharon's confidence in me was vindicated before about fifteen hundred participants, the maximum the college's main auditorium, and our security folks, could accommodate. An equal number had signed up for the live stream as if it were an international soccer match.

With great exposure had come great responsibility. And, in the end, significant applause. The English Department chair was smiling when she stepped onto the stage and walked to the podium where I stood, while the names of my students scrolled on both projection screens.

"Thank you to literature professor Mimi Jones and our very skilled tech team for these reminders that poetry is all around us—we just have to listen for it," Sharon told the crowd. "We're going to take a twenty-minute break before launching into the various morning workshops. If you need help finding yours, there are students ready to assist you. Some of them are from Mimi's class, if you want to continue to explore the theme of poetry as protest. Please plan to be at the first workshops promptly at 10:30."

I smiled at those who waved from the audience and chatted with a few people about my keynote. But did I breathe easier? No way. I still was expected to sit in on at least a couple of the workshops, as well as attend the luncheon—an all-hands-on-deck mixer in which the faculty would circulate among festival participants—plus the 4:30 p.m. announcement of this year's Mary Irene Jones Poetry Award winner. Too many moments in which to be on my best behavior on behalf of the college in front of scholarly types from other schools, members of the public, and very observant reporters.

With no 10:30 workshop to lead and no office to hide in, I took my time gathering up my notes and laptop. I had my back to the auditorium when I heard an unexpected voice call my name from the balcony, where overflow seating had been set up.

"Mimi, Mimi, up here! I want you to meet my husband." Jen Dill waved a scarf at me. "Give us a minute to get down there, okay?"

"Sure," I shouted. Wasn't she supposed to be on her way to South Carolina? Wasn't he supposed to be down there already, waiting for her and Liam to arrive? I eased up onto the table next to the podium, wishing I could take off my shoes. I'd had to stand throughout the introduction and the whole keynote presentation in these brand-new heels.

Foot traffic up the aisles and out of the auditorium had subsided by the time the couple appeared. Jen climbed the few steps onto the stage and pulled her husband toward me.

"Thanks so much for waiting. I thought for sure we'd miss getting to see you after your speech. It was fabulous, and you look great. Mimi Jones, this is my husband, Conor Tilden. I've been telling him all about you.

Conor put his hand out for me to shake. "I feel like I've already met you, Ms. Jones. Jen refused to leave town without hearing your presentation. It was good, she was right."

He sounded sincere enough. I mentally slapped my forehead for equating "systems engineer" with a "no art in his soul" kind of guy.

"Thanks, nice to meet you, Conor. I feel guilty for holding up your move though, since Jen and Liam were supposed to be on the road by now."

"Change of plans. I found a cheap flight here," he said. "I figured I'd drive back with them, though the dog makes things a bit tight."

"Yeats is not that big," Jen said, her voice registering some annoyance.

"We'll have to stop more frequently," he said. I suspected he had made that argument a few times.

"True," she conceded.

Add a disrupted schedule to a dog and a toddler in a cramped car, depending on how many belongings Jen and Conor were trying to move on their own, and I was thinking Mr. Tilden wouldn't be a fan of mine for very long. My deduction must have been obvious to him, because he immediately tried to make nice.

"We're staying for one workshop, then we have to pick up Liam and Yeats from the babysitter's. Any suggestions?" Conor asked.

I racked my brain to remember who was speaking on what, and quickly consulted the program Jen was holding. "There's a session starting in five minutes about environmentally conscious poetry. Mary Irene Jones has several famous poems in that category, if you're interested in what your neighbor wrote. Or maybe you're already familiar with her work—"

Conor smiled. "I am, I studied her when I was a kid. But it's still a great idea." He tugged at Jen's arm. "We'll have to hurry if we want to get seats."

She waved. "Wish us luck!"

Again, I turned my back to the auditorium, thinking I might scoop up my gear and closet myself in the English Department conference room with Mary Irene's manuscripts for a few quiet minutes. Sister Marlene's thirty-day probation clock had ticked down to twenty-eight, and I hadn't looked at the binders since she had issued her command that I try to find something that explained MIJ's disappearance. But I was only midway to the auditorium's main door when two figures blocked my path: Jordan Lisle and a man in a suit with an envelope in his hand.

The man thrust the envelope at me and said, "M. Irene Jones, you've been served." My arms were full, which made accepting anything difficult. And once I understood, there was no way I was taking those papers. "Sorry, no hands," I said, and pushed past him. Lisle scrambled after me.

"Ms. Jones, I intend to gain possession of Mary Irene's manuscripts to prevent you and your cronies here at the college from profiting from them while she isn't here. That document is an order restraining you from any contact with those manuscripts until a court of law decides the issue."

Outrunning these guys wasn't possible, not in the heels I was wearing. Nor would it settle my debt, so to speak, to Sister Marlene.

"Have you spoken to Dr. Bernstein and delivered this legal update to her, as well? I take my orders from her and the college administration, not from you. Now, if you'll excuse me, gentlemen, I have to prepare for the day's crowning event: the Mary Irene Jones Poetry Award, also known as your client's life work, Mr. Lisle. Four-thirty, right here. Unless you've arranged for someone to videotape that for you too."

I marched into the auditorium's lobby, expecting Lisle and the process server to chase after me. Instead, Lisle shouted at me, "What were those two doing here, the Dill woman and her husband? Seems awfully convenient. Are they in on the little scam, too?"

An odd question, coming from him, but I wasn't about to waste time thinking about it. I hustled out of the building and as soon as I hit the quad, I texted Martin, asking him to meet me at the English Department conference room, stat.

I unlocked the door and pushed the box with the manuscripts into the corridor, not caring that the security camera would see what I was doing. Contempt of court was contempt of court, but leaving Mary Irene's work to her sketchy lawyer would be more criminal, and would surely muddy that transparent chain of custody Quinn wanted.

Ten minutes later, the manuscripts were loaded into the trunk of the Town Car and on their way with Martin to my mother's condo. I texted her to say he was dropping a box off for me from the college, and that I'd pick it up sometime soon. The less I told her, the better, though she would figure it out.

"A little notice would have been nice. You're lucky my stylist canceled my hair appointment," Cass replied. "Your Mr. Hernandez can stash the box in the guest bedroom. Make sure you have your key when you come for it, so I don't have to wait around for you too."

Eventually, she would be happy I had included her in the plan, assuming she, Martin, and I didn't land in jail.

Sharon's office was locked, so I scribbled a note and slid it under her door. "Won't be working in the conference room." She might not immediately understand the message, but she'd recognize the handwriting.

More than halfway through the workshop I had recommended to Jen and Conor, I ducked into the lecture hall and took a seat in the back row. A poet with connections to the University of Pennsylvania was discussing environmental degradation as a consequence of conflict, as reflected in the works of writers in Afghanistan and South Yemen whose English translations had been published in the past three years. The topic was related, in a way, to my dissertation forever in progress, and I wished I weren't so distracted. Martin said he would text me when our troublesome package was delivered safely to the condo. Even afterward, sitting through the rest of the festival program was going to be torture.

"Why so twitchy? Your speech was a big hit. I watched online, for obvious reasons. Wouldn't want to get too close."

And yet Quinn was there behind me, very close to my ear. I forced myself not to turn around. "We need to talk," he said. "Meet me at the loading dock behind the English Department in five minutes."

No way did I want to be seen anywhere near that building. "Meet me at my car. I'm in the last row of faculty parking, along the fence near the gate."

"Awfully public."

"Everything on this campus is public today. You're here anyway."

He ran a finger along my throat and tapped twice. For "yes," I guessed—correctly, since I found him standing in the lot a few minutes later.

"This isn't a good idea, Mike, unless you're trying to add to the list of reasons we should be fired. What do you want?"

The toll of the last few days showed on his face. He looked tired and sad. "I'm sorry for what happened at Lisle's office. And I'm sorry about the video."

"Apology accepted. If that's all, I'll just hurry back and catch what remains of that workshop." Not that I gave a damn about the workshop.

"The only way we can fix this is together, Mimi, you know that."

"Please define fix, Detective."

"Fix your job and mine. Fix us."

The manuscripts *were* my job. Whatever motivated her gift of those binders, Mary Irene wanted me to have what they contained. I couldn't put Quinn in the middle of a custody battle over them, especially after I just had them smuggled off campus.

"There is no us," I said, deflecting away from the missing poet. "The college has placed me on a thirty-day probation, with no union to protect me the way the Fraternal Order of Police will protect you. That keynote speech you just streamed is the only reason I'm still employed. So, for my sake, please take your own advice and go home."

Hard for him to refute that, right? In case he tried, I retreated a couple feet and fisted my hands at my side.

He moved closer, swallowing the space between us, as if he couldn't care less who might be watching. "Tell me you, of all people, don't think I've been playing you to gain an investigative advantage. I'm not, I swear. I wouldn't do that. If the department officially tosses me off this headache of a case for inappropriate conduct—"

"I don't think you've been playing me. I should have known better than to play, period."

His breath was warm near my cheek, tempting me to slide my arms around him. But, no, that had already landed me in a huge mess. I unlocked my car, squeezed past him and got behind the wheel, and drove away, circling the lot until I saw that he was gone. I wanted to believe Quinn, but I had to trust my instincts. As I passed through the area designated for festival parking, I saw Jen and Conor drive toward the main gate, toward the state highway that would take them back to the house in Upper Roxborough they would soon be leaving for good.

One luncheon, two afternoon workshops, and one awards ceremony still stood between me and my departure from this campus today. And until I resumed my quest for MIJ's truth, more searching for my own would have to wait.

Chapter Fifteen

On my coffee table sat two manuscript binders I had retrieved from my mother's condo sometime after 11 p.m. After the poetry prize had been awarded, and the winner honored, and the finalists lauded for their exceptional work. After the festival committee ran the numbers: tickets sold, calculations of expenses versus revenue, totals of pledged and outright contributions to next year's event. After surprisingly enthusiastic praise for my keynote address from committee members representing the college's board of trustees. After Sharon congratulated me, saying, "Good work all around today," leaving unspoken whether that included moving Mary Irene's box off campus.

Barrett tiptoed along the back of my sofa, not purring but evidently reassured that I had come home to stay. He stopped often and stared at the closed drapes that blocked his view of the street. Was he dreading another night of media commotion?

"We're not the top headline anymore. You can relax, buddy." He nudged my shoulder, reminding me that some attention was just fine, in his opinion. Yeah, yeah, and there was no such thing as bad publicity.

Sleep seemed unlikely— I was too wired. But I couldn't muster the strength to revisit the bits of poetry contained in the binder labeled, "Now," so I opened the one labeled, "Since."

The first entry comprised seventeen lines, written in MIJ's neat penmanship on a page torn out of a spiral notebook then slipped into a plastic sheath.

Wanting peace and never finding
always reaching, always striving
Cycle.
Sitting home, yet always leaving
always seeking, always questing
Cycle.
Always leaving, never lasting

> *always searching, never ending*
> *building this, yet always yearning*
> *wanting peace and never finding*
> *Cycle.*
> *Always lonely, always tearful*
> *always waiting, always fearful*
> *always watching, never seeing*
> *wanting peace and never finding*
> *always hiding, always seeking*
> *Cycle.*

I turned the page and saw a date, also in MIJ's handwriting: May 1, 1974. She would have been thirteen years old, but that didn't ring quite true. The words ached in a much older voice, carrying a weariness that seemed seasoned much longer.

The next sheet in the binder offered the same poem, this time typed on the same thin paper Mary Irene had used for most of the pages I'd examined thus far. None of the words had changed.

"Same stuff, different day, is that what you're telling me?" The poem quietly screamed disappointment. Disillusionment. Disenfranchisement, as if she had no vote on her life's direction. I knew how that felt, though I couldn't say what had prompted her to write the words. I tried to imagine being *that* Mary Irene Jones in 1974, or even seven weeks ago.

Barrett curled next to my left hip, not caring about the meaning of it all. I scratched his back, hoping to soak up his wisdom. His solace.

Solace, that was it. In this poem, MIJ seemed inconsolable. I snuggled Barrett to my chest and cried, frustrated for her and me. But I had run out of time for tears. I had only twenty-seven days left, minus pet-sitting stops, to sort through the two binders here and the three I hadn't yet touched.

The next half-dozen pages in "Since" brought short poems more suggestive of a teenage girl: overwrought lines about love and giving oneself up to it; eternal devotion, then hurt feelings, and righting oneself after the emotional storm. Themes universal enough that a poet of any age might consider them, but these verses leaned heavily toward loss of virginity, loss of innocence, and the realization that trust could be betrayed, that the writer had been betrayed. No dates accompanied these pages. Perhaps they represented moments Mary Irene wanted to forget, or perhaps she wrote these poems as her way back to them. None of her published poetry was about love or the naïveté of youth; very little of it was personal or individual.

On a neon-pink sticky note I wrote in big block letters, "SINCE" WHEN? "SINCE" WHAT? "SINCE" WHO? Jostling Barrett off me, I reached for the most recent MIJ biography I owned, one of several stacked precariously on the edge of the coffee table.

I would either come away enlightened or finally get some sleep.

The tinkling crystals of my phone's ringtone startled me awake about five in the morning. I squinted at the number: Was that the area code for Virginia? Did area codes still apply the same way they did when people had only landlines? A call could be from anywhere.

I answered, fat-fingering the call onto speaker mode.

"Jennifer Dill is calling Mary Irene Jones," a robotic voice rang out.

What the hell?

"Jen, is everything all right?"

"Ms. Jones? My name is Marianne Rossi, I'm a social worker at a medical center just outside Richmond, Virginia. Jennifer Dill is a patient in our emergency room, and we got your number from her. Just a moment please, I'll put her on."

A muffled voice in the background warned that the phone's battery power was low, and that the call would need to be short. Another voice insisted that someone in the hospital must have a phone charger and gave orders to locate it.

"Mimi, hi. God, is the sun even up yet? There are no windows where I am. I'm not sure how they knew to call you. We were in an accident on I-95. Conor was trying to push through before we stopped for the night, maybe he got sleepy—"

"Are you guys hurt? What happened?"

More background voices and beeping and squeaking followed. I took my phone off speaker, which made things slightly better on my end.

"What did you say?" Jen asked. "Oh, wait, they found a charger and are moving the bed closer to an electrical outlet. Okay, I'm hooked up now, sorry about that. Yes, we're mostly all right, I guess, though the car isn't. Conor misjudged a guard rail as we were pulling off the highway to get coffee. He clipped the rail hard on the driver's side. They're pretty sure he has a broken left wrist."

"What about Liam?"

Jen sounded calm, if a little confused, understandably. "He was scared in the ambulance, of course, and he cried as they poked at him and me, but that was actually good because they needed him to be awake during the exam. And then, poor baby, he was really afraid when they took Conor away to X-ray. He finally just fell asleep in a crib here next to me in the ER. Sounds like they're keeping us under observation for concussions but otherwise we're okay."

Sounded as if they would be staying put for a day or two, at least. "So, stuck in the hospital, and basically without a car."

"Right, so I need a really big favor, Mimi. Can you drive down here today and get Yeats? They have him at a rescue kennel the local fire department runs, but he's putting up a fuss. He's had so much change in his life lately, no wonder he's freaking out. But he knows you."

I did a quick search on my phone. Richmond was about six hours away by car. If I got moving about seven, I could be there by early afternoon.

"I'll take care of Yeats, he'll be fine. Put Ms. Rossi back on the line and I'll get the contact information and directions from her. Just concentrate on taking care of Liam and Conor and yourself, okay?"

"You're a lifesaver. Thank you, thank you, thank you."

Jen relayed what I would need. I could hear the social worker's assurances that she'd take it from there.

"Hi, this is Marianne again. I'll text you the directions to the kennel and the number there. The person I talked to earlier said the dog's identification chip was registered to Mary Irene Jones, but the number listed on the registration wasn't picking up. How lucky that Jen had this number in her phone contacts."

Lucky for Yeats. I wasn't sure about me.

"Oh, before I forget," she said, "you might want to check if something's wrong with that other number. Conor, Jen's husband, also has you listed as his emergency contact under it."

That made no sense at all.

"I'm sorry, I'm not quite awake yet. Can you repeat what you just said?"

The social worker laughed. "This is a lot to digest without caffeine, I'm sure. I just happened to be on call this morning, or else I'd also be totally out of it at this hour. Anyway, you are listed as the sole emergency contact on Conor Tilden's phone, but the number doesn't seem to work. It's the same number that's on the dog's ID chip registration. Maybe it's a line that can't receive text messages?"

Her text pinged my cellphone with details about the rescue kennel. "I'll try to get on the road in the next hour," I promised.

"And now you have my office number too. Text me when you get to the kennel, please."

"Got it. Will do."

"Just one more question before I let you go." Marianne Rossi giggled. I prayed she hadn't seen the make-out video. "Are you *the* Mary Irene Jones? You know, the famous poet?"

What was the right answer to that? What did she consider famous? And under the circumstances, if I said no, would Yeats be stuck at the rescue kennel until Jen and Conor were able to travel again?

"I'm the one you want," I said. Or close enough. She probably assumed there could be only one Mary Irene Jones in Conor and Jen's lives — and in their phone contacts, emergency or otherwise. Unless you knew, you wouldn't know.

The way I didn't know this: What connection existed between Conor and Mary Irene? Why would he want her contacted before anyone else, even Jen?

At the moment, however, the more urgent, far more upsetting, question was: How could I manage a six-hour drive back to Philadelphia alone with a dog? Just thinking about it sent my stomach twisting. It was too early to call my pet sitter colleagues to see if anyone was willing to ride along with me and, eventually, Yeats.

I knew of one person, though, the one who swore that he had been honest with me and was eager to help find a way out of our mutual Mary Irene Jones dilemma.

Quinn picked up on the first ring.

Pennsylvania and Delaware faded in the rearview mirror. By the time we crossed the Maryland border, silence had perched itself on the console between us in Quinn's SUV.

I had already spent the better part of an hour on my phone, talking first to the rescue kennel, confirming that we were on our way and estimating an arrival time of early afternoon. Then I ascertained the location of Jen's car from the state police barracks in Virginia that had responded to the accident.

Fortunately, I had snapped that photo of her license plate. That, plus Marianne Rossi's name and contact information at the hospital, were proof enough that I needed to know where the car had been towed. The garage was open when I called, thank goodness, and so I was able to learn that the crate MIJ, then Jen, had used for Yeats was intact, as were his dog bed and toys. The owner said his repair shop was near the kennel, and that he would have everything waiting for us.

My head was pounding, and I was already exhausted. Quinn pulled onto a ramp leading to gas, coffee, and bathroom facilities, at least two of which were becoming critical needs. I studied his face as he filled the tank, maybe cringing at the price per gallon, or maybe at the prospect of several hours more with me before we picked up Yeats and turned homeward. But he caught me watching and smiled. Seemed he was hoping to make nice. I was the one who had been avoiding conversation, though I was also the one who had asked for his help.

We walked wordlessly to the rest area. I dawdled in the bathroom, re-brushing my hair into a ponytail and repositioning the Phillies cap I'd thrown on seconds before Quinn picked me up. Appropriately, I looked like someone the tow truck had dragged in, and no amount of lip gloss was going to help that, so I finally ventured back out to the lobby.

Quinn handed me a bottle of water, a large takeout coffee, and a white bag. "Creamers and sweetener in there, along with a chocolate croissant. Let's roll," he said, and headed for the car. I stopped first at a table to fix my coffee, then peeked into the bag. The croissant was huge. At least I wouldn't starve or dehydrate.

Before crossing the parking lot to his SUV, I ducked into the mini mart, where I bought an overpriced supply of ibuprofen. A hundred tablets might be enough. I shook the bottle as I opened the car door.

"Speak now, Detective, before I swallow them all."

He held out a palm. "Two please. And thanks."

"I mooch the ride, you get the pain relief. Well, as much relief as you can get as long as I'm the one mooching the ride."

He spit out his coffee laughing. "You're funny, Mimi Jones. It's one of your few redeeming qualities."

I had at least one. Good to know.

The mile markers made for fascinating reading as we zipped along about ten miles over the speed limit, keeping up with Sunday morning traffic on the highway. Places to go, a dog to retrieve.

"What's the plan once we get Yeats back to Philly?"

Damn cops, always with the questions.

"Guess I'll have a new roommate. I think Barrett misses the reporters staked out at my house. With Yeats inside, things should liven up considerably for him."

"You hate dogs, Mimi."

"I don't *hate* dogs, I'm just not comfortable around them, which they understand, and so they go out of their way to persuade me I'm wrong. I'll mostly be working from home the next couple of weeks. As long as I renew my anti-anxiety meds and Barrett doesn't eat Yeats, all will be well. Unless you want Yeats—he likes you."

Quinn passed a tractor-trailer and gunned the SUV until he could safely change lanes again. "Why are you working from home? No poetry manuscripts waiting for you at the college?"

"I said mostly working from home. We're on summer break."

"Uh-huh," he muttered skeptically and reached for the radio dial. "I'll tune it to classic rock if you don't tell me what's going on. Spill it, Mimi, or I'll torture you with Black Sabbath."

"What makes you think I don't like classic rock? My dad was a Black Sabbath fan. I spent my childhood listening to records with him on Saturday mornings. I miss those days, honestly. You don't scare me."

Quinn grunted.

"And who," I asked, "were your father's favorite rockers?"

He must have seen that one coming, but Quinn stared at

me for a minute, thought for a few more. "Rolling Stones, Bowie, Pink Floyd. I can't pick just one because he never could."

Fair enough.

"The manuscripts aren't at the college," I confessed. "Jordan Lisle tried to serve me with a restraining order to stay away from them. I wouldn't take it. I told him to serve it on the college. Too much depends on what's in them."

"When was this exactly?" The traffic as we approached Baltimore was the heaviest we'd seen all morning. Quinn concentrated on the road, but I could feel a third eye staring me down.

"Just after my festival keynote. I didn't even make it out of the auditorium before Lisle and the process server confronted me. I wasn't sure if you knew. Wasn't sure if you would want to know."

"About the court order, yes. About where you stashed the manuscripts, no, don't tell me. Where was the order issued?"

"No idea."

Quinn picked up his phone and dictated three texts to me, what turned out to be two civil court websites, plus one username and password.

"Check those links," he said. "And remind me later to change that password."

My mother lived in Montgomery County, not too far from Lisle's law office. I hoped his choice of jurisdiction would keep Cass out of my legal snarl.

We got lucky.

"The order was issued in Philadelphia County. Says I have thirty days to respond."

"You, or you and the college?"

"Just me." I was glad I hadn't told Sharon where Martin had taken the box.

"The manuscripts are safe?"

"Best guard I could summon on short notice."

Quinn glanced my way, trying to puzzle that one out. "As soon as possible, you need images of every page in those binders—photograph them or scan them, whichever is quicker. Photograph the box from all angles, too. Get a lawyer to file a response and appeal the court order. You don't need the originals to do your job, and that box has to get back to the college before someone figures out that the chain of custody has been breached."

Lisle's parting question to me in the auditorium seemed more significant now, in light of the morning's events. Quinn was the only person I could talk to about it.

"There's something else, isn't there, Mimi. I can hear you thinking."

"Lisle asked me about Jen and her husband, whether they were in with me on my little scam, as he put it. Then, not twenty-four hours later, they're in an accident on an interstate highway in the middle of the night."

Might be a coincidence. Maybe Conor did doze off at the wheel. Maybe Jen was asleep and didn't know what was happening until after they hit the guardrail.

"The hospital social worker who reached me said Mary Irene Jones was listed on Conor Tilden's phone as his only emergency contact. Not me, of course, but why not his wife, or his employer—"

Quinn moved into the passing lane again and hit the accelerator. Then he asked the digital assistant on his phone to call the Virginia State Police barracks responsible for covering I-95 just south of Richmond.

"Hi, this is Detective Michael Quinn of the Philadelphia Police Department. I'm heading your way to collect the dog of a couple who were injured in an incident on an off-ramp early this morning, before dawn. Driver's name is Conor Tilden. C-O-N-O-R T-I-L-D-E-N. He was driving a car belonging to his wife, Jennifer Dill, Jennifer spelled the usual way, D-I-L-L. PA license number …"

I checked my photo of the plate and read off Jen's number, which Quinn repeated. "If an accident investigator can give me an idea what happened, that would help. There's a possibility the crash is related to a missing-person case I'm working on."

Quinn shook his head, acknowledging that small bit of fiction regarding his current status as investigator. "Contact me at this number," he said. "I'm hoping to hit Richmond mid-afternoon. Appreciate it."

I half-expected him to put a flashing light on the dashboard to get us down there faster, but Quinn settled for speed and strategic jockeying between travel lanes.

"Tell me again about Jen and Conor's emergency contacts. What did the social worker say?"

I reconstructed for Quinn my conversation with Marianne Rossi, noting that I made her repeat things to allow for the fact that I'd been startled awake. This time, I could hear *him* thinking.

"How did Jen describe what happened?"

"*Misjudged* was the word she used. Conor had *misjudged* the distance to the guardrail as they were getting off the highway; she said maybe he had gotten sleepy. But she was a little distracted by what was going on in the ER around her when we spoke, I think. She said Liam had just settled down and she was worried about Yeats. I'm not sure how much she saw of what happened until she felt the impact."

We were well past Baltimore when Quinn's phone rang. The accident investigator said he had just filed his report. Quinn put the call on speaker.

"A missing-person case?"

"A well-known poet named Mary Irene Jones. Jennifer Dill and Conor Tilden were her neighbors. The dog I'm picking up belonged to Jones. What can you tell me about the accident?"

The investigator more or less read directly from his report. Traffic cameras picked up Jen and Conor's car about five miles from the off-ramp, the driver drifting toward the road's right shoulder, then correcting and straightening the car. A white van was traveling close behind the car, the cameras recorded seconds later.

A second set of cameras near the ramp showed the white van speeding up and clipping the car just as it moved into the exit lane. The van squeezed past the car on the right, crowding the car into the guardrail on the driver's side. The car hit the rail at a fast enough speed that it bounced back, tire marks on the ramp indicated, but neither the front nor the side airbags engaged.

"If anyone on the ramp had been really close behind these two vehicles, there would have been one rear-end collision at least and the potential for more injury," the investigator said. "Fortunately, the next few drivers picked up by the ramp camera took it slow and were able to squeeze by the Dill car. The 911 center got several calls reporting the accident. What's interesting, though, is that the on-ramp camera at that same interchange shows the white van returning immediately to the highway, entering via the northbound ramp rather than heading south again. We're checking the cameras on the other side of the road to see where the van might have gotten off. The registration showed it's a rental out of Bucks County, Pennsylvania."

"Did anyone take a statement from Tilden or Dill at the scene or at the hospital?" Quinn asked.

"Not at the scene. First responders said Mr. Tilden was bleeding from a cut over his left eye and cradling his left arm in pain when they arrived. Ms. Dill was in the back seat between their little boy and the dog. The child was crying, and the dog had vomited. They checked everybody, stabilized Mr. Tilden's arm, and got them into an ambulance. The fire company picked up the dog. I'll text you my report. Give me a call if you find out this is more than an accident. I'll do the same."

The call went dead. A text pinged through a few seconds later, and Quinn picked up his phone, triggering the facial ID feature. "See if the report came through."

It had.

"Text it to Steve Cahill, he'll be in my contacts, then give me back the phone."

Done.

Quinn dictated the next text: "Yo, Steve, run the registration on the van in this report. Ask the rental agency if it was returned, and, if so, by whom. Tell them it's part of a missing-person case. Forward the info to me when you get it. I owe you one."

He flipped the phone into the console. "Now what?" I asked.

"We drive. Oh, and we wonder why you didn't tell me about your conversation with Jordan Lisle *before* we got on the road. Intel that you were dragging me into another Mary Irene Jones drama would have been a nice professional courtesy, Mimi, since we're keeping things professional. Did you conveniently forget I'm off the case because I'm under disciplinary review?"

"Of course not," I said. "This trip was supposed to be about the dog."

What neither of us said: It wasn't about the dog now.

Chapter Sixteen

Marianne Rossi's notes from our phone conversation were in the file, Quinn and I discovered when I invoked her name in the lobby of the suburban Richmond medical center where Jen, Conor, and Liam were being treated.

Quinn flashed his Philadelphia Police ID and a text containing the accident investigator's report. "Ms. Jones is a friend." He managed a smile at me for his audience. "I'm along for the ride and whatever I can learn about what caused the accident. We're here to see both Jen Dill and Conor Tilden."

The woman staffing the reception desk made a call, gave us visitors' passes, and pointed to a sitting area nearby. A quarter-hour later, we were told by the person who led us upstairs that we could see Jen and Liam, but that Conor was with a doctor who was splinting his left wrist.

We found Jen reading a story to Liam, who lay tucked against her in bed, half-asleep. She nudged him a little, and he squinted at her, then at us. "Look who came to visit us, sweetie. It's Yeatsie's friend Miss Mimi and Detective Quinn. Yeats isn't with you, is he?"

I pulled a chair close to the bed. "We're on our way to get him, but I know Yeats misses you guys. We told the rescue people that we wanted to see you first so we could tell Yeats that you miss him, too."

"Blow kiss," Liam said, and slipped his hand into mine.

"I promise to blow a big kiss to Yeats for you. Should I tell him you're feeling okay? Not all ouchy, are you?"

The little boy shook his head and squeezed my fingers.

"We're being very brave today, especially Yeats and Daddy," Jen said. "Daddy has a broken thumb and a broken wrist, and we'll have to leave our car here so it can be fixed. We'll get a rental, and Mommy will drive it to our new house. Maybe in a week or so, we'll be able to come back to Philadelphia to get Yeats."

I pulled a pack of pink sugar-free bubble gum from my pocket. "When I feel sad, I try to make bubbles with my gum. Do you want to see, Liam?" I unwrapped a stick, chewed like mad, then poked my tongue through the gum and wiggled it. Liam found that very funny.

"Hey, I didn't say I could make bubbles, I just said I try. Should we ask Mommy if she wants to try too?" Liam lifted his arms and let me set him onto my lap.

"One stick," Jen said, clearly grateful for anything that would divert her two-year-old. "I'm glad Liam and I slept through the crash. Conor says some idiot in a van forced us into the guardrail."

Quinn opened the accident investigator's report on his phone for Jen to read while she chewed. "I asked a fellow detective in Philly to find out what he could about the guy driving the van. If you were asleep, I guess your husband is the only one who saw him coming. Doesn't sound like he'll be in any shape to fill in some of the blanks while we're here, though."

Jen blew a respectable little bubble, eliciting giggles from her son. "We decided to leave Philly late, so Liam would sleep through most of the trip. But I guess we were all way too tired, and this happened. Could have been a lot worse. We're so glad that the social worker reached you, Mimi. And thanks for your help too, Detective. We all know how Mimi is about dogs."

Would Quinn bring up the emergency contact thing? Should I? Just because it seemed like the wrong time didn't mean asking was a bad idea.

"Dogs are a no-go all right," Quinn said, sticking to pups and the people who fear them. "I'm the first person Ms. Jones called when she learned about the accident and realized she'd have to drive a long way with Yeats by herself. You'd think he was some big, vicious thing instead of a little fur ball."

Quinn checked his watch. "We should head to the rescue kennel before it gets much later. Hope your husband is able to travel soon, and you can get your new life started."

I set the little guy back on the bed and blew a fair equivalent of a bubble, which I preserved with a tissue. Vowing that I would show my bubble to Yeats, I did a mini-high five with Liam and followed Quinn into the hallway and out to the parking lot. We climbed into the SUV, Quinn asked me to search for a pizza joint, and we roared away.

Within the next hour and a half, we retrieved Yeats and picked up a large pepperoni-and-mushroom. We devoured the pie and took the dog for a quick run at a park the kennel folks recommended—or rather, Quinn took Yeats for a run while I collected our paper plates and soda cups. Then we headed back toward the highway. Yeats began to howl after I sat up front. Quinn pulled over after a block and all but lifted me into the backseat.

"Karma is a bitch," he said, favoring me with an evil grin. "She's all yours, Yeats."

During the return trip, Quinn blasted classic rock, relenting only after we had exited the main roads and were approaching my house. By then, Yeats had licked my fingers raw, but what was a little drool among travel buddies, especially when both of us were taking friendship where we could get it.

At my place, Quinn deposited Yeats, still in his crate, and the other doggy paraphernalia in the foyer. He stepped around a disgruntled Barrett and let the door bang behind him as he departed.

How many ways were left to convey how annoyed he was with any and all Mary Irene Joneses?

Chapter Seventeen

Hissing and growling woke me as the sun rose on the Monday morning after the Sunday from hell. I managed to get Yeats out of the crate without Barrett attacking him, and we walked through the neighborhood for twenty minutes, a baseball cap covering my hair and an oversized hoodie covering my pajamas. I thanked the gods that while we were married Daniel seldom noticed that I borrowed his clothes, much less remembered to claim them when we split up—a happy outcome for his mother, who never missed a chance to skewer my fashion choices or his.

My rowhouse was hardly the ideal place to keep Yeats, who was used to having a grassy backyard, however small, to roam. I'd have to call in a pet-sitter favor and have someone foster him for a week or two. In the meantime, as we wandered, dog and non-dog lover, I snapped a few pics of Yeats sniffing flowers and trees. I even took a selfie of us, which earned me a slurp on the face that I didn't love, but truthfully didn't hate as much as I would have a month ago. I texted the photos to Jen, figuring she and Liam would appreciate knowing the pooch was doing all right.

Back at home, I separated and fed the animals, exiling Barrett to the basement with orders to behave while I showered. Then I photographed every sheet of paper in the two manuscript binders I had brought from my mother's condo. Cass would not love my camping out at her place long enough to tackle the contents of the remaining binders, but it was a better alternative than sneaking them out a few at a time. Involving her further in manuscript smuggling was not an option.

In the five years I had worked for Sharon Bernstein, she had demonstrated extraordinary mind-reading skills—or maybe I just had zero ability to bluff. Her call as I was driving to my mom's condo surprised me not at all.

"Where can we meet? You have to catch me up on what's going on."

I suggested a spot located between the college and Casa Cass, calculating that I could easily lose Sharon if she tried to follow my car afterward. What this diner lacked in ambience it also lacked in decent sandwiches, though the baked goods and coffee were excellent, as I recalled.

"Where are the manuscripts?" Sharon asked as soon as she saw me, her social graces gone where I was concerned. "You don't have them at your house, do you?"

"No, and I'm not telling you where they are, either. There's a court order with my name on it, but not the college's, at least not yet. I need to create a copy of every piece of paper in the seven binders, then figure out a way to return them to campus. While I'm doing that, I can't study the poems, which is supposed to be my priority."

She ordered a cranberry walnut muffin and coffee. I skipped the sweet snacks—this rendezvous wasn't helping my appetite.

As if each bite brought with it a revelation, Sharon chewed very deliberately. "I've got it," she finally said. "Martin can help copy the manuscripts. I know you, Mimi, I bet you stashed them at your mother's. And probably with his help, if I know Martin. He's already stuck in the middle of this MIJ adventure, so why should today be different?"

Should anyone ask why Martin Hernandez, second-in-command of college security, was spending time at my mother's condo, Sharon suggested we speculate that they were dating. He was single; she was single. Sharon failed to note that Martin was easily fifteen years younger than Cass; that little lie would please at least one of them to no end.

Tearing my attention away from fictional romance, Sharon asked, "You've been through four of the binders so far?"

"All of two, parts of two more. It's hard to know what to make of the work I'm finding. Some is polished verse, though different from her other poems. Other pieces are unfinished; still others are immature. And whatever thread connects the poems in some of the binders isn't always obvious."

Sharon was thinking what I was thinking: that my deadline was getting closer, though my understanding of what MIJ intended in leaving me the manuscripts was not.

"Sister Marlene is not happy, Mimi, which I realize makes three of us."

"She should read the manuscripts," I proposed. "She's known Mary Irene better and longer than you have, while I don't know MIJ at all. Maybe Martin could bring her to take a look."

It wasn't the worst idea, Sharon conceded. "Today's budget meeting was rescheduled to tomorrow so they can work the poetry festival numbers into the plan for next fiscal year. She should be available."

Sister Marlene was exiting the college's Town Car at my mother's complex when I pulled into the visitors parking space next to it. Martin sent a "Don't you love a clandestine meeting?" wink my way as we mounted our invasion of Casa Cass, though Mom was not at home. I'd called her from the diner parking lot and politely requested that she clear out for a few hours, explaining again that the less she knew the better, and that the college president was dropping by. For once, my mother had not argued.

Handing Martin my phone, I asked him to start with the binders I had yet to study. "Every page of each binder, both sides, and the front cover please." I suggested that Sister Marlene begin her manuscript scrutiny with the "1999" file.

She read slowly through every draft of the single poem it contained. "I'm confused why this is labeled '1999.' This doesn't sound like Mary Irene back then."

I offered her a glass of the Italian sparkling water Cass bought by the case and waited for her to continue. Sister Marlene sipped, and spoke, thoughtfully. "In all the time I've known her, Mary Irene has been intelligent and incisive and sensitive, all the things that produced wonderful poetry, but almost never calm, and seldom relaxed. There's a peace in these words that doesn't fit with the woman I knew in 1999."

That was it, the intangible quality of this binder's contents I couldn't articulate. MIJ didn't just write the words, she possessed them in a way I had not experienced in her poetry before.

I placed the "1999" folder next to the ones Martin was working on. Sister Marlene produced the cigarette she always carried, opened the door to the balcony, and stepped outside and actually lit it. When I joined her, she protested, as if I'd walked into a private space, then quickly apologized.

"Martin tells me this is your mother's home. You have more right to stand here than I."

"Cass might argue that point. We don't always agree."

She extinguished the cigarette against the building's brick façade and brushed the ashes away. "Daughters and mothers can be like that. Sons and mothers, too, I understand." She blew on her fingertips. "I don't have brothers, or sons obviously, but, boy, did I have a mother. If she were alive, she'd still be complaining about how I hadn't told her in advance that I would be entering the convent, as if a grown woman needed her approval."

Didn't I know that feeling. I also knew grown women sometimes wanted their mothers' approval anyway.

"Sister, do you know Jennifer Dill and Conor Tilden?" I asked, trying to ease into the topic. "They were Mary Irene's next-door neighbors until a few days ago."

She hesitated before answering. "I've never met them," she said. But something in her voice told me there was more to it.

"Conor's cellphone has Mary Irene Jones listed as his emergency contact, with the number we've been calling unsuccessfully for weeks to try to reach her. That seems odd, doesn't it?"

Conveniently, Sister Marlene's own phone rang. "On my way," she told the caller then walked inside.

"Martin, we need to pack all this and get it back to the campus."

I hurried after her and started loading binders into the box. Martin shook his head. "Only about a dozen pages to go," he said.

"Do it in the car. I'll drive. The judge just extended the restraining order on the manuscripts to include the college," Sister Marlene said, quietly seething.

Minutes later, she swept them out of Casa Cass like a warrior queen.

Evidence of my neglect greeted me at home, the sour stink of urine assaulting me the minute I entered. Barrett had busted out of the basement and was perched atop the crate, tormenting poor Yeats. In his misery, the dog had wet his bed. I scooped up the offending feline and sentenced him to time-out in the powder room, dragged the malodorous dog bed to the washing machine downstairs, and put the leash on Yeats. A walk would do us both good.

The local dog park was empty. I let Yeats off the leash to wander over to the toy box. He fished out a rubbery critter, maybe a chicken or a duck, and shook it by the leg. I longed for hand sanitizer or some dog-friendly disinfectant as he dropped it at my feet in hopes we could play fetch. I threw, the bird flew, Yeats brought it back.

A tennis ball rolled in front of us. "Somebody left this in my SUV. Think I can guess which one of you."

Yeats greeted Quinn with happy yips and offered his paw to shake. He knew a true comrade when he saw one—both of them were on my you-know-what list. But today, everyone was.

"He peed in his bed. Bring him back when you're done bonding. I'll be home doing the laundry."

The sleep-deprived, job-endangered, writing-blocked poet in me wanted to throw a rock at something, but property damage was not what the situation required. I jogged home to handle the doggy housekeeping, hoping that exercise would enhance my mood, and that Barrett had not decided to emulate our new roommate by missing the litter box. I got each of my wishes.

On reflection, it hadn't been *such* a terrible day. A copy of every MIJ manuscript in the box now awaited transfer from my phone to my laptop. Thirteen unread text messages represented the pages Martin scanned as Sister Marlene drove, hustling the binders back to the college. I vowed to buy Martin the best dinner I could afford, hoping my meager funds would allow better than drive-through burritos.

The dog bed thudded through the wash cycle. My brain thudded too—I felt like one of those whiteboards you see in TV police shows, layered with Venn diagrams and sticky notes and multicolor threads stretched between disparate people and pieces of evidence. Maybe that's what I needed to do: make one list of what I already knew about MIJ's poetry based on her published works and one of what I had learned from the four binders I'd spent time with so far. I rummaged through my office supplies and found two legal pads and blue and red pens. Eureka! I was set.

Quinn and Yeats found me hunched over the "What I Already Know" list. Yeats snagged one of the pens and ran into the kitchen with it. I wrestled it out of his mouth and lured him into his crate with a bowl of kibble.

"Behave, buster," I commanded. I was having none of this.

I walked down the creaky basement stairs to wrestle the dog bed into the dryer. As I set the timer, Quinn sat on a step about halfway down.

"I filled his water bowl. I gave Barrett some water, too, after he hopped up on the counter to drink from the faucet."

Quinn gave me a "Sweet puppy, sweet kitty" smile. I wanted to simultaneously punch him and kiss him.

I needed peace and quiet to work on the manuscripts. The old typing paper MIJ used did not enhance image quality, based on the few reproduced pages I had looked at. Tough to read, combined with tough to fathom, would mean many days cooped up with the missing poet's "gift."

"Not to be inhospitable or anything—"

"--Heaven forbid—"

"—but I really need you to get lost, Detective."

He peered around me for a better look at the timer on the dryer, as if that were some previously agreed-upon window in which to speak. "I heard about the court order being extended to the college. My buddy Steve Cahill is temporarily assigned to Mary Irene's case, such as it is. Somebody saw to it that he got a copy of the order."

"Okay, good to know."

"Turns out a credit card from Jordan Lisle's law office was used to pay for the rental van whose driver took issue with Jen Dill and Conor Tilden down in—"

"Did they arrest them both?"

"Nobody's been arrested, not yet. We're trying to confirm where the driver returned the van. Stay tuned."

Certainly could have been Lisle who made sure the Philly P.D. got a copy of the court order, but what linked Lisle and the manuscripts to Jen and Conor? Would it take a cop to teach a poet to see the world the way an investigator did?

Would it take a poet to teach a cop to notice certain nuances?

"I think Sister Marlene knows more than she's saying, Mike. She knows Mary Irene better than anyone."

Quinn looked puzzled, as if what I'd said didn't register. So I laid it out for him.

"The president of the college, Sister Marlene St. Vincent de Paul Flaherty? The woman responsible for bringing Mary Irene Jones to the United States and our little corner of Pennsylvania? I'm telling you, she either knows or has her suspicions about what happened to MIJ. I asked her about Jen and Conor, and she said she'd never met them—not that she had never heard of them, or that she didn't know they existed."

"And you think that's significant why?"

I opened the dryer and checked the dog bed. Still damp. I set the timer for sixty more minutes and stepped around Quinn on the stairs. "It's a long story, in case you have somewhere better to be."

"On indefinite desk duty, unless they decide to suspend me. Time, I have."

Or he did until a text summoned him to Philly's northern suburbs.

"Looks like I'm suddenly back on the case and heading to Bucks County," he announced. "You can tell me that long story between here and the Bensalem Township Police Department."

"Bensalem? Did they find Mary Irene at the casino up there?"

Quinn glowered at me. "Switch off the dryer already. They picked up the guy who hit Conor and Jen's car in Virginia. Maybe he's someone you'll recognize."

Would that be a good thing or a bad thing? My mind raced through the possibilities for the next forty-five minutes, give or take.

Chapter Eighteen

Quinn mumbled a quick introduction to the Bensalem police detective who met us at the front desk.

"This is Mary Irene Jones?" the detective asked.

"This is the Mary Irene Jones who got the call to come to Virginia after Conor Tilden and Jennifer Dill ended up in a hospital, allegedly because of whomever your boys picked up at the rental agency," Quinn oversimplified.

"I thought she was an older woman. In her sixties, your guy Cahill said."

"*That* Mary Irene Jones is the subject of my missing-person case. It's complicated. I'm hoping Mimi here will recognize our driver."

I was beginning to understand why Quinn was off desk duty and back in the investigative trenches. Cops in their right minds wanted to stay as far away from this case as possible, was my guess. The Bensalem detective, seeming more than happy to avoid complication, parked me behind a two-way mirror and handed me a headset. "Listen through this. One of us may pop in at some point, to see if there's anything you need to tell us."

About ten minutes later, a uniformed officer led a tall man, maybe in his late twenties, into the interrogation room to face Quinn and his detective counterpart. The man didn't look at all familiar to me.

"I'm Detective Jim Lascala. This is Detective Michael Quinn of the Philadelphia Police Department. Tell us your name please."

"I'm being questioned by two cops? What's up with that?" the man asked. "All I did was return a van to the rental place up the road."

"A van that was involved in a hit-and-run on Interstate 95 near Richmond, Virginia, on Sunday morning. Maybe you'd like to tell us about that, after you tell us your name?" The Bensalem detective, Lascala, might not know a lot about why we were there either, but he sure didn't let on.

"Am I under arrest?" the man asked. "I want to call my lawyer."

Quinn smiled. "Would that be Jordan K. Lisle, Esquire?"

At the mention of Lisle's name, the man looked from one detective to the other. "No one is under arrest, we just have a few questions," Quinn said. "Your name is Peter Yastremski, according to your driver's license. Is the Warminster address on your license current, Mr. Yastremski?"

Yastremski nodded.

"But the van was rented under someone else's name, or rather someone else's business. Jordan Lisle's, in fact. Tell us about that please."

"Don't you need to read me my rights?"

"Only if we decide to arrest you," Lascala said. "This is just a conversation."

Yastremski seemed to weigh his options, deciding to go with the conversation.

"Someone contacted me a few weeks ago from Lisle's office, offering to pay me a thousand bucks to tail a car from an address in Philly to some point on I-95 between that street and the South Carolina border. I was supposed to keep the car in my sights, give the driver a hard time for a little bit, then get off the road and turn back north."

"Did this person specify how you should give the driver a hard time?" Quinn asked. "Or was it left up to you?"

Yastremski chewed on a thumbnail. "Harass him, I guess. Make him uncomfortable."

"No instructions beyond that?" Lascala asked.

"Nothing else."

Quinn looked at some paperwork supplied by the rental agency; the company logo was big enough for me to distinguish even upside down.

"Someone contacted you about this job. Did that person identify himself, Mr. Yastremski?"

"Herself, it was a woman. Older-sounding, with an accent. If she said her name, I didn't catch it."

"What kind of accent?"

"I don't know, she was hard to understand. Russian maybe?"

Lascala leaned over the table. "Lots of people left the old Soviet Union and settled in Northeast Philly and Bucks County. Some neighborhoods, everybody might sound a little Russian; there are Ukrainian families, and Uzbeks. Seems awfully convenient, Mr. Yastremski."

If Yastremski was expecting any help from Quinn, I foresaw quick disappointment.

"Maybe she had a Spanish accent or Vietnamese?" Quinn asked. "Jamaican? French? Irish? Anything ringing a bell here, Peter?"

"How should I know, I'm from Warminster? If I could, I'd tell you, man. What difference does it make anyway?"

"I'm trying to put myself on your end of the phone call," Quinn said. "You accepted a job from someone you describe as hard to understand. What was this offer you apparently understood well enough that you couldn't pass it up?"

"Hey, a thousand bucks is a thousand bucks, seemed like a quick score. She said she was with Jordan Lisle's law office in Montgomery County, explained what the job was, and said she would handle the rental arrangements. She asked for my email and said I would get something confirming the reservation and the date I was supposed to pick up the van before driving to the street address she specified in Philly."

"Did she email you the Philly street address?" Quinn asked.

"No, she texted from the same number she called on. Made a point of reminding me I needed to bring the rental agency's confirmation email and my ID when I picked up the van. I gave her my payment information so she could deposit the money after I returned the van to the rental place."

"But you trusted that you *would* get paid, even though she was hard to understand. Had you ever worked for Jordan Lisle before?"

"Nope. Never heard of the guy. No reason I should worry about getting paid."

"How did Lisle's office find you?"

Yastremski cleared his throat, asked if he could have some water. Lascala filled a paper cup from the black plastic carafe sitting on the table. "I do occasional courier work. Some investigative stuff too."

"So you're a private investigator?" Quinn asked.

"No, but sometimes I do surveillance for a friend who's a PI. I figured Lisle's office got my name through him. I mean, this sounded like what I usually do: follow somebody around for whatever amount of time. In this case, a guy and a woman and a kid and a dog got into the car and drove off from the address Lisle's office gave me, and I followed them, per the terms of the deal. Got a real late start though. I waited for, like, three hours outside their house before we all got rolling."

Quinn poured himself some water and sipped slowly. "I need to check in with my department," he said after a couple minutes. "Be right back."

He ducked out of the interrogation room and into the space on the other side of the two-way mirror. "Anything, Mimi?"

"Never saw him before, sorry."

"Does Lisle have a secretary?"

"You saw his office: There was barely room for one desk, let alone two. It's possible he hires someone when he needs to, I suppose. Maybe someone with an accent."

Quinn massaged the left side of his neck, as if trying to work out a kink. "I better get back in there."

He poked his head into the interrogation room. "Detective Lascala, can I have a word? We shouldn't be too much longer, Mr. Yastremski."

Lascala joined Quinn by the door. Yastremski put his head down. After what I guessed was just enough time to make Peter uncomfortable, they resumed their places at the table.

"You said you were hired to give the people you were following a hard time," Quinn said. "To intimidate them?"

"Yeah, that's what I took it to mean," Yastremski replied.

"So you were hired to ram a car with a woman and a child inside into a guardrail on an exit ramp around dawn on a Sunday morning?" Quinn asked.

"No, no!" Yastremski shouted, waving his hands. "I was just going to squeeze him over toward the rail. But he was weaving a little on the road beforehand, I think he was falling asleep at the wheel. On the exit ramp, I think maybe he hit the gas when he felt me bump his car, he went into the guardrail kind of hard. But that wasn't the idea, not at all."

"So you didn't plan to break Conor Tilden's wrist and thumb and threaten the lives of his wife and his little boy?"

"No way, honestly! I called 911 to report the accident, in fact."

"And then you left the scene."

Yastremski stared down at the table. "I want to call my lawyer now."

Quinn stood. Lascala followed his lead. "I don't see an immediate connection to my missing-person case, Detective. Unless you see a need to hold Mr. Yastremski, I'm done here."

Lascala nodded toward Yastremski. "You're free to go for now. We'll be in touch. I'll walk you out to the sergeant's desk so you can retrieve your belongings."

Once they were gone, Quinn checked something on his phone, then began typing. Several minutes went by before he motioned me to meet him in the corridor.

"Virginia emergency-dispatch records confirm a call did come in from the phone number Yastremski gave us. He was telling the truth about reporting the accident he caused. That seems odd since Lisle hired him, unless Peter also was telling the truth about the intimidation plan succeeding way beyond his expectations. I need to contact the accident investigator we talked to Sunday, to see what Conor had to say in the follow-up interview."

I remembered what Jen said about the crash. "If Conor confirms he was asleep at the wheel when the van hit the car, does that mean there's no case against Yastremski?"

"May not be. Time for me to get you home either way, Mimi."

We took the outer lanes of Roosevelt Boulevard through Northeast Philadelphia, then cut westward toward my neighborhood. Quinn parked in front of my house but made no move to get out of his SUV.

"You're sure you've never seen Yastremski before?"

If I had, he didn't make an impression—unless someone else did instead.

"The day the fire alarm went off in the college library, the security cameras in the lobby and at the checkout desk would have captured people streaming out of the building."

Quinn eyed me skeptically. "You're the one who pulled the fire alarm. And our pal Pete doesn't fit the description of the guy you think was stalking you that day."

"But what if the big man I saw wasn't alone? Yastremski said he sometimes worked surveillance jobs for a friend who's a private investigator."

What if Yastremski was a face in that crowd? Someone I had walked right past.

Chapter Nineteen

About a week after the visit to the Bensalem Police Department, I called my co-conspirators to an MIJ summit in Sharon's office. Well, most of them: Sharon, Martin, and Quinn, but not Sister Marlene. I risked her potential displeasure in the name of a quick, productive mind meld as free of personal history and emotional baggage as possible.

It had taken several days for Martin to pull all the surveillance footage I requested: security camera video from the day I was stalked in the library, as well as everything available from the day of the poetry festival, all of which we would turn over to Quinn for facial-recognition wizardry by whichever forensics folks he could enlist.

I had also asked for whatever surveillance tapes could be had from the last day Mary Irene was on campus, whenever that was. Sharon's pre-summit assignment was to go through old meeting minutes and anything else she could lay her hands on that might help fix MIJ's movements as close as possible to the date she was last seen. Sharon also dug through her files for any email or correspondence the college may have had with Jordan Lisle in his capacity as MIJ's attorney in the last six months.

In the meantime, Quinn hit every database he could for information about Jen Dill and Conor Tilden. He also started contacting South Carolina real estate agents, none of whom had yet been able to find a house for which the couple signed a lease.

As we gathered, Sharon pushed a thumb drive and a stack of papers toward me. "Why are we doing this, Mimi? Have you found something in the manuscripts?"

Articulating that was no longer as tough as it once was. Whether my theory was correct remained to be seen.

"Until now, we've been working on parallel tracks. The police have been looking into Mary Irene's disappearance, and I've been looking at the contents of the box she sent me. The two had to be related, but how wasn't clear."

I handed Martin and Sharon copies of the poem I'd come to call "Cycle." Quinn had seen it earlier.

"When was this written?" Sharon asked minutes later, pushing her reading glasses up into her hair.

"It's from the binder Mary Irene labeled 'Since,' though I don't know what she meant by that. There was a handwritten copy of the same poem, too. The other side of that paper had the date May 1, 1974, also handwritten, but this doesn't read to me like the work of a thirteen-year-old girl."

Sharon rushed to the substantial bookshelf on the other side of her office, pulling down a volume I recognized from its cover as the latest MIJ biography, considered the most comprehensive to date. One I had not yet read.

"There was a bombing in Belfast that day," she said, quickly turning pages. "I knew Mary Irene's mother, Sarah, had died of injuries suffered in a bus station blast. This new book says her mother was among more than a dozen victims not identified for almost forty-eight hours after that bombing. The many casualties, plus concerns that not all the explosives had been located and disarmed, complicated efforts to rescue, then retrieve, bodies."

Quinn joined her at the bookshelf. "What else does it say?"

Flipping to the index, then to the middle of the book again, Sharon scanned and summarized. "Sarah Jones was thirty-eight years old. She was heading back to her family's home outside the city from a food market when a bomb attributed to the Irish Republican Army exploded as she boarded the bus. Her husband was known to have alcohol issues, and suddenly he had two young daughters to care for alone, thirteen-year-old Mary Irene and her nine-year-old sister, Anne Elizabeth. Things did not go well, this biographer maintains. But he also notes that most information about the daughters' lives afterward comes from second- and third-hand sources, and that Anne Elizabeth Jones died of cancer in Wales about five years ago."

Sharon carried the book back to the table where Martin and I sat. "Mary Irene has never been one to write overtly personal poetry, so it's been hard to know what effect this period of her life had on her."

"'Cycle' is likely significant for that reason," I conjectured. "It's as if Mary Irene is finally telling us, revealing herself. Also, the box of manuscripts was first sent to me in April, just weeks before the anniversary of her mother's death."

"It's one poem," Sharon protested. "She's written about a thousand."

And my theory was based largely on gut instinct born of the years I'd spent reading MIJ's famous work, as well as these previously unknown scraps of verse and a few comments made by Sister Marlene.

"Despite the dates Mary Irene assigned to some of the binders, I don't think the few finished poems they contain are from the past. They're recent, written within the last twelve to eighteen months, I'd say, though some of the scraps of paper and false starts at poems do seem to be little bits she saved, in some cases from when she was a young girl." I paused, to give my audience the opportunity to digest the possibilities.

"I've gone through all seven binders at least three times now, and I'm confident Mary Irene never intended to publish any of this material. There's something valedictory about it."

I had written a report saying as much. I offered the lone copy to Sharon, anticipating that she would have more questions, and would want some corroborating evidence.

"Did the police forensics team ever determine how recently the old typewriters in Mary Irene's house might have been used?" I asked Quinn. "I think we'll discover I'm right about the timing of the manuscripts, based on the ribbons and the inking on the keys. We can check the pages against them."

He sent off a text. "Checking now."

Martin had taken it all in. "I didn't know Mary Irene Jones very well. We only exchanged a few pleasantries back when she was on campus regularly. She wasn't a bubbly person, but she was friendly enough. Something seems different in this 'Cycle' poem. She seems regretful."

"There's definitely a change here," Sharon agreed. "Some of her most famous poems are positive, about finding the brilliance in the plain, but Mary Irene was never a happy person. I'm not sure she was comfortable with the notion of joy."

Bingo. That was the perfect way to describe it.

"Did she think she wasn't entitled to joy, and hadn't been since her mother's death?" I asked. "Was there a significant event in her life recently that reinforced that, and—"

Quinn's phone buzzed and interrupted me. He looked at the number and left the office to take the call. My phone pinged almost immediately with texts from him:

"From VA state police."

"Dill supposed to pick up repaired car. Didn't."

"Tilden discharged after thumb and wrist surgeries, hospital says."

"Didn't show for accident follow-up interview. Cellphones go to voicemail."

I turned to Sharon and asked her the same questions I had posed to Sister Marlene. "Do you know Jennifer Dill?"

"She's Mary Irene's neighbor, isn't she, the one who was taking care of Yeats?"

"She's married to Conor Tilden. Do you know him?"

"I've never met either one of them," Sharon said, an answer remarkably similar to the one her boss gave me. True in Sharon's case maybe, but …

"When the college gave Yeats to Mary Irene, did he have an identification chip?"

"Yes, I ordered the chip myself and included her contact details," Sharon said. "I knew Mary Irene wouldn't think to get one."

"Then why would the phone number on the dog's ID chip also be in Conor Tilden's phone, listed as his only emergency contact?"

Sharon went pale and started turning the pages of the MIJ biography in front of her. "Conor was Mary Irene's father's name. Sarah Tilden was her mother's name before they married."

Quinn stepped back into the office. "Conor Tilden and Jen Dill are not where they were expected to be today, and they're not answering their phones. There could be a simple reason why, still—"

Still, if we were inclined to jump to conclusions, this was the MIJ script playing out again, and nothing about her was as straightforward as it seemed.

"How old is Conor Tilden?" Sharon asked.

I knew immediately where she was going. "If his online profiles are truthful, he's twenty-four, maybe twenty-five by now, so he could be the mystery child."

"What if he is?" Quinn asked. "Does it mean Conor knows where Mary Irene is, or just that he's looking for her, too?"

We'd have to locate Conor to find out, which was in Quinn's job description, not mine. He signaled to me that we needed to talk. I followed him into the corridor.

"I have to walk a fine line here, Mimi. Police in two states still have no grounds to conclude that a crime occurred in which Mary Irene Jones was a victim, and there's no solid evidence that the Virginia crash involving Jen and Conor was intended to do them harm. The best I can do is try for data from their cellphones for the last twenty-four hours. If they called anyone, we might be able to determine where they were when the signal pinged a tower."

Where would help. It was better than nothing.

Martin was sitting at the secretary's desk, eyes on his phone, when I returned. "I need to get back to my office. Call if you need me," he said.

I hoped no more surreptitious movement of files would require his services. A hearing on who was the legal custodian of MIJ's unpublished manuscripts had not yet been scheduled, motions filed by the college having thrown an obstacle into Jordan

Lisle's path. For now, the box remained in the locked English Department conference room, pending the judge's decision. I had surrendered my key to Security, as had Sharon, her secretary, and the janitorial contractor.

I found Sharon where I had left her, sitting at the table, looking at the printout of my report on the binders' contents.

"Hard copy only. Interesting."

"There's that court order. Safer this way."

But she knew that wasn't the only reason. "Marlene's schedule for today is wall-to-wall meetings. I'm sure that must be why you didn't include her on your guest list for this. I'm trying to decide whether that was a good call."

"When in doubt, don't. So I didn't."

"I'll keep this report to myself for now. But when she asks for it, and she will, you'll have to deliver it, Mimi."

Sister Marlene, a Ph.D. with a focus on the Romantic poets, had hired a Shakespearean scholar to succeed her as English Department chair. The presence of Mary Irene Jones on the faculty and the rising profile of the poetry award and festival had made Sharon Bernstein a surprise pick for the job thirteen years ago. The academic gossip machine had been agog; I had even heard about it up at Syracuse at the time.

Sharon was a good hands-on administrator and a quick study of all things MIJ—she'd had to be to work with Mary Irene directly while she still taught classes here, as well as on poetry prize and festival matters. Yet Sharon's relationship with her boss was a complex one, based on what I could see.

"Do you think Sister Marlene knows anything?" I asked.

"She's connecting the same dots we are, I'm sure of that. What she's suspected about Mary Irene's child or knows for a fact, that's another thing. A lot of don't ask, don't tell exists between them. Mary Irene doesn't seek permission or forgiveness very often. Marlene chooses not to ask it of her, in my experience."

"Sister Marlene told me she was one of the few friends Mary Irene had left."

Sharon flexed her neck, then nodded. "Talk about loving our friends for who they are, not who we'd like them to be. Mary Irene pushes people away if they get too close. Marlene hasn't let her, despite everything."

I was aware of some of that "everything." Was MIJ trying to push her last friend away for good this time?

Chapter Twenty

I suddenly felt very guilty about Yeats, whose desire to love seemed limitless. On my way home, I called the pet sitter friend who had taken him in temporarily and asked if I could visit. She was as surprised as I was.

But first, I detoured over to the block where Yeats had lived since he was a puppy. The house Jen and Conor had been renting now featured a "For Sale" sign on its lawn. Something about that tripped my curiosity alarm. I slowed down and took a picture of the sign. My sister, Trish, worked for a real estate brokerage that had been around for decades in Northwest Philly. I texted her the address and asked if she could find information about the seller.

Next door, at MIJ's house, a man was pushing a gas mower along the grass. My alarm tripped again: In all my visits to this block the last couple months, I had never once seen a lawn-care worker at Mary Irene's property. I shot a picture of the name on the side of his truck, too.

Maybe I wasn't the trusting soul I had once been, or maybe the timing of these two events was too coincidental. I texted Trish again and asked her to run the real estate records on MIJ's house as well.

When I pulled into the driveway at his temporary digs, Yeats was sitting in a window. He spotted me and started jumping like a miniature kangaroo. At the front door, he pawed at my legs and licked my hands. He was doing fine, my friend said, playing with her two pups and taking frequent walks with them to the dog park. I told her we were having trouble reaching the people who had been caring for Yeats, and paid her for another week of fostering. The food supply Quinn and I retrieved from Jen's smashed-up car was still ample, she assured me—the huge bag of dry food and case of canned meaty varieties the Dill-Tilden household had purchased ahead of the move to South Carolina ought to last through seven more days.

Lucky thing. Since I had no summer classes and no idea whether I'd ever teach again at the college, it would take a few pet-sitting jobs just to keep Barrett and me in kibble. Which I mentioned to my friend, who mentioned that she had passed along my number to a couple with three cats who might be needing my services soon. I thanked the gig-economy gods for word-of-mouth recommendations.

We hung out in the backyard for a while. I tossed Yeats a chewed-up ball, which he guarded from the other dogs so he could be the one to bring it back to me. Then the five of us strolled to the dog park, where the canine crew got some off-leash time. When missed-call notifications cascaded onto my phone's lock screen, I said my farewells and walked back to my car alone. The cat parents in question had left me a voicemail; the pet-sitting agency I worked with was also trying to reach me. Promising developments I could follow up on almost immediately.

Or not, since Trish texted repeatedly as I was unlocking my front door.

"Outfit called UJJ LLC owns the rental house. Same tenant for about two years. If you look at the link I sent, you'll see it's in good shape. Not staged attractively, but whoever lived there apparently took good care of the place. Listing's only thirty-six hours old. Should be a quick sale in this market.

"UJJ also owns the other address you asked about. That house hasn't been on the market since 2000. Exterior looks to be in decent shape. Sent you a link to that one too.

"Now's not a great time for buyers. Few starter homes, small inventory of replacement homes if you sell and cash out equity. Prices and interest rates higher than everyone wants them to be. Let me know if you need anything else."

I opened the first link, which offered about two dozen views of the interior and exterior of Jen and Conor's house. The stagers had installed minimal furniture, evidently anticipating the speedy turnover Trish predicted. I saw nothing I recognized—Jen and Conor's corporate movers had left nothing behind. No surprise there.

That was in the second link, which opened to a photo of the house MIJ lived in until she went missing in April. Fresh flowers smiled for the camera from a tall vase centered in the window visible from the street, something I had missed completely. Was this house being readied for sale too? Was Mary Irene connected to UJJ LLC? A state registry of such details existed, but I wasn't sure who could get access to it.

I forwarded both of Trish's links and the information she found to Quinn, and hoped he could clear up the riddle du jour.

"You home? I'm outside."

Odds were good. My car was parked on the street, the lights were on in the house, and my laptop was blasting the protest song playlist we posted online for MIJ Fest.

"Only if you're in disguise, Detective."

"Open your drapes and see what the reporters standing here on the sidewalk with me are seeing."

"Very funny."

I met Quinn at the door. No pizza, no telltale signs he'd been at the gym, but he was carrying a six-pack and a bag that smelled like buffalo wings.

"You've come bearing food. You may enter, Sir Michael." I curtsied, because I was so tired of being serious I was ready to scream.

He reached into his back pocket and handed me a roll of paper. "Printouts of the info you requested. But food first. Your little confab earlier forced me to skip lunch."

I dropped the printouts onto a stack of junk mail and walked past Quinn to collect placemats, napkins, and dishes, which I set on the dining room table. A little formality seemed like a good idea in case the media did decide to visit, though I hoped Quinn and I were last week's stale gossip. He opened containers of chicken and celery and bleu cheese dressing, while I fetched myself a glass and the bottle of wine I'd been dipping into.

"This is oddly proper, Ms. Jones," he said, rather informally clutching a tiny drumstick in one hand and a bottle of dark beer in the other.

"I miss Yeats. How weird is that?"

He put down the bottle and felt my forehead. "Are you feverish? Has the stress gotten to you?"

I selected a wing and a small drumstick and slathered a stalk of celery with dressing. "Good theory, stress. I do feel like a lab rat, bumping into the walls of my little maze while some scientist squints at me and takes notes. There must be a design to this experiment that I'm part of, but I still have no idea what it is."

"Unwind for a little while, Mimi." He poured some wine into my glass. "Get drunk even. As for me, it's moderation time. I'm due in early tomorrow, under orders to finish all the paperwork I ignored because I was working on the Case of the Disappearing Poet even when I was barred from working on it. Pray for a slow day."

I had a mid-morning interview on tap at the three-cat household. Turned out the owners were leaving this week, which would help with cash flow but also meant I had to be clearheaded and on my best kitty-friendly behavior to win the job. So we ate more, imbibed less. Quinn complained about how boring baseball games could be despite rules intended to jazz them up, and about over-analysis of pitchers' statistics by micro-managing managers, and I lost track of what else because I couldn't take my eyes off him as he did his best to act like he wasn't trying to get me my out of my funk. I leaned over and kissed him, which stopped him in both endeavors.

"Damn, I've been thinking about that all day," he whispered when I let him come up for air. "I wish there weren't so many reasons I need to stop thinking about it."

We were good at distracting each other from the person who had us distracted most of the time. Could be that's all we were doing. I pushed away from the dining table and walked to the junk mail stack where his printouts sat. The rubber band around them snapped as I picked them up.

"Tell me what I'm looking at."

"Fictitious-name registration for UJJ LLC, owner of the two houses, Mary Irene's and the one Jen Dill and Conor Tilden were renting. UJJ *is* Mary Irene Jones, according to the 2000 filing with the state by, guess who, Jordan K. Lisle, Esquire, so the timing lines up with what your sister found. I didn't dig deeper into the filing or the sales history of the rental house, but I wouldn't be surprised if UJJ bought both houses around the same time—one for Mary Irene to live in, one for the rental income."

Quinn walked to the fridge and opened another beer. "Also in there is a copy of her will as drawn up by our friend Mr. Lisle, which I gleaned from the FBI's financial search on Mary Irene. It looks legit, it's notarized as it should be, and says her house is to be sold upon her death."

Which might mean one of two things, if I understood this correctly: Either MIJ was taking care of business remotely, or Lisle was.

"Lisle gets to bill hours to UJJ whether Mary Irene is alive or not, yes? Is he legally allowed to put the rental house on the market without knowing whether she's alive? If he's not, that could mean he knows she's not dead and where she is. How can we find out?"

Barrett jumped onto the table, nosing the takeout box for chicken. I grabbed another wing, tore some meat into small pieces, then placed them on a napkin and set Barrett down on the floor.

"Can't keep a hungry cat down, you know. You were about to say, Detective—"

"I'm no expert, but from what I know a limited liability company, an LLC, sets its own rules for its business and who signs off on decisions. Those names could be in the rest of this filing, which I didn't print out but can check if I can get it to open on my phone."

"So Lisle could theoretically list the rental but not the other property?"

"No, it's conceivable he could list and sell both on behalf of UJJ. What happens afterward to the money made from the sales is another matter, especially since one might involve providing proof that Mary Irene Jones was dead."

That was a chilling thought.

Quinn stood and carried his phone into the kitchen, where the light was better. The link finally opened, and he scrolled through it. "What are the odds Mary Irene knows more than one Marlene Flaherty?"

I joined him at the counter. Quinn stepped behind me, positioning the phone screen in front of both of us. Sister Marlene was part of UJJ too. The filing listed her as chief operating officer, to Mary Irene's chief executive officer.

"That could explain her current displeasure with MIJ and her odd reaction when I mentioned Jen and Conor. Could be the only connection she knew of between them and Mary Irene was the lease on the house, but that wouldn't explain the emergency contact information on Conor's phone. If he had been living in Philadelphia alone, in a place where he knew no one else, maybe his landlord would be the emergency go-to, but even that's a stretch. He had his wife and child here with him, and an employer here."

Definitely, this called for a lawyer conversant in estate and corporate law writ small. Also more wine, my best intentions aside. I ducked under Quinn's arm and returned to my glass, which was sitting a safe distance away.

"Chicken," he accused.

"Fox, henhouse," I responded, which brought lots of eyebrow-raising and fake mustache-twisting, mixing the metaphor but at least we were clear where we stood. He'd pounce if I let him. I wanted to, but a certain poet kept getting in the way.

Quinn paced for a bit, giving us both some space, and weaved around Barrett, who kept darting into his path. Eventually, he scooped the cat into his arms.

"Let's imagine I'm the judge who issued the restraining order on the manuscripts," he said, giving Barrett his unsettling detective stare. "I'd want to know, wouldn't I, about recent developments suggesting that Mary Irene Jones might still be alive, and that there was a business relationship between a college official and the company that owned real estate mentioned in Mary Irene's will—real estate whose sale would benefit the poetry award based at the college whether she was dead or alive, as directed by Mary Irene Jones herself? And as the judge, I would be pleased, wouldn't I, if the attorney for the college brought these matters to my attention, especially in light of the fact that the lawyer for the other side, who has a financial interest in all things Mary Irene, hadn't mentioned them? Not that it would necessarily make a difference as I mulled my decision, but it might."

Barrett wriggled free. "The cat isn't impressed, but I am, Mike. Did you go to law school?"

"You'd be surprised what you pick up on this job. No law degree, but someday I may just have an MBA. At the rate I'm chipping away at it, I'll retire from the force first."

"An MBA? In what?" Because I had to ask, I knew so little about him and his non-cop life.

Quinn grinned a wry little grin. "Logistics, what else? I like figuring out the best way to get from A to B, even if it's not always the quickest."

Hidden depths, how interesting! Lucky for the detective, who rarely divulged such personal tidbits, that his transcript was not my principal concern just then. When Mr. Play It Close to the Vest steered us back to the topic at hand, I didn't squawk.

"Jordan Lisle batted this thing into the civil court ballpark," he said. "I can't ask a district attorney to get involved, not without more substantive evidence that Lisle was behind the crash in Virginia. For now, there's only a credit card transaction and an alleged phone conversation with a woman who spoke with an accent and said she represented Lisle's office. If Conor and Jen don't press charges against Peter Yastremski, I have nothing, and that seems likely since they blew off the follow-up interview with the state police down there. If the college security tapes put

Yastremski on campus, that would be something, but it could be days before we know."

Quinn knocked back what remained in the beer bottle. "Text me Sister Marlene's personal cell number, Mimi. It's time for her to come clean."

Not before I sent her my report about Mary Irene's manuscripts. I would have to eventually, given the court case about them, and she should be fully informed when she fired me after hearing from Quinn. I opened my laptop and emailed the analysis to my boss's boss. I cc'd the file to Quinn as well.

While I was at it, I located my post-NYU, post-divorce resume. All it needed was a little updating and a link to the video of my MIJ Poetry Festival keynote address. Might as well jump on those fleeting fifteen minutes of fame while I still could.

Chapter Twenty-one

No way was I invited to the meeting between Quinn, Sister Marlene, and the college's attorney. If any big revelation came out of it, it would be news to me.

Nor was I invited to the meeting between the college's attorney, Jordan Lisle, and the judge who had issued the order restricting my access to the manuscripts. The judge liberated them at a subsequent hearing—one I was urged by the college not to attend, lest Lisle seize on my presence and persist in his efforts to keep me away from them. I could analyze the manuscripts as I saw fit, the judge ruled, and could publish them as long as financial compensation was provided to the appropriate parties as stipulated in any contract, estate, or other legal agreement governing Mary Irene's literary output. In the courtroom, as I was subsequently apprised, the judge challenged Lisle to find grounds on which anyone's lawful claim to the manuscripts superseded mine. In ultimately sending the box to me through the college, MIJ had made my employer and me an inseparable legal entity, the judge said, preempting any attempt by Lisle to take further steps against me as an individual.

All that was dandy—well, absent an appeal. Also if you enjoyed being rendered a puppet unable to move too far without the college pulling back on the strings.

I didn't, even if it brought me job security.

I was less consulted than informed that I would be made available for interviews with both scholarly and mainstream publications to discuss the intricacies of studying the manuscripts left in my care by a superstar poet who by now had ostensibly been missing for several months. What I would be saying about those manuscripts was not explicitly decreed, yet I was advised that though comments about their tone were acceptable, speculating about Mary Irene's state of mind was not. As the college's PR representative began inviting the media to have at me, I also was instructed repeatedly to emphasize that a timeline for the poems had not yet been established, and that doing so was my priority.

As the legal machinery was grinding, I had been tending to some cat and guinea pig clients (summer being peak season), Yeats was still being cared for by one of my fellow pet sitters, and Jen and Conor remained as missing in action as Conor's possible birth mother.

Sharon, who had been briefed by the college's attorney, called me to dish about the latest wrinkle, Mary Irene's residential properties—and who was and was not authorized to dispose of them. *Enlightening* was the word she used to describe that situation.

"UJJ apparently stands for Ulysses James Joyce, how Mary Irene is that?" Sharon marveled while I was en route from pet gig to pet gig. "Anyway, it's a real quandary. Sister Marlene has the authority to sell the properties on her own, but she may not want to yet in the hope that MIJ turns up. Meanwhile, Lisle is allowed to keep the rental house on the market and press Marlene to sell if a good offer is made, in the interest of the company, which is also in the interest of the poetry award. He gets a fee either way, whether the house sells or continues as a rental."

The judge's ruling on the manuscripts meant Lisle was unlikely to get much out of them, Sharon said, unless MIJ's longtime publisher became involved through contracts Lisle had previously negotiated. "Neither you nor the college are obligated to work with that publisher, so I'd guess Lisle is pressing hard for action on the real estate."

"Have there been any offers on the house Jen Dill and Conor Tilden lived in?"

"Not sure. Our attorney says he's backed away because the college has a conflict of interest in the property matter because of Marlene and the poetry award—he just got involved because Detective Quinn brought it to his attention. Honestly, Mimi, the only good thing to come out of the legal wrangling is that I get to keep you. And the lawyer says we've resolved the question of future whistleblower issues."

"Say *what?!*" I nearly rear-ended the car in front of me. From the silence on the other end of the line, I deduced that Sharon shouldn't have let that slip.

"So that's how this works? I get the promised associate professor post in exchange for my silence on whatever embarrassing MIJ-related secrets might be uncovered about the college? It's not enough that the college will co-opt me in a 'We own your work' fashion, and that anything I ever publish about Mary Irene will have to credit my time here?"

More silence. I ended the call, wishing I had an actual receiver to slam down on Sharon and Sister Marlene and everybody else. My job was safe for all the wrong reasons. I felt contaminated and exploited.

Wary, too, because the college security tapes showed that both Peter Yastremski and the goon from the library incident had been on campus frequently since MIJ dropped out of sight, including on the day of the poetry festival.

According to Quinn, neither he nor Detective Lascala had asked Yastremski yet about why he was on campus, but Yastremski did give them the name of the private investigator who occasionally threw work his way. Quinn had checked the PI's license—the ID photo on it was not Library Man. Lisle emphatically denied knowing either of them or the PI, or hiring Yastremski to harass Conor and Jen on the highway. Lisle had, in fact, produced for Quinn a series of emails disputing the rental-car charge on his law firm's credit card and notifying him of a pending refund. If MIJ's lawyer wasn't behind the men's presence on campus or in Virginia, who else could be?

After my last pet visit of the day, I drove to Mary Irene's block, grateful I had nothing with me to hurl at her house. The "For Sale" sign was still up next door. I called Jen's cellphone. It rang and rang, cutting out without going to voicemail. I called again and again, and again and again, with the same result. She knew my number. She knew it was me.

She surprised us both, I think, by answering on my tenth try. I laid on the guilt.

"Where are you? Remember, I traveled to Virginia and back to take care of Yeats for you."

"I don't have to tell you anything," Jen whispered.

One idiocy demerit for me. Maybe dumping the pup had been the plan all along, and I was suddenly the best way to handle it.

"You and Conor and Liam landed at the only hospital on the planet with a social worker on call before dawn on a Sunday morning, and *that* person tracked *me* down."

"The rescue people would have found a place for Yeats, Mimi, and everything would have worked out as soon as Conor could travel—"

"—If not for the efficient Ms. Rossi's second effort on everybody's behalf when she found a different Mary Irene Jones number in *your* phone. Does Conor's mom know what happened to Yeats? Someone told me the world-famous poet loved her dog. Oh, that was you, wasn't it, Jen?"

The line went dead. But she had said all I needed to hear. I called Quinn immediately.

"I just spoke to Jen Dill," I told his voicemail. "Can you figure out where she is by tracking that call?" I recited her number and pulled away from the curb as the now-less-frequent police patrol drove by.

Seconds later, a text beamed across my lock screen, but it wasn't Quinn responding. It was a reporter from the Philadelphia region's biggest newspaper seeking an interview about MIJ's manuscripts. College PR had told me to expect her call.

"Would love to talk," I dictated in reply. "Driving now. Available in twenty minutes."

I ignored my phone long enough to get home without a traffic mishap. A text from Quinn beamed in with the words "Myrtle Beach" as I unlocked my front door.

When the reporter called, she had my full attention. We arranged for her to come to my house to chat.

"I've examined and reexamined everything in the seven binders Mary Irene Jones sent to me. I haven't yet pinpointed when she wrote each of the completed poems in them, but I can say with some certainty that these poems are contemporary. We may not have a timeline, but Mary Irene did not write them in the distant past. I'd say she wrote them in the last year to eighteen months."

As a photographer took still images of me and shot video, the reporter looked at selected photos of the manuscript binders I had sent her earlier.

"What about the poems made them seem more present-day?" the reporter asked.

"The subject matter is different, and her writing style has evolved. Mary Irene's oldest work—her best-known poetry—is nothing like this. These poems reflect the times in which she has lived, but there's a maturity to them. An older, fuller voice, if you will. She's experienced life, and we see in these poems how it has affected her."

But the manuscripts looked old, especially so because of the paper, the reporter noted, adding that Mary Irene Jones had used one, possibly two, vintage typewriters, based on an analysis of the pair found in April during the first police search of her house.

"Do you think Mary Irene Jones was trying to trick us into thinking this was poetry from an earlier era?" she asked.

"We all hold onto things that remind us of who we used to be," I said. "Creatively, I think that's what Mary Irene wanted as she composed these poems on those old machines—to be immersed in yesterday while writing today. No trick, just going back to the way she might have set down the same verses in an earlier time."

We covered all the boilerplate issues: Who MIJ was and how she came to live in the Philadelphia area. How it was that I knew her work so well. Our identical names, and how I had won the Mary Irene Jones Poetry Prize, and my job at the same college where she once taught, although we had never actually met.

"Why do you think she sent you her manuscripts, Mimi?"

"She was familiar with my work, and I believe she respected it. She trusted me to treat her manuscripts as they deserved to be treated. And she knew that I would never try to pass her work off as my own, because I had spent my whole career showing the world which Mary Irene Jones *I* really am."

Finally came the question we all wanted answered: Why did Mary Irene Jones disappear?

"I think she's alive. I hope to God I'm right about that, because she's my idol. But I also think she simply doesn't want to be Mary Irene Jones anymore. I think she wants something else for herself—the privacy her fame has made next to impossible for decades."

The reporter sat quietly for a minute, as if letting what I said sink in. "The police have spent weeks and weeks watching her house, following up leads, and looking for Mary Irene Jones. What happens if they find her?"

"I don't know." That much was true, I didn't. No idea what laws Mary Irene had broken, or circumvented, by vanishing in such a public way. And I didn't dare mention what I had good reason to suspect— that she was, indeed, alive—because I had no concrete proof.

Early the next morning, the Philadelphia police released a terse update on the search for Mary Irene Jones. Authorities in Pennsylvania and South Carolina, in hopes of concluding their investigation, were working to corroborate a report that she had been in contact with a relative near the South Carolina coast, the news release said. It offered no further details.

My newspaper interview, with accompanying video, went live online within minutes of the update. I drafted a letter of resignation, just in case the college demanded that I go down with the inscrutable woman whose name I shared. I dropped a check off with my fellow pet sitter to cover another week's care of Yeats, dropped Barrett off at my sister's, and dropped a bathing suit I borrowed from Trish into the suitcase in the trunk of my car.

I was flying to South Carolina, bound for Myrtle Beach. Trish called it the dumbest move ever. I began to regret telling her the reason for my trip.

"Mimi, you have no actual idea where Jen Dill is right this minute, let alone where Mary Irene Jones might be. All you have is Jen's phone pinging off a tower in Myrtle Beach within the last twenty-four hours. Why rush down there?"

"Why not? Why wouldn't they hide in plain sight, in a place where people come and go all the time? If they're not in Myrtle Beach, I'll hunt deeper into South Carolina, all the way down to Hilton Head if necessary."

It wasn't as if I was trying to find a single needle in this haystack. There were four of them, a young couple and a toddler and a sixty-something-year-old woman who would have rented or bought at least one house. Only Conor had a job, that I knew of; the others might have searched for work, and maybe looked for a preschool.

"I have parsed every line of poetry that woman left me, and followed clues she might not know she was leaving. Acting dramatically and impulsively is exactly what *that* Mary Irene Jones does. If that's what I have to do to find her, so be it."

Without a doubt, Trish would call our mother, and one of them would call Quinn. I wasn't about to wait around for his reaction.

He got off the same plane I did, though I never saw him during the flight. Quinn was ready either to join me on the next leg of the trip to Myrtle Beach or drag me by my hair back to Philly. Coin toss which it would be.

"Trish or Cass, who called you?"

"Your sister. She said your mother would be impossible to live with if she didn't."

A frequent motivator among us Jones girls.

"Plus, Trish is worried that you've lost your mind. Don't know where she's been, I figured that out the day I met you." Quinn winked. "I'm here with the permission of my boss, butyou're in charge. Your instincts about these people have been good so far. Can't wait to hear what your next move is, Mimi."

What *was* my next move? We had already lost a lot of time. I imagined Mary Irene finding a place to live shortly after arriving here, and Conor and Jen adapting their situation to hers, again living near, but not with, MIJ.

"We go to real estate offices and inquire about properties available at least through the end of the year."

Quinn pointed to a car-rental sign. "We'll need wheels. Picking up something here in my name will give the department a paper trail for our little undercover operation."

Undercover wasn't exactly what I was thinking. More like, go in as Mimi Jones or M. Irene Jones, drop the names Dill and Tilden, and see if anyone reacts. Get people talking.

As for a paper trail, at least a digital one, my text messages from Sharon were into the double digits.

"Where are you?"

"Call me immediately."

"The board of trustees is not happy with you."

What about the college president, who could no longer hide her involvement with her friend's financial affairs? Had she decided to put as much distance as possible between herself and MIJ now? Too bad.

"Get Mary Irene to end this charade," I texted Sister Marlene.

"I've tried," she replied instantaneously, as if she had been waiting, phone in hand, to hear from me.

"Try harder."

Sister Marlene was the shortest route between me and the truth, but the longer route wasn't going to scare me off.

Quinn had detoured to a coffee kiosk, returning with two cups. He glanced at my phone screen, which still displayed the exchange. "Thrown down the gauntlet, I see."

The coffee was terrible, a lot like my mood. "Is there a company with a name like UJJ LLC registered here in South Carolina? If not listed through Mary Irene's name or Sister Marlene's, then under Sarah Tilden? Can you check?"

Quinn pulled out his phone. "It might be on that FBI financial report—the Pennsylvania LLC was, but Mary Irene's real estate holdings weren't on our radar at the time. If it isn't and I can't get access to local fictitious-name records, the people on the case here in South Carolina can."

Intuition told me Sarah Tilden was the name to look for. It was MIJ's mother's name. Her death affected the course of Mary Irene's life. She was determined to change course again.

Quinn texted someone, then stepped into line to rent a car.

Chapter Twenty-two

Fueled by frustration and adrenaline, until long past midnight I collected names of real estate agencies where we might inquire about long-term rentals. Morning sun was sneaking into my motel room through the vertical blinds when I woke to find myself on top of the bedspread, in the clothes I'd worn on the plane. I stared at the popcorn ceiling for a while, watching the fan whirl above me, mesmerized by its simple task—rotate and refresh. Some of each would be a good idea for me too. I needed to get my bearings, so I could formulate a strategy.

I took a long shower and stepped outside about 8:45. The car Quinn had rented was still parked in the space in front of his room next door. A glimpse through the window of the motel's breakfast room showed he was not there, so I walked several blocks to a stretch of stores that we'd driven past the night before. Window-shopping was always a good way to clear the head.

I had no sense of this town, whether there was a higher or lower end, a touristy district for day trippers and vacationers versus places the full-time residents frequented. These shops were a blend of Bohemian and beachy, the sort I'd idle in if this were a leisurely visit. Seizing the opportunity, I ventured into a clothing boutique with an impressive array of flowing retro sundresses and a nook offering sea-inspired décor—shells and anchors, life preservers and nets. Farther along the block, a café beckoned. I needed coffee, and I desperately hoped I could find it at a business called Chamomile.

Vintage tea services filled a window display, six shelves arranged pyramid-style. Some of the sets bore time-honored patterns I recognized from my honeymoon in England with Daniel. Iridescent bone china and imaginative painted pottery, with teapots and sugar bowls and creamers, cups and saucers, and small labels indicating their prices. I sat at a table outside and ordered, twisting to study each shelf while I waited for my cappuccino and croissant, sort of regretting that this wasn't a time for making memories and buying souvenirs.

Inside, shelves with tea sets covered every wall. Behind the cash register, an undistinguished white teapot caught my eye as I paid for my breakfast. From a few feet away, it looked like Mary Irene's, but also like one I bought for a dollar at a flea market a few years ago. Barrett had knocked it off the counter during a thunderstorm, smashing it to bits.

"The tea sets are a lovely touch," I said as I put my credit card back into my purse. "What a great variety!"

The barista laughed. "They're all garage sale finds; the owner loves to hunt for treasures. And every one of them is for sale."

"Except that white teapot behind you." I gestured to it. "There's no price tag."

"Oh." The barista seemed surprised. "I guess she's hoping to find random pieces that match it. The rest of the set was broken, I think. Shouldn't be too hard, because it doesn't have a maker's mark on the bottom."

Neither did mine. Neither did the one MIJ owned. I took a business card from the counter and crossed the street. In front of a bank branch and a not-yet-open ice cream parlor, I pulled from my purse the notebook I always carried with me. Inspired by the teapot, I wrote.

> *Ceramic, white.*
> *Unembellished.*
> *Unchipped.*
> *Complete in what it lacks.*
> *No initials to proclaim it an artisan's lone creation.*
> *No stamp to signify mass production.*
> *Teapot, lid, and spout and handle,*
> *willing to serve if recruited,*
> *unnoticed until then.*
> *Tip it, it pours, as mine does, as hers does.*
> *Anonymous, as she always wanted to be.*

As she wants to be again.

From the bench where I sat, I could see a real estate office on the corner, pages of listings covering the lower half of its window. I considered going in, but doing it together with Quinn would be the better approach. Not that we were together in that sense.

Back at the motel, I texted Trish to see how Barrett was adjusting and called the pet sitter tending Yeats, my best canine pal. Reports were good on both boys. My friend forwarded a video of Yeats frolicking with her dogs in a backyard kiddie pool.

On a well-followed Philadelphia poetry blog for which I was a contributing writer and editor, I posted my few lines of just-written verse under the title, "No Names, Please." As soon as it published, I forwarded the link to the reporter who had interviewed me. "Please add this to your story," I requested. "It's relevant."

Quinn knocked on my door, poking his head in when I opened it. "Duty calls, Professor Jones, if I may call you that now. Bring your list."

I gathered my notes and off we went, the happy couple in search of a rental home to settle into for a few months.

I did the talking. Quinn played the strong, silent type constantly on his phone for business, which gave him the chance to run searches on every real estate office we visited and check for messages from his South Carolina police counterparts.

The agreed-upon script went like this: We were looking for at least three bedrooms and two bathrooms, a pet-friendly rental with space for entertaining and a yard good for a dog. It should be situated in a walkable part of town and be available at least through January, because we were hoping to bring family down for a destination wedding at Christmas. At the last minute, when I thought I would be making this trip alone, I had packed the engagement ring Daniel gave me years ago, which I flashed at every agent we met. Quinn turned out to be the ideal prop fiancé, affecting for the real estate pros a mix of boredom and eagerness to do whatever it took to make his future bride happy.

Our rental price range was flexible, within reason, I said. We filled out forms as truthfully as possible—I was a college English lit professor, he was an investigator—counting on no one checking anything we told them until we were "ready" to sign a lease.

"A move and a wedding this year, how exciting!" was the typical reaction, along with assurances that great houses were available, we'd just have to pick a few to start with and go from there.

It was a lot to take on, I acknowledged, gazing lovingly at Quinn, who smiled and squeezed my hand. But we were so looking forward to beginning our new life. "I bet a lot of people tell you that."

"Oh, for sure—couples like you, but also older people looking to retire," was the typical response. "Let's see what's listed."

I would drop in references to acquaintances from Philadelphia who had just moved here, a couple in their twenties named Jen and Conor who had a cute little boy, along with an admission that I couldn't remember which part of town they had mentioned.

"My girl is a little distracted," Quinn would offer. "The semester just ended at her last job, and now she's planning the move."

"And he's not always as present as he could be," I'd counter. He would put his phone down as a sign of his devotion.

We spent about an hour with each agent, four of them by mid-afternoon, by which time I was starving, my face hurt from smiling, and we had gotten approximately nowhere.

"These agents are chatty enough and eager to please, but there are fourteen real estate offices total on my list. If I get any sweeter with these people, my teeth will fall out."

My fake fiancé leaned in for a kiss. "Please don't get sweeter. I'm on assignment here."

Quinn's boss wanted him back in Philadelphia by the end of the week. Allowing a day for the return trip, that gave us only two days on the ground.

"So we hit a few more agencies today and ask specifically if they have relocation experts who can refer us to couples who recently moved here. Emphasize the urgency, the wedding angle, and if we get any leads we ask to see the houses first thing tomorrow."

"You have the ring, Mimi. Turn on the tears and go full Bridezilla if you think it will work."

It might not be the best idea, but I didn't have another one. Didn't think he did either.

"Still nothing on an LLC?"

Quinn steered me into a little lunch place and waited until we were seated and given menus. "I asked for a pretty broad search, from the start of this year and for five names: Mary Irene Jones, Marlene Flaherty, Jennifer Dill, Conor Tilden, and Sarah Tilden. No idea how long that could take."

We ordered, and I checked my phone. Not surprisingly, Sharon had fired a salvo as soon as my post went live on the poetry blog. "Really, Mimi, you've gone too far. I'm surprised you didn't put it up on the college website," her first text read. If only that had been another quick option for my pressure campaign.

Had Sister Marlene read my new poem? If so, she wasn't saying yet. But poetry was our lives, so of course she'd see it eventually. I was counting on MIJ seeing it too. Mary Irene had helped launch the blog—I first read it as a grad student in upstate New York.

After lunch, Quinn and I visited more real estate offices. I returned calls from two agents from our earlier rounds and set up house tours for the next day. Hitting half the fourteen brokerages on the list was probably the best we could accomplish.

A busy schedule awaited us over the next twenty-four hours. I was already beyond tired, but also totally wired. The black bathing suit I'd borrowed from my sister looked good on me; a swim ought to chill me out. A few teenagers were testing their diving skills at the deep end of the pool, so I parked myself on a lounge chair and picked up the magazine a previous occupant had left behind. (The cover story was about decorating your beach/lake/mountain house to stand up to summertime guests. All-weather fabrics and flea market finds were the solution!)

What I lacked was a glass of wine.

"Come here often, Ms. Jones?"

I knew there was a reason I liked Mike Quinn, who arrived with a bottle of white and two plastic cups.

"Not often enough. Pretty relaxing here. I think I've forgotten how."

He pulled over a chair and poured. We sat in silence for a long time. He watched the diving teens. I flipped through the magazine, a little chilly but warmed by Pinot grigio and the knowledge that doing something was better than passively letting one woman turn many lives, including mine, upside down.

"I've decided I don't like Mary Irene Jones very much."

Quinn looked up at the twilight sky. "You've never met Mary Irene Jones, or talked to her in person."

True enough. "Okay, based on recent experience, I don't like her. She seems self-obsessed to the point that she can't see how what she does affects others. Assuming her actions are not being dictated by some abductor or by delusions resulting from mental incapacity, she has put her son, daughter-in-law, and grandson, as well as her oldest friend, at personal or professional risk. Worst case scenario, Jen and Conor could go to jail for obstructing police investigations, and then what happens to Liam? The reputations of the college and her esteemed poetry award could be tarnished. I can't even speculate whether her publisher has anything to lose, and who knows what Jordan Lisle's agenda is. Maybe he *is* just working for an eccentric, demanding narcissist of a law client."

"I was worried the outrage was diminishing. Glad to see it isn't." Quinn felt for my hand. "Angry Mimi gets things done."

Instead of Wallowing Mimi, the me I had been for the past five years, letting what other people did define me, rather than defining myself.

"I am Angry Mimi, and Defiant Mimi, and, damn it, Mimi the Writer. I knocked out a poem today and published it to a Philly blog. It's been forever since I did that. It was about Mary Irene, naturally. Someday, not everything will be about her. That day can't come soon enough."

Quinn stroked my knuckles. His hand was warm, comforting—a comfort I shouldn't count on, any more than I had counted on Daniel's. That had to come primarily from me, I was finally learning.

I shook out of his fingers, walked to the pool's edge, and slipped in. The teenagers had dispersed at last, so I swam one lap, then two, then ten. Quinn was waiting for me with a towel when I emerged from the water. He wrapped it around me, picked up the almost-empty wine bottle, and said good night.

Pounding on the door and a text notification woke me. My phone read 3 a.m.; the text read, "Mimi, let me in." I greeted Quinn in my latest MIJ Poetry Fest T-shirt and boxer shorts.

"Sorry, couldn't sleep." He took a deep breath and showed me an email.

It said: S & C Tilden Associates LLC, doing business as S & C Tilden Myrtle Properties and Chamomile. I pulled him and his phone inside and turned on another light.

"Chamomile is just up the street, a tea shop in that little strip of stores. I had breakfast there yesterday." I fished around in my purse for the business card. "There's a white teapot behind the cash register. That poem I told you about, I wrote it just after I saw it."

I tapped into the blog site and showed him. He ran a search on S & C Tilden Properties' recent transactions.

"My South Carolina counterparts sent me a link and a login for this county's real estate records. Looks like S & C owns two houses." He searched on a national real estate site and found the listings. They were modest-sized dwellings not unlike MIJ's Philadelphia houses, probably a bit larger but similarly priced, with nice yards perfect for a small child and a dog.

I flung my arms around Quinn's waist and tried to slow my heart down, breathing in and out slowly, the cotton of his Philly P.D. T-shirt rising and falling under my cheek. He wrapped his arms around me.

This was it. We were so close to finding Mary Irene Jones.

"We need to get some sleep so we can think clearly tomorrow, though I swear I haven't thought clearly in months now. Not since Mary Irene Jones vanished and I met you, Mimi." He kissed the top of my head and sighed. "Set your alarm, I'll be back at seven o'clock."

I was astounded I had guessed right so far, and eager to see where the trail would lead. But I was torn, as well. Yes, I felt manipulated by Mary Irene and ensnared by the elaborate web of misdirection she was spinning. The decision to untangle it had been mine, though. It wasn't as if she had killed anyone. She hadn't even abandoned her dog, not really—in the end, I took care of her manuscripts *and* Yeats, however indirectly.

Still, someone had triggered a highway accident in Virginia that injured Conor. His wife and child were in that car. There had been repercussions MIJ either didn't anticipate or underestimated. At best, she seemed reckless. At worst, she seemed not to care who suffered because of her.

No way I could sleep. As soon as the sun slipped above the horizon, I got dressed and walked down to Chamomile. I aimed my phone's flashlight through the window at the shelf behind the register.

A certain white teapot was gone.

Chapter Twenty-three

The two houses were about a mile apart. S & C Tilden Associates, established in October of last year, had closed on one house the following January, the other in February, both at what seemed to be low prices for a resort town.

A second, coffee-assisted study of all the online listing photos showed the houses had suffered what looked like storm damage. Roofing shingles littered the ground below, and windows had been shattered.

"Sad fixer-uppers Mary Irene could renovate," Quinn said. "That could account for the cash she withdrew gradually from the one Philadelphia bank account. The FBI never found a paper trail for that money through other bank or investment accounts in her name. S & C Tilden Associates obviously had an account it used to purchase the houses here. An estimated second-quarter tax form the company filed with the state of South Carolina was signed by Conor Tilden, who is listed as chief financial officer."

"So Conor would have been the one to move funds into and out of the company's bank account."

"Correct," Quinn said. "There was also some insurance money involved, a less than $10,000 payout on each Myrtle Beach property, but the previous owners apparently opted to move rather than spend time repairing the houses and signed over the proceeds to S & C Tilden."

Selling even one of the two Philadelphia houses would go a long way toward paying off the repair debts S & C Tilden incurred in Myrtle Beach. Chamomile had not opened for business until May of this year, according to a mercantile license Quinn found. It probably barely covered its expenses, let alone helped with cash flow to the renovation projects.

"Can you pull up the real estate records for the building where Chamomile is located? Does S & C own that?"

Quinn searched for the address listed on the tea shop's business card. "Nope, that's a rental. The landlord owns the whole building—the first-floor retail space, full basement storage, and an apartment on the second floor. The entire property is described as being under a three-year lease that started in January."

I strained my brain to remember the regional poetry conferences to which I had offered myself as a speaker last year. When *the* Mary Irene Jones also offered herself for these symposiums, my bids were routinely rejected, or just as often simply ignored. There had been an event in early November, I recalled, but that was in Georgia, not South Carolina. Still, one speaking engagement plus one scouting trip could have added up to her vanishing point of choice.

"Mary Irene is living over the tea shop." I was sure of it. "I passed by there this morning, and the white teapot was gone. I bet she knows someone was in Chamomile asking about it. She might be aware of the poem I published, too."

Quinn read further into the S & C Tilden file. "This LLC doesn't appear to have real estate involvement in South Carolina other than the mortgages on the two houses and the building lease, so she could well be living over Chamomile, maybe hoping to flip the second house."

"If one house was habitable again by sometime in May, wouldn't that be the place Conor and Jen were going to move into with their son and, if everything had gone according to the original plan, Yeats too? Can you call up views of the streets to see whether either house looks occupied now?"

His laptop worked its search magic. The house bought in February had an SUV in the driveway and a small sliding board in the backyard.

"Let's go," Quinn said, tossing me the room key card I had dropped onto a table near the door. "If no one is home, we can cruise by the other place and see what shape that's in."

The SUV was gone and the backyard empty when we pulled onto the street. The exterior of the February house was still being repaired. A work crew was transferring siding panels from a flatbed truck in the driveway to a stack in the side yard. In that regard, the house fit right in with others on the block, many of which also had what looked like wind damage and were in some stage or another of reconstruction. We drove around a couple of times to get the 360-degree view. The sliding board must have been moved inside. Looked like no one was home.

At the January house, a rebuild of the roof was underway. A tarpaulin covered a substantial section to the left of the chimney; the right side had new shingles. Workers leaned against a pickup truck in the driveway, coffee cups in hand. They glanced over both times we drove by. I took a photo of the roofing company sign, as if I were just another neighbor checking out a prospective contractor.

A frustrated Quinn pulled into a nearby park with a food truck that offered coffee and pastries. We found a shaded area with a picnic table, where we could eat breakfast and cancel the home tours we had scheduled.

"Jen may have taken Liam to day care, that could explain that, but where is Conor? He's a systems engineer, you'd think he could be working from home." Or a diner. Or a tea shop, though that would be too much to hope for.

"The company Conor lists in his online profile has a brick-and-mortar office a few towns over, assuming that's still his employer. But it's not like I have jurisdiction to go there and demand to see him, Mimi. Hell, if it weren't for the Virginia crash and the Mary Irene Jones connection, my bosses wouldn't give a good goddamn about Conor Tilden or Jen Dill. As it is, they're making me take this time here as vacation days. Everything about this trip is only as official as it has to be."

That, I did not know. "You're here because I'm here, following my hunches."

"Tell me I'm not an idiot. You'd be the first person today."

That Quinn was tired of searching databases and watching roofing tar cure was clear. We had less than twenty-four hours left to our stay, but we couldn't keep driving around the February house waiting for Jen or Conor to return. And confronting Mary Irene at the tea shop was the last thing I wanted right now, assuming she was, indeed, there. We still didn't know her reasons for wanting to disappear, and even with the FBI's financial analysis we still had no idea how much money she might have stashed away or how she planned to live out the rest of her life.

Was I furious with her? You bet, but I didn't want to ruin her or expose her whereabouts to the world. What I wanted was for the woman to own up to the unnecessary upheaval she had caused and help set matters right herself.

I located the water-frolic video of Yeats that my dog-sitting friend had texted me. I forwarded it to what I hoped was still Jen's phone number. I was not above piling on the guilt.

"You said you would take care of Yeats, remember?" I typed. "Big fail."

Three hours since my text to Jen, and no response. Six and a half hours since we left the motel, and no sightings of her or Conor, despite our repeated passes by the house we figured they must be living in, as well as the closest day care center. We had entered the realm of paparazzi and stalkers.

We ate a second meal at the picnic table in the park. The food truck's hot dogs weren't bad once you loaded them up with mustard and pickle relish and sauerkraut and swished enough diet cola in your mouth to tamp down the disturbing vinegar aftertaste.

I reached into my purse for my notebook and a pen.

"If you start writing a poem, I will lose it," Quinn growled from under the brim of a Phillies hat. "I've been on two-week-long meth lab stakeouts that were less boring and way more productive."

I ignored him and drafted a letter I planned to send Mary Irene, or rather Sarah Tilden, in care of her Chamomile tea shop. I described what I was trying to achieve, while also acknowledging that our perspectives on the matter were vastly different. I pointed out all the negative results of her actions. Also the positives, because she would have heard by now that this year's poetry festival was a huge success financially and artistically. Professionally for me as well, in one way—I had gotten more attention in the last month than in the ten years since I'd won her poetry award, and she would be aware of that. She'd be aware of my conclusions about her manuscripts and could no doubt see in them a new approach to my dissertation. She might not agree, or care, but she would know.

Mary Irene Jones was brilliant and eccentric and paranoid, but also, I hoped, able to be reasoned with via snail mail. I had covered two pages on both sides when I pushed the notebook over to Quinn to read.

"Very nice handwriting," he said.

"Twelve years of Catholic school, plus I am a teacher myself, remember? Blackboard ready."

He finished and passed the notebook back to me. "Now what?"

"They sell cards in that home décor shop across the street from Chamomile. You can drop me off there to buy one. I'll find a post office, mail this return receipt requested, and meet you back at the motel."

In dejected silence, we drove past the February house again. It looked no more alive than it did the last time. Did Jen and Conor know we were watching it? Did it worry them that we were? I'd hate to think that was true.

Conor Tilden was a grown man. His mother would do what his mother would do, according to her own plan. That had been the pattern throughout his life, based on what I'd learned about Mary Irene. But he evidently had decided to stand by her choices now.

Wouldn't I do the same if I got the chance to be with my mother openly for the first time since the day I was born? If an end to the chasing around and secrecy Mary Irene insisted on presented itself, wouldn't I seize it?

Rather late, yes, for me to be having this epiphany. There was no denying how I'd failed to see things from all sides. I had let my raging at the fates get in the way of understanding why these people might go to such extremes to be together. My letter to Mary Irene would acknowledge what I knew and how I knew it, and then I had to let it go. I might be out of a job, but at least I would have my self-respect.

And I would have Yeats. I intended to bring the dog home to live with me and Barrett. I wouldn't shirk that responsibility any more than I had my role as keeper of the manuscripts. Others could decide for themselves whether I acquitted myself well in either capacity. All I wanted now was to say truthfully that I'd given it my all.

My missive dispatched, I found my way back to my motel room, and back to the pool. As he did the night before, Quinn found me, wine bottle and cups in hand.

"Here's to us and our first investigation. No matter how it turns out, it's been some adventure." He tapped his cup against mine.

That he described it as our *first* investigation gave me hope. Quinn had never once called me an idiot whenever we ran around from state to state, only himself.

"From what I hear, it's fallen short of a meth lab stakeout for excitement, but I'll drink to it if you will."

As I did, he touched my left hand, caressed my ring finger. "This is looking naked. I was getting used to taking credit for that big shiny rock. Your ex had good taste in diamonds."

The ring had belonged to Daniel's grandmother, who died shortly after I met him at Syracuse. He wanted me to keep it after the divorce, he said, because I was a lot like her. Putting it on again had been like slipping into an out-of-shape old sweater—comfortable, but no longer something I wanted to wear.

"Fancy jewelry isn't my thing, as I'm sure you've noticed. More substance than style, that's me. Cass has been trying to, shall we say, elevate my wardrobe for years without much success—as I'm sure you've also noticed."

Quinn topped off my cup and his. "Do you call your mother Cass to her face?"

The wine was tart, a dry Riesling, the label read. "Sometimes. It's an inside joke, the name thing. My sister and I know she's really ticked off when she starts calling us Mary Irene and Mary Patricia, and when we're annoyed we call her Cass. I don't think either one of us has ever called her Mary Catherine — that would involve a whole new level of maternal interference. What might set her off like that, I can't imagine."

My falling for a cop? No, Mom would be fine with that, she had been worrying for so long that I still wasn't over Daniel. As if you ever got over a person you'd loved for that long. As if she had gotten over my father in the years since he died.

"You're pensive, Mimi Jones, usually a dangerous sign. What's going on in that busy brain of yours?"

Oh, lots of random things whirled around in there along with my feelings for one Michael Quinn and my utter ambivalence about the keeping-things-professional rule I had told him I wanted. Add together everything else and it might someday equal a full professorship in English literature, but I doubted anyone but me cared about that. What I mostly was thinking just then was that I wished I wasn't thinking at all.

"I hear Myrtle Beach has an actual beach — sand and waves and ocean breezes with that sharp salty tang. I'd like to soak up some rays, read a romance novel or three. Go to a nice restaurant afterward. Dance under the stars. Stuff I don't typically do — make that stuff I *never* do. I'll have to add those things to my online dating profile. You know: 'Describe your perfect evening.'"

He was lying back on a lounge chair studying the evening sky, which was still too bright to see much more than the setting sun coloring the spaces between the clouds. "What about you, Detective Quinn? Where is your busy brain taking you?"

He pointed up. "I wanted to be an astronaut. Fly to the space station. Learn Russian and whatever engineering I'd need beforehand, so I could conduct experiments and repair the heat shields. Come to find out I wasn't much of a science and technology guy. I was good at finding answers to questions, just not the ones the cosmos posed. Struggled to pass high school physics, though it was my favorite subject."

I was no psychologist, but it sounded as if we both wanted to escape. Swimming would have to do; we had the pool to ourselves. I walked to the diving board, jumped once, and went in headfirst, which was the way I did everything lately.

I flipped over onto my back and floated toward Quinn, who eased into the water and kissed me. I offered no resistance whatsoever.

"If I asked you to share that perfect evening with me, would you, Mimi? I promise to take you dancing."

I wrapped my arms around his neck. "That would be lovely, whenever."

Whenever we were no longer preoccupied with a poet from Northern Ireland who had decided merely staying in the shadows wasn't enough.

Chapter Twenty-four

Freelance reporters called constantly. I did one or two interviews a week with writers for academic journals scrambling to make MIJ the cover story for their fall issues. Their hard late-summer deadlines made it easier for me to skirt questions about Mary Irene's disappearance and steer the focus to what I believed I had gleaned from those seven binders of unpublished manuscripts. No one wanted an article that could be out of date before it hit actual and digital mailboxes.

A *New York Times* reporter, informing me she needed to turn her article around in less than seventy-two hours, set up a preliminary interview via video chat. Right out of the gate, she wanted details about my recent visit to Myrtle Beach with a Philadelphia police detective investigating MIJ's disappearance, a man with whom I also was believed to be romantically involved. No idea how she knew about the trip, but I danced around her questions.

"We didn't travel there together. For me, it was just an impromptu vacation," I said.

"You stayed at the same motel on the same days, my sources tell me."

"In separate rooms," I replied.

She smiled a knowing "Bet I can get key card data" smile, then proceeded to negotiate arrangements for the in-person interview about the poetry matters at hand.

Although it contained a dearth of juicy information about either MIJ or me, the *Times* article found a considerable online audience, according to the college's marketing team. The buzzy headline, "Did Poet Mary Irene Jones Hint She Might Vanish?" had a lot to do with that, our search engine optimization expert said. Who was more pleased with those thousands of clicks, my boss or my mother, was a toss-up.

Sharon was understandably thrilled by the publicity for the college and the spotlight the article shone on a scholarly undertaking by its newest associate professor of English literature.

"You dazzled them, Mimi. Dazed them a little too, of course, analysis of poetry will do that. But we'll take it," she said.

Since the more substantial interview with the *Times* reporter took place in and near my house—I suggested that one photo of Yeats appear with the article, because who doesn't love a cute dog in their news feed—Cass had been able to flash her style chops nationwide, with an assist from Trish. My sister had staged my home, while our mother quickly rehabbed me.

"You're beautiful, Mimi. I just wish your wardrobe didn't come from the Salvation Army," Mom lamented as she rejected outfit after outfit. "Though I admit you have a flair for thrifting interesting furniture."

That the article ultimately elicited high praise from both my parent and her academic surrogate was phenomenal indeed.

Daniel sent a bouquet of sunflowers and gerbera daisies. "Still my ray of poetry sunshine," the card read. Whereas in response to the article link I sent Quinn, I received a short voicemail saying he was slammed with new cases and would read it as soon as he could.

We hadn't seen each other since the week after we returned from Myrtle Beach, and then only for an update from his fellow investigator there. Conor and Jen were definitely living in the February house; their new state driver's license applications listed the address. More proof that my hunch about them had been correct. Sarah Tilden did not apply for a license this year, per the South Carolina motor vehicle records, though the previous year's files were still being checked. My partner in sleuthing had delivered these facts during a half-hour walk through the dog park with Yeats as chaperone. I tried not to let the brevity of his visit bother me.

For my part, I had texted Quinn the day I received confirmation that someone at Chamomile had accepted the letter addressed to Sarah Tilden, which offered concrete evidence of little other than successful mail delivery to the tea shop.

Between press opportunities, I had been pretty slammed too. I accustomed myself to dog ownership—some online talk therapy helped temper my fears. I tended to a few September cat-sitting clients. And, because my mojo was working again, I submitted a revised dissertation proposal to my Ph.D. adviser up at NYU.

The start of my expanded fall teaching schedule lay ahead, with courses about the Romantic poets and Shakespeare added to the semester's workload. The syllabi, prepared by Sister Marlene and Sharon years ago, were familiar—I'd taught both classes before—but there were still lectures to prepare and class assignments to devise. So no idle hands for me, yet the devil got into my head anyway, tempting me to search my mail, my inbox, my texts, my social media notifications, my favorite news sources, anything that might bring word about MIJ.

Instead, this morsel arrived courtesy of Jordan Lisle, in a voicemail that said: "Your favorite poet's lawyer here. The house next to Mary Irene's has sold, going to settlement end of this week. If you want to get inside, let me know ASAP. You've probably snooped around there before, what's one more time?"

I couldn't imagine what might be left at that house to see. Jen and Conor had moved out how long ago now? But absent a response of any kind to my letter from either Mary Irene Jones or Sarah Tilden, being there might yield some insight. Lisle agreed to meet me that afternoon.

"Dill-Tilden house sold," I texted Quinn. "Lisle invited me to look around. We'll be there at three o'clock."

We included Yeats. He knew the place better than the rest of us. He also would recognize his old house, that is, Mary Irene's old house. I counted on his tugging me in that direction, so I purposely arrived a half-hour early. The dog bounded across the front lawn as soon as I freed him from the car.

I was reasonably certain the Philadelphia Police Department had ceased extra patrols in the neighborhood, so I let him into Mary Irene's backyard. Yeats nosed into every corner, finding yet another disgusting tennis ball and dropping it at my feet. I tossed it for him and wandered over to the screened porch where Yeats and I first met. The dog supplies were gone, of course, though the cooler Jen had put there to store water remained. It was empty, but next to it, still under the rock Jen had used to weigh it down, was the note she wrote months ago informing MIJ that she had taken Yeats to live with her.

At the bottom, in green-ink block letters, this had been added: "We must take good care." Care in what sense, that writer did not say.

The dog nudged past me and squeezed into the porch through a hole in the screen. "Get the ball," I commanded as I pitched, and Yeats scampered out onto the grass again. I reached in for the note and pocketed it.

I chased Yeats down and carried him to the sidewalk, where I found Quinn and Lisle staring. "I thought he might be helpful," I said innocently, "but I couldn't keep him out of the spot where he used to play. He sniffed out a tennis ball he'd lost in the shrubs."

Both looked skeptical. "Fine," Lisle muttered, "as long as you clean up any mess he leaves." I waved two plastic grocery bags at him.

Quinn took the dog and set him on his feet. "I'll walk this backyard with Yeats for now while you go inside." I gave him the bags and a smile and followed Lisle through the front door.

The walls wore a fresh coat of gray paint that read as pale lavender in the rooms with more shade than afternoon sun. Other than that, what little I'd seen of the house looked the same. We covered the first floor, then ascended to the second. A dinosaur mural remained in what had been Liam's room. It had been hand-drawn, the giant reptiles rendered friendly in soft shades of green and grayish brown.

Up another flight, the attic was bare, dust moving through the sunbeams. Down three flights, the basement was newly swept, nicely dry, ready for its new owner.

"Nothing to see," Lisle said as we climbed to the kitchen, "but I figured you hadn't taken my word for anything. Why would you start now?"

"Thanks for inviting me," I said, fingering the paper in my pocket as I glanced through the window at Quinn and Yeats outside. "He'll want to look around too. I'll take the dog off his hands."

Mid-yard, Yeats circled my legs, trailing his leash. Quinn gave me the tennis ball.

"You're next for the house tour, Detective. It's quick and pretty dull. A nice change of pace when Conor and Jen are involved."

"No sense in not taking Lisle up on the offer, after what's gone before. Thanks for the tip, Mimi."

Quinn winked that killer wink. I waved, and we departed, me with the just-discovered note, Yeats with whatever canine nostalgia kicked in as he watched his former homes fade into the distance.

The nation's most influential poetry publication had been pushing aggressively for an interview with me and, if possible, for permission to print an excerpt of MIJ's unpublished work. Others would have to weigh in on the legal particulars. The interview was mine to accept, or not.

After Myrtle Beach, I had made a pact with myself as keeper of the manuscripts: I gave only the interviews I chose to give; I refused to let anyone else mess with me because of them; and I vowed not to interfere publicly with MIJ's new life. Since Mary Irene had not responded to my overture in the mail, it was a one-sided commitment, yet one I felt bound by. This interview request gave me pause, mostly because people I considered more impressed by academia's politics than poetry wanted it so badly.

My hesitation in granting the august journal its wish brought immediate accusations of petulance, immaturity, and disrespect. Its leader went over my head to Sharon, Sister Marlene, and the president of the college's board of trustees, demanding that I be given my comeuppance. That put each of us in an awkward position—or I should say another awkward position, in what had been a months-long contortion.

I had said all I was willing to say on the subject of Mary Irene Jones, to pretty much everyone who still cared enough to listen and publish it. The only good reason for doing this interview? It was one more opportunity to coax her out. Not that the previous interviews had succeeded, but this was probably my last high-profile chance to signal that the game was up, and that it was up to her—not me—to tell the world what she intended.

As Yeats rambled around the dog park near my place, romping with a tiny poodle and a chihuahua, I turned the sheet of paper I'd just filched from MIJ's screened porch over and over. There was absolutely nothing in those five words written in green ink that proved Mary Irene had been at that house after leaving it in April. I could say pretty much the same about the mysterious removal of the white teapot from her kitchen the following month, but at least the initial police inventory supported the fact that it was missing. Right now, it would be my word against the world's that MIJ had been in Philadelphia more than once since her supposed disappearance, like a ghost haunting her longtime dwelling.

I whistled twice for Yeats, his cue that it was time to go, and he obediently trotted over and allowed me to reattach his leash. We weren't best buddies, that hadn't happened, but he was a cute little guy who was just as intimidated by Barrett as I was by him, and we were adapting. I wasn't taking the anti-anxiety meds anymore, which was amazing when I stopped to think about it.

What I hadn't considered was that one anxiety-inducing police detective would be waiting outside his car when Yeats and I returned home. In the window facing us, Barrett paced and screeched so loudly behind the glass that we could hear him.

"Better get inside before your cat has a nervous breakdown." Quinn distracted Yeats while I looked for my key. Barrett did his best flying-squirrel impersonation as he saw me enter.

"Give me a minute to feed the menagerie. You know where to find the wine, unless you're on duty."

"Too many long days lately. I decided to clock out early today."

Quinn squeezed past me and the food bowls and gathered a bottle of white and two glasses. "I thought the next time I arrived here unannounced I would sweep you away for that perfect date, Mimi. Then I remembered another spontaneous road trip was not what you had in mind, and that the nearest beach was about sixty-five miles away in New Jersey."

Seemed farther lately, as if much more than sixty-five miles lay between him and me, despite the obvious chemistry and incremental kissing.

"You know, Michael Quinn, I have no idea where you live. Own or rent? Mansion or hovel? No idea if you have brothers and sisters, or whether your parents are alive. No idea when or why you decided to go to the police academy. I know your phone number, what you drive, and that you're divorced. Oh, and how you take your coffee. Meanwhile, you have a file *this thick* on me."

I slapped a bag of cat food on the counter and put my hands on hips. "Makes me wonder, Detective: Do I know you well enough to date you?"

The cork broke, as perfect a metaphor for the moment as you could get. Part of it was wrapped around the corkscrew in Quinn's hand; part of it floated down into the wine bottle. Obsessively, he fished it out, and then took his time pouring. Between him and Mary Irene, I was oh-for-two with one-sided relationships. I couldn't get either of them to open up.

"I guess I do know this about you: You've been terrible at maintaining professional distance since I met you, from that first little kiss on my arm the night Barrett scratched me, through our viral video and a few other stolen moments. Not that I've been a shining example either." I lifted a wineglass. "Shall we drink to first dates that will never be?"

He raised the other glass. "Let's toast second dates instead. Let's call everything that's happened up until now one long, messy first date. You want details about me, I'll fill out a questionnaire beforehand. Pick a day, pick a restaurant, I'll make a reservation, we'll get dressed up and put ourselves out there. We'll be the opposite of Mary Irene Jones, the opposite of private and paranoid. I'm tired of her disappearance standing in our way."

I clinked my glass against his. "Hot dogs are a deal breaker. Make it a French restaurant, and I'm in."

An alternative occurred to me, though. "What do you think about flea markets?"

"Fleas are much too small to make a meal out of, so I don't go to the markets much."

"Now you're going to deny me my perfect second date?"

To shut me up, he kissed me. Little did he know, he might take my breath away for a while, but he couldn't distract me indefinitely.

Chapter Twenty-five

I plotted a route that would take us along the Delaware River north of Philly, to the land of upscale fleas, antiques barns, and vintage shops. If I found what I wanted early, we could while away a sunny Saturday and drink margaritas on a deck somewhere.

I gave Quinn a printout of a photo. "Keep your eyes open. If you see something that looks promising, holler. Four eyes are better than two."

He looked over his sunglasses, projecting an "Aren't there alternatives to digging through old dishes?" glare before a table with baseball cards caught his eye and the gender stereotyping commenced. I picked my way through acres of china and glassware. He rooted through scuffed-up mitts and autographed balls.

I towed a hard-sided rolling suitcase behind me, filled only with bubble wrap at the start. Eventually, I collected two cups with saucers that didn't match but were close enough, and a sugar bowl lacking a lid. The advantage of these gems was that they were not chipped, and that they had no marks disclosing their origin stories. They were nothing but white, and I had spent only three dollars on them. If I had to fill the suitcase with miscellaneous dishware to get the additional pieces I wanted, so be it. If I could find cake plates, even better.

An air-conditioned shop beckoned, Quinn texted me. "Go ahead, I'm the middle of buried treasure, give or take a few bug carcasses," I replied. As it turned out, the treasure chest didn't have what I sought. I looked around and guessed the rest of my search party, Quinn, was still inside.

He saw me before I saw him, a height advantage and the detective training working in his favor. "I'm three vendors' booths away. See me waving?" I looked up from my phone and joined him.

On a table covered with a cloth made of intact, if not pure white, Irish lace was a modest tea set of ideal proportions. No mark on the bottom. Thicker, more serviceable ceramic, possibly restaurant quality. Four cups, four saucers, four cake plates, and a teapot, but no sugar bowl and no cream pitcher, all priced at forty dollars. Much too much.

"Will you take thirty?" I asked the dealer. We negotiated, and I got the partial set for thirty-three bucks.

Quinn helped me wrap the pieces and gently position them in the suitcase. "I'll grab us some drinks, then where to?" he asked.

Back the way we came, just one aisle over. He rejoined me holding two bottles of water. "What's your budget for today?"

"Trying to keep it under forty dollars. One small pitcher, maybe a lidded sugar bowl, and we're done."

But it wasn't to be, and nothing even close presented itself at the flea market up the road. By then, we needed food and a reapplication of sunscreen. We wedged the suitcase between an elderly sleeping bag and a pile of half-ripe gym clothes in the back of Quinn's SUV and found a spot for lunch al fresco. It didn't serve French food, but the French fries and margaritas made up for it.

Hours later, we arrayed our haul on my dining table and judged which of the pieces looked better together.

"The pricier set looks best. I guess you expected that." Quinn set aside the cheaper cups and mismatched saucers. "What will you do with these?"

I set the pricey teapot next to them—Mary Irene didn't need it. "Those are for me. I'll get a box and paper and mailing labels on Monday and send the rest to Chamomile."

A good faith offering for Mary Irene, postage paid and insured for next-day delivery in care of Sarah Tilden. But also one for me and whatever Quinn and I could become. All further activity concerning MIJ would be related only to my career, I hoped, and no longer to Mike's.

It wasn't the perfect ending. There was no cream pitcher to complete the tea set. Sometimes, we had to accept that certain things would elude us. But when consecutive nights of insomnia followed my trip to the post office, I decided Mary Irene Jones would not remain one of them.

The card listed business hours as 6:30 a.m. to 5 p.m. About 7 o'clock Thursday morning, I called the number. The phone rang several times before a woman answered.

"Chamomile," she said.

"I'd like to speak to Sarah Tilden. Tell her it's Mimi Jones. She's been expecting my call."

"Hold on, please, she's in the kitchen."

I heard the woman shout Sarah's name and mention mine. The tea shop was long but not wide, I recalled from my visit to Myrtle Beach. I had not been able to see the kitchen when I stood at the cash register at the front counter. There was a phone on the counter, perhaps the only one. Was she ducking out a back door now to avoid me?

I paced my living room, zigzagging around Barrett and Yeats, who snoozed as I fretted. When an undeniably Irish accent materialized on the other end of the line, it startled me to a stop. I recognized Mary Irene's voice immediately from the many recordings I had heard of her Poetry Festival speeches and others.

"This is Sarah. What can I do for you?"

"I appreciate your taking my call. I think you're quite aware what you can do for me."

"Ah, yes, thank you for the tea set. It's lovely. You shouldn't have."

"We both know that's not why I'm calling, Mary Irene."

She hesitated, forcing me to wait as she crafted her reply. "That person exists only in myth now, as a matter of convenience. The poetry will live on and, as a result, the award encouraging young women poets."

"Very altruistic. Also very convenient, indeed," I said, more irritated than I expected to be whenever I had only imagined this conversation. Lack of sleep had increased the cranky quotient.

"Mimi, I owe you neither an apology nor an explanation for choosing to live the rest of my days on my own terms, rather than those imposed by the grand career I never sought."

True enough, she owed me nothing, and had given me much. But there was a story behind MIJ's actions over these last months, and I wanted to hear her tell it.

"Why was all the subterfuge necessary? Why did you hide your family and force them to lie about everything, from picking the lock on your porch to behaving as if they were just neighbors? Why did you leave Sister Marlene to clean up after you?"

"No one lied for me. I shared details with them as I saw fit."

"So that what they didn't know couldn't hurt *you*. But sins of omission, dissembling—your son and daughter-in-law and your longtime friend did those things for you, and in return you jeopardized their safety or put their professional reputation at risk."

Silence hung between us. I was demanding answers from her as she stood in a public place. I could hear the bustle of the tea shop around her, and the sounds of the cash register as patrons paid for their breakfasts. She told someone that she needed a few minutes to finish the call.

"I did nothing to put anyone at risk," she finally said. "I would never put those I love most in danger."

"Semantics, Mary Irene? Really? Your son was injured when someone rammed his family's car on the highway. Your sweet little grandson, Liam, was in the backseat right behind Conor. He could have been hurt, too—and you've scarcely gotten a chance to know him. In the meantime, Sister Marlene is turning herself inside out to untangle a knot you designed. And you left Yeats behind with no one to care for him."

More uncomfortable silence followed. I envisioned her waiting until people stepped away from the counter so she could speak in her defense.

"Still on the line, are you, Mimi Jones? Then know this: Yeats was Sharon's idea, not mine. He would have been taken care of, I had seen to that, if you hadn't gotten in the middle of it. You and your friend Quinn."

Was it possible Jordan Lisle had no clue even after she set the plan in motion? "You were the one who put me in the middle, Mary Irene, and it was your lawyer who involved the police."

"You've said your piece, asked your questions. But I have a business to run and a new life I have worked very hard for —"

"No more puzzles. No more red herrings. I don't intend to play along anymore."

"Then don't. Live your own life, and we'll all be better off," she said.

Then she hung up.

Chapter Twenty-six

More like a nook, the space was scarcely big enough for a desk and two chairs, but it was mine. At last, I had an on-campus office of my own.

Bookshelves dominated one wall, as befit a professor of English. I had inherited dozens of ancient volumes from the office's past occupants, which gave the place a Masterpiece Theater vibe. Winnowing the old tomes would take some time, and considering the dirt I removed from their covers, I deduced that it had been decades since anyone had touched them. I squeezed some of my own collection onto a thirty-six-inch-long, eye-level stretch of wood and lined others up along on the sill of a small window overlooking the quad. Nice view, though definitely more Philly suburbs than Regency-era London.

On the wall space that remained hung my undergraduate and graduate degrees from Syracuse University, my Mary Irene Jones Poetry Award, and framed portraits of Elizabeth Barrett Browning and the cat I had named for her. Places of honor also went to the photo I'd taken on my honeymoon of Dove Cottage, Wordsworth's home in the Lake District, and an enlarged version of the first selfie I took of Yeats and me. Once a pet sitter, always a pet sitter, though I no longer had the time or an urgent financial need.

I didn't hear Sister Marlene knock on the open door. She tapped my shoulder as I was running a hand-held vacuum cleaner, scaring the life out of me.

"You know, this used to be my office. Still smells a bit musty, good luck getting rid of that. Books come here to decompose, I think."

"Can I interest you in undecayed translations of *Plutarch's Lives* or the *Aeneid*? I have at least three each."

She laughed and sat on the newly cushioned guest chair, leaving the one behind the desk for me. We hadn't exchanged more than twenty words since I finally agreed to the poetry council's interview request. She had said zilch about my remarks in that article or any of the earlier ones. Had she even read my analysis of the unpublished manuscripts? But now, it seemed, we were going to have a chat.

Sister Marlene looked around the office at the little touches I'd added so far, such as the chair cushions and a quill and ink pot. "We're having an estate auction. Based on what I see here, you'll like what's on offer. I emailed you an invitation to the in-person preview."

"Who died?"

"Not an estate per se," she corrected herself, "but rather the contents of Mary Irene's house." UJJ LLC owned the house and had sold it, as permitted under the company's bylaws, Sister Marlene explained.

"It was either that or rent it. As chief operating officer, the decision was mine to make, and I held off for a while. But it's a seller's market. I had to take advantage of it."

How could she just sell off MIJ's belongings? "Don't you have to put her things in storage, in case she should return and want them back?" I asked. "Also, Mary Irene had a will …"

"The company owns the contents of the house; under the bylaws, Mary Irene rented the property furnished. Her will reiterates that UJJ owns everything in it as well as the stipulation that, where possible, proceeds from their sale are to be used to help set up an endowment that will indefinitely sustain the poetry prize at the college."

Quite precise, every move calculated, with nothing that could be thwarted by failure to produce proof of her death. Mary Irene's decision to send the unpublished manuscripts to me made more sense by the minute—issues of ownership, however complicated I had inadvertently made them, ultimately would not be tied to her estate. As for the fate of the more mundane things MIJ surrounded herself with all those years, it appeared that would be determined with help from her legion of devotees.

Me among them.

"We have to keep the poetry prize going," I said. "Of course, I'll come to the auction preview." No guarantees I'd buy. I already carried more Mary Irene Jones baggage than most people, with the possible exception of the woman sitting across from me.

She had anticipated my reaction.

"I haven't heard from her, if you're wondering." Sister Marlene paused and struggled to keep her voice from catching. It was as if to speak might mean also shedding tears in front of me, and that, I believed, she would not do. After several minutes, she stood, more composed, and walked over to the photo of Yeats and me.

"UJJ has set up a crime victims compensation fund, to be administered by my religious order and seeded by a percentage of the home and estate sale proceeds. The city has been persuaded that it would be an appropriate way to reimburse the Philadelphia police for the effort and expense of investigating Mary Irene's disappearance. We will do the same in Delaware and Virginia, on a smaller scale. As the company's COO, this was also my decision to make. Mr. Lisle is drawing up the papers now."

An impressive strategy motivated, I was certain, by Sister Marlene's sense of guilt.

No doubt she was a formidable negotiator, but I had to ask: "Lisle? Is that a wise move?"

She turned toward me and shrugged. She had picked her battles.

"I have no desire to reinvent the wheel, and Jordan has been warned. If he submits so much as one billable hour or anything else to UJJ that I haven't authorized, I will have him charged with embezzlement. The police in Virginia have apparently left it up to Conor Tilden and Jen Dill to press charges or not against the man Jordan quite likely hired to run them off the road, though he continues to deny that. To my knowledge, no charges have been filed against Peter Yastremski, no matter who hired him."

Counting Lisle in along with Yastremski, Conor, and Jen, four out of four loose cannons had effectively been silenced.

Intuition told me Quinn had guessed correctly when he asked Yastremski at the Bensalem police station whether the maybe-Russian-sounding woman who hired him over the phone could have had an Irish accent. I'd lay money on Mary Irene as the one who gave Yastremski his orders. The one who hired the library goon who had spooked me, too. More misdirection by a woman who was proving to be a master of it.

Outside, the clock on the administration building tolled the hour. I had a class to teach. Sister Marlene had a college to run. Yet she lingered as I gathered what I needed and locked my office behind us.

"You've handled all this so well, Mimi," she said.

A strange compliment, if ever there was one.

Shakespeare devised so many intricate plots, so many ways for his characters to get into the messes they did and out of them. Under the circumstances, I felt singularly prepared to teach a course on the poetry in drama and the drama in poetry.

"Our aim is to take a critical view of William Shakespeare, Poet. But we're not doing the sonnets or the big plays this semester. The idea is not to have you spouting the balcony scene from *Romeo and Juliet* or Hamlet's soliloquy — those are part of the soundtrack of your lives. You already know all the hooks, all the bells and whistles."

Groans rose from students I recognized, some of my snarky "Poetry as Protest" collaborators on the MIJ Fest keynote speech.

"Instead, we're going to listen to the rhythm of Will's language, the flow of his words off the page into our ears and our collective consciousness, and also how they propel his stories forward. How many of you have read or seen a performance of *Pericles, Prince of Tyre* or *Timon of Athens*?"

Oh, the silence.

"They may not be Shakespeare's most famous plays, or his best, but we're going to study what works in them, and what doesn't, and why he might have made the decisions he made in writing them. It will be exciting."

More groans.

"Fine, maybe you'll discover it isn't so exciting. But if you want to write poetry that moves people, it doesn't hurt to examine a great poet's process, not just delight in the final product. I don't plan to be boring. I've waited too long for the opportunity to teach this course my way to be boring."

"Can we get that in writing, Professor Jones?" one of my cheeky collaborators shouted.

"You draft me an agreement in iambic pentameter, and I'll take it under advisement." I bowed in service to that promise, as a character in Shakespeare might. I also winked knowingly—it would never happen.

"Meanwhile, scholars of the Bard that we are, let's pick two other relatively obscure plays. We've got a comedy and a tragedy. We need a history and a name-your-own-adventure entry. You're in control."

Two students stepped up with their "complete works" e-textbooks and grabbed pieces of chalk, more than willing to run the show. What the heck, this might work. I was getting used to flying by the seat of my pants. People told me I was good at it.

One of those people met me after work for drinks in an actual public place. Kissed me at the bar, too.

"Mmm, you've started with a mojito. Tasty." Quinn licked his lips as if Little Red Riding Hood were sitting on the stool next to him. "In a good mood, Professor?"

"I am, Detective. I had a good first Shakespeare class, and Trish and her kids offered to go by my house to walk Yeats. What could be better?"

He ordered a stout and started nibbling from the bowl of nuts in front of him. "You heard about Sister Marlene's agreement with the city?" Even though nothing had been officially announced, Quinn, naturally, had an inside track.

"She visited my new office earlier today. Not a win for everyone, this deal, but it sounds awfully close to it."

I remembered the email Sister Marlene said she'd sent me and pulled it up on my new college-issued tablet. The estate sale offerings were enumerated in an eighty-page attachment. "Plus, there's this."

Quinn scanned the list, which was more than I had done. "Interesting. Are you going to the preview?"

Was not going an option?

"She didn't make it a command performance, but raising money from the sale of the house and its contents was a principal topic of discussion. I'll put in an appearance to support the cause. Poetry Fest forever!" I raised my fist in mock solidarity.

Quinn did too. "I'll be in court, so I won't be able to make it. Would be cool to eyeball the crowd, though, and see what catches their interest."

I had eyeballs, and I certainly knew the local poetry players, as well as some of MIJ's eclectic celebrity fans. The auction would take place online the following day, but, yes, it could be cool to see who else showed up for the in-person preview.

We decided to eat at the bar, across from a bank of televisions tuned, sound muted, to late-season Major League Baseball and a midweek NFL game. My linguini and mussels in white sauce consumed my attention, so I didn't immediately notice Quinn texting. Seconds later, my phone pinged.

"Just sent you a file with some follow-up paperwork Conor T. submitted in South Carolina as designated chief financial officer of S & C Tilden Associates. He had to produce a birth certificate or passport as further proof he is who he says he is," Quinn said. "Apparently this U.S. passport, which is about to hit its ten-year expiration date, shows a number of trips back and forth to the United Kingdom. Two visits per year, sometimes more, mostly arrivals and departures at Heathrow Airport in London, going back to when he was fourteen years old."

Quinn got another text, so I waited to look at the file.

"According to the person who sent me this, on another document Conor writes N/A, for not applicable, when asked to list his father's name. Maybe a custody situation with the phantom dad was behind those trips across the Atlantic."

As if we knew anything definitive about the circumstances of Conor's birth and upbringing.

"When I asked about the picture of Conor and Jen I had seen in Mary Irene's house, Jen told me they were visiting some relatives of his who lived in the U.K., in the Lake District. Sister Marlene once told me she and Mary Irene were never closer than during a time they were both in that same part of England."

Which reminded me I needed to accept the auction-preview invitation the college president had personally extended. I clicked on a link, and within minutes, a confirmation email appeared in my inbox.

Chapter Twenty-seven

Like the tea shop in Myrtle Beach, MIJ's Philadelphia house was charming and modest, though imbued with significance now only because she wasn't there. Left behind were the simple things she had lived with for years. The woman whose work was the antithesis of epic poetry had also put on no decorating airs.

In advance of the auction preview, to get a sense of what might have been excluded from the sale, I spent some time studying the photos I took at Mary Irene's house before I turned over the key, as well as the comprehensive inventory that resulted from the police search back in April.

Missing from the auction catalog, based on my cross-referencing, were a handful of first editions of Mary Irene's American-era collected verse, plus books of poetry inscribed to her by some of her well-known, late-twentieth-century peers. I could see Sister Marlene squirreling those volumes away for a second auction. Not surprisingly, since there were high hopes for this sale's proceeds, the minimum bids for first editions of each of Mary Irene's earliest poetry collections were set quite high, north of $30,000 in some cases.

Also purged pre-auction were personal photographs and photo albums, several boxes of letters, and the contents of MIJ's desk. Sister Marlene might have been a collaborator in all this, but she was also Mary Irene's friend, even if she alone hoped the friendship would continue. In any event, the items were likely to become more valuable the longer MIJ stayed off the radar, all to the advantage of the future beneficiaries of her poetry award when that second auction came to pass.

Perhaps because they were considered unlikely to sell, the catalog did not list certain household contents that might otherwise have fallen into the auction's category of "Northern Ireland keepsakes." Among those were what the police inventory described as a "yellowed cashmere shawl" and "two young girls' dresses."

However, the vintage typewriters were listed in the auction catalog, as were the doghouse and the boxes of printer paper and the green suitcase I'd seen in the hall closet. All the mismatched dishes were available. Some pieces of fine Waterford crystal also were included, and so were the plaques Mary Irene received as international poetry prizes. What she valued was evident, and the rest stood as witness to her choice to abandon this house.

I had participated in enough estate auctions to know that most of what was on offer was priced to move—except for the first editions, the minimums were set low, even for the appliances and larger pieces of furniture. Deals could be had for the savvy bidder, aficionado of all things Mary Irene Jones or not.

The morning of the preview dawned sunny and breezy, on the cool side for mid-September, which made standing in the queue to get in pleasant enough. I had arrived about an hour after the proceedings began, to avoid a still-longer line.

Next door, at Jen and Conor's former home, a family with little kids had moved in, judging from the tricycles outside, but the new owners evidently had better things to do than observe these festivities. A few neighbors gathered across the street to watch a TV news crew videotape those of us waiting to enter. The block would probably be a lot quieter once the MIJ circus folded its tent.

Inside, everything was tagged with a catalog number. On my prior visits to her house, I hadn't paid much attention to the oriental rug in Mary Irene's kitchen, a long, narrow piece priced at a minimum below what Ikea might charge for something similar. It looked authentic enough, so I checked the underside for a label, on the outside chance MIJ had bought it in Morocco or the Middle East. There was none, and also no obvious machine stitching or one-side-only dye that suggested the rug was a mass-production piece. I wrote the number down in my always-present notebook.

Cabinets stood open to reveal dishes and pans and glassware. I inspected a plain white serving platter for chips along the edges; finding none, I made a note of that, as well.

The typewriters sat side by side on a table in the living room. I needed another old typewriter like I needed another hole in my head, Grandmother Mary Irene's Olivetti occupying a similar spot in my living room, but I noted their numbers and minimum prices for quick reference anyway.

I spotted Sister Marlene in MIJ's office, sitting behind the desk, now devoid of its owner's personal effects and available for purchase.

"I'm sure Mary Irene's biographers are unhappy that her papers were excluded from this auction. Maybe a future one?"

She looked confused for a minute, then recovered. "Right, you were here when the police first searched this house. Checked the catalog against that inventory, did you?"

I tipped an invisible hat. "Mimi Jones, Girl Detective."

Space near the window offered me a view of prospective bidders as they wandered in and out. One couple removed about thirty books from a bookcase that matched the desk, lifted it with difficulty, and scrutinized it from all sides. "Mahogany," the forty-something man said. Sister Marlene smiled as they repositioned the books, rolling her eyes after they moved on.

"That bookcase has been very popular today. We should have taken more pictures for the catalog. Who knew?"

I ran my hand across the wood and made note of the catalog number. "It's beautifully made. You could have raised the minimum price by at least a hundred bucks, but a lower one might mean someone buys both it and the desk. I can imagine someone hoping Mary Irene's greatness would rub off."

If only it worked that way. I knew better, as did Sister Marlene. "With the greatness might come the rest," she said. "Anyone who's spent extended periods with Mary Irene soon recognizes her unique ability to make those who love her insane. I'm sure her son has. His wife, too."

So many questions clamored to be asked, but voices in the hall interrupted us. More prospects. A group wanting to know more about the desk. I ducked around them and wandered into the bedrooms, then downstairs and into the screened porch. Imitating the bookcase people, I lifted the doghouse and examined its condition. Wasn't sure I had any room for it except in my basement, but it was in decent shape, and I was sure Yeats and Barrett would like it. I noted the catalog number and moved back into the house.

Some pottery in the china cabinet caught my eye. I opened the breakfront and checked the bottom of a cream-and-blue cake plate for a mark. "Wetheriggs Penrith," it said. British, from the Lake District; I had a plate like it at home.

A few of MIJ's higher-minded biographers had offered extensive details about her travels in the U.K. over the years, as I recalled, documenting that she was a frequent speaker at poetry symposiums at universities throughout England, Scotland and Wales, as well as her native Northern Ireland. Notable speeches were quoted, as were noteworthy poems published close to those appearances. Several cited Mary Irene's 1997 collection, *Gaia*, written during a months-long fellowship in York, calling it enlightened and triumphant. Not favorites of mine, the poems in *Gaia* always seemed forced to me, as if she were badly imitating herself. Was York another crossroads, like the one at which MIJ stood when she first met Marlene Flaherty in the Lake District?

I settled in at Mary Irene's dining table and watched the last of the preview participants pass through. At 4 o'clock promptly, the auction company representative asked those of us still in the house to leave, while also reminding us of the latest moment we could register for the online auction. I slipped upstairs to MIJ's office again, to catch Sister Marlene as she wrapped up for the day before the private security guards hired to watch the property hustled us out.

"Is there somewhere we can talk?" I was hoping she didn't need to dash off to a meeting.

"Drive me to the train? My car is at the college."

"How about I drive you directly there?" She had to recognize my gambit, but Sister Marlene agreed. I opted for a no-highway route through towns bordering Philly, counting on school buses and early rush-hour traffic to slow us down. They did not disappoint.

"Are you optimistic about the auction tomorrow?" I asked, going for a soft opening.

"Mary Irene Jones fans and academics will bid on something just so they can say they did. But the auction isn't why you're playing chauffeur. What is it you want from me?"

The truth, or some portion of it, would do.

"Conor Tilden's passport shows he visited the U.K. often as a teenager. Trips lasting weeks at a time. Was that the only opportunity he got to spend time with his mother?"

"Not necessarily."

I wanted to scream. "You told me you first met Mary Irene in England, when you were both at a crossroads. It seems as if she never really found her way."

Sister Marlene looked out the passenger side window, so I could not see her face. "She was overwrought then. She often was, I learned over time."

These were not her secrets to reveal, Sister Marlene had made that clear. I pressed anyway.

"When Mary Irene gave birth, did she drop out of sight for almost a year because she wanted to keep him a secret? Is that the reason she didn't show up at the college and you were fired, because you had promised she would be the new poet-in-residence then couldn't deliver her on time?"

"Mary Irene Jones did not have a baby."

I slammed the brakes. The driver behind me swerved into a left-turn lane to avoid rear-ending my car.

"Then who did, Sister? Surely not you."

"Absolutely not!" she shouted, as I ignored the resulting ache in my right knee and kept driving. "I told you, Mimi, I knew what my vows meant when I swore them more than thirty years ago. No lovers, no children. I agonized over the decision that spring in the Lake District when I first met Mary Irene, but once it was made I never wavered from it."

"Then what are you telling me now? Jen Dill offered no denials when I confronted her about Mary Irene Jones being Conor's mother. And just a few hours ago, you referred to Mary Irene's son and his wife."

I blew past the campus, preoccupied with connecting this constantly shifting set of dots. Sister Marlene didn't seem to notice I had missed the turn. I drove into a shopping center parking lot farther along the road and stopped the car so I didn't risk an actual traffic accident. The pain in my knee wasn't helping my mood any.

"Conor Tilden supplied his passport to the state of South Carolina as proof of identity, rather than his birth certificate. Do you know if one exists? Does it name his mother, or his father for that matter?"

"Why would I know any of that? I've never met the man, I told you that."

She didn't have to meet Conor Tilden to be acquainted with the intimate details of his life. "I *have* met Conor. His wife introduced us in May at the poetry festival—Jen insisted on it after I gave the keynote address Mary Irene failed to provide this year. You didn't know he was in the audience, observing? Probably reporting back to his mother?"

Out came the cigarette Sister Marlene always carried. She opened the window next to her and lit it, not saying a word.

"Even before meeting him, I knew that Conor was a systems engineer with a couple of Ivy League degrees; that's on his social media profile. But I've learned a lot more since then. As of the weekend of the poetry festival, for example, Conor listed Mary Irene Jones as the person to contact in case of emergency, his cellphone showed that. Growing up, he did a lot of trans-Atlantic traveling, his passport showed that. And it turns out Conor has a business relationship in South Carolina with a woman named Sarah Tilden—they own a real estate company together, like the one you and Mary Irene own here in Pennsylvania. The incorporation records for the business showed that he has the same authority over their holdings there as you have here. He's not Mary Irene's little boy anymore, so he's old enough to take on that responsibility."

I started the engine and turned out of the parking lot in the direction of the college. "I know Mary Irene Jones and Sarah Tilden are the same woman. Mary Irene confirmed it—I called her at Chamomile, the tea shop she owns in Myrtle Beach, and she knew there was no point in denying it."

Still, I was certain Sister Marlene had not just lied to me.

"All these things about Mary Irene and Conor, I will never make public, I swear, Sister. I've made that promise to myself, and I respect that you want to keep her confidence. What I don't understand is why you invited me to the auction preview today. Did you want a witness, someone to watch you tie up the loose ends for her? Or is there still more to this story?"

Medusa might have been jogging alongside my car, staring into it. Sister Marlene had turned to stone.

Chapter Twenty-eight

Yeats and Barrett made the doghouse their new hangout. The thing wasn't especially heavy, but it was bulkier than it had seemed on MIJ's screened porch. My brother-in-law, Bob, helped me with some basement redesign, and we created a space for it plus a path to the washer and dryer that my furry little beasts couldn't easily disrupt.

The bookcase was another species of monster — the solid, expensive, four-foot-tall variety. My winning bid was seriously more than I wanted to spend, and you might have thought I had paid by the pound, with shipping extra, of course. It took superhuman effort for Bob and me to carry the bookcase from my front door to its permanent spot in my living room. Someday, someone would have to demolish the house around it, because I was never moving it again. Filling a portion of its shelves with my own published work, as well as a not inconsiderable number of books written by *the* Mary Irene Jones or about her, felt right. All three MIJs would be represented in it: me, my grandmother, and the poet whose name we shared, especially once Grandma's typewriter found a new home atop the piece.

Offsetting my bookcase splurge, I scored a great price on the oriental rug, which further research suggested was, indeed, made in Morocco and bought by MIJ on a trip there in the mid-1980s. It now adorned my kitchen, as it had hers. I bought the white serving platter for a few dollars above its minimum price, for no other reason than I was both sentimental and conflicted about Mary Irene and the odd adventure I had taken with her.

Once all parts of my auction haul were set in place, I got a little weepy, to be honest. MIJ's house in Upper Roxborough had been a fixture of my life for several turbulent months. I couldn't see myself driving on that street again without thinking of her.

A therapist likely would advise against the immersive approach I had adopted in redesigning my home, seeing in it obsessive behavior. Then again, I had always been the kind of writer who would endlessly move a comma from place to place, reading the line aloud repeatedly to hear how each different placement of the punctuation affected the tone or the emotion I was trying to express. Surrounding myself with the physical Jonesiana couldn't hurt—I had gotten my dissertation mojo back, thanks to my involvement thus far with her more ephemeral goods.

I'd always figured that I had inherited whatever creative gene ran in my family, while Trish inherited the logic gene. Yet I had discovered one thing about myself during these MIJ-saturated months: I was good at solving puzzles. Eventually, if I kept moving the words around, maybe I would solve this one, too: When Sister Marlene told me, "Mary Irene Jones did not have a baby," what was she actually saying?

Michael Quinn, investigator extraordinaire, wasn't much help, though admittedly I hit him with the question again mere minutes after he walked into my house after a three-day conference in Pittsburgh about interviewing witnesses, followed by the four-hour-plus return drive across Pennsylvania.

"You could kiss me, Mimi, and tell me how much you missed me. But, no, you ask for a consult."

I gave him a really good kiss. "I did miss you, so much—and not just because I had no one to bat this around with."

"Translation: Your brain is on Mary Irene overload of a new kind now. The auction stuff looks great here, by the way, nice touches."

In all these months, I still hadn't seen Quinn's apartment. It was my way of avoiding what the nuns in catechism class used to call a near occasion of sin. So I had no idea what to make of his decorating commentary except to interpret it as, "Time to let it go, Mimi." Whatever, he was entitled to his opinion.

As he played with Yeats and allowed Barrett to crawl on his back, I opened a bottle of Pinot grigio, ordered a white pizza with vegetables, and tried to think of anything but that conversation with Sister Marlene.

Didn't work. The pizza arrived, we ate, and Quinn described the highlights of the Pittsburgh conference. But he knew the discussion was coming, it was just a matter of time. He employed delay tactics. He cleared the table and loaded the plates into my dishwasher, stashed the remaining slices in my refrigerator, and refilled our wineglasses.

"Go ahead, have at it," he conceded at last.

I recounted yet again what Sister Marlene had said the day of the auction preview, both at MIJ's house and in my car, hoping that hearing me recite the conversation verbatim in person, instead of in a phone call, would stimulate our weary brains to new insights.

"When you first told me Conor had used his passport for the South Carolina LLC filing, the simplest explanation seemed to be that the passport was more accessible, that Conor didn't have a copy of his birth certificate and getting one would take time. But, Mike, there was something in Sister Marlene's tone when she said Mary Irene didn't have a baby. I couldn't see her face, I was driving, but her voice was flat—that's what struck me. It was as if she were a little kid in school parroting back an answer, or someone spouting a set script for the thousandth time."

"Not what she said, but how she said it." Quinn understood.

"It's also interesting that she mentioned again that she had never met Conor Tilden. That may be accurate, but maybe that's all it is," he said. "If Sister Marlene's other statement was equally accurate, Mary Irene Jones might not be the name on Conor's birth certificate. Could be the name Sarah Tilden is."

I wanted to know if that was true, but also didn't. It would only lead to my lugging around more pieces of a secret that had already weighed too many people down for too long.

Yet I had to ask. "All this time, could Mary Irene have had a second passport and a second Social Security number? And now, a second active existence on two continents as Sarah Tilden?"

They said everyone had a double somewhere. Who would have given a second thought to Sarah Tilden's comings and goings?

"It's not the worst theory in the world," Quinn said. "If something unexpected, say a health scare, doesn't trip them up, and if there isn't something else involved that's bigger than they are, like a criminal investigation, and if identity theft isn't a factor, people do get away with it."

That was a lot of ifs.

"Add in a good friend who's always watching out for you, ready to hold the net steady beneath you no matter which new stunt you attempt, well. ..."

He raised his wineglass and tapped mine with it. "The Great Poet is gone. Long live the Tea Shop Owner."

I drank to that.

Sleep eluded me. MIJ and Company weren't responsible for this round of insomnia, though, Quinn was. The detective and I had spent a lot of hours in each other's company, days at a time on the road, yet our relationship remained undefined. Not an "Are we exclusive?" kind of undefined as much as an overall "Who is this man and where I am going with him, if anywhere?" lack of clarity. Another case of my wanting to know, but not wanting to know.

We were seeing each other publicly, at least. We had incredible chemistry, which was both fabulous and frustrating in light of the never-quite-closed MIJ case file. Quinn respected my ideas and trusted that following where they led was worth the trouble. Hell, he seemed to trust that *I* was worth the trouble.

"Just have to wait and see, Mimi," I counseled myself, as the old song "You Can't Hurry Love" repeated in my head.

No sense lying there and staring at the ceiling. Yeats was snoring undisturbed in the dog bed when I rose from mine.

Barrett meowed groggily but followed me into the living room, snuggling next to me on the floor as I contemplated MIJ's bookcase. I turned the skeleton key and opened it, fussing with the slim volumes of my poetry I had dared to position for now on the bottom shelf, directly below her first two published collections. I was no slave to symmetry, but even I could tell that something about the shelf was off-kilter, and that the books' spines didn't line up properly on it.

One by one, I pulled all the books off the shelf and propped them up in a line on a stretch of hardwood between my sofa and the area rug. Height-wise, I'd done it right the first time—the books were in the perfect order. All four legs of the bookcase also were sitting on the hardwood, off the rug. In a ninety-eight-year-old rowhouse, wonky floors were common and furniture could be hard to balance, but the bookcase itself was sitting level, which I verified with both an old tool of my dad's and the level on my phone's utilities app. I turned on the phone's flashlight and searched for the possible problem.

I ran my fingers along the lower shelf, from the side wall of the bookcase to the center, where the left-hand glass door met the right. An extra piece of wood seemed to overlay the shelf, causing a definite tilt. I grabbed a butter knife from the kitchen to see if I could lift the wood.

It took some maneuvering, and a prayer that I didn't jostle the piece and send the books on the upper shelves crashing through the glass doors and Grandma Mary Irene's typewriter tumbling to the floor. But I finally wedged the knife in enough to see between the wood and the shelf underneath.

A thin black binder peeked back at me.

Chapter Twenty-nine

Jordan Lisle's office was cluttered, and then some. Stacks of accordion files squeezed between covered white boxes with case names and dates scribbled on the side. Law books crowded onto shelves, occupied chairs, or rose from the floor in lopsided towers.

Clear, however, was the top of the desk, a grand mahogany addition to the suburban space I previously had barely seen from the hall beyond. Almost blocking the office door was a three-drawer metal filing cabinet that now squatted on the stair landing.

Lisle waved me in through the doorway and extended his hand, a gesture of peace, I supposed. I offered the fingertips of my right hand.

"Your bid won the matching bookcase from Mary Irene's house, I understand. Just as well, would have been no room for it in here, as you can see." Lisle relocated several books, creating a spot for me to sit. "So, what can I do for you, Ms. Jones?"

He knew exactly what I wanted—details about MIJ's literary estate. I had left a voicemail with precise questions about what rights publishers had to her early work, and what steps I would have to take in acknowledging those rights in the book I was writing about Mary Irene's unpublished manuscripts.

Lisle had called back and invited me to meet with him at his office immediately, if I were available. He saw dollar signs, I guessed. I saw a chance to ascertain how much he knew about MIJ's secrets.

"As I mentioned in my phone message, Mr. Lisle, I'm expanding the analysis of the unpublished manuscripts I did for the college into a book that will also serve as my doctoral dissertation at NYU. Needless to say, in addition to getting every citation correct, I want to be sure I cover all the legal bases. The situation is obviously not as clear as it would be if Mary Irene Jones were known conclusively to be dead."

Lisle produced a legal pad and a pen and began to make notes. "Sister Marlene Flaherty is, of course, administrator of the properties owned by the company she and Mary Irene founded, as well as its chief operating officer. She is also designated as administrator of the will Mary Irene made, which addresses her literary estate. But that will cannot be enforced without a declaration of death—which complicates matters, as you mentioned."

He reached for a file on a shelf just behind him. It was labeled *Unpublished/Mimi Jones/College.*

"You should have received a copy of this agreement on ownership of the unpublished manuscripts, Ms. Jones. In light of the judge's decision, I have stepped away from estate matters relating to any material Mary Irene left in your care via the college. The attorney who represented the college can explain the fine points to you."

No explaining was necessary. I knew that I could do what I needed to, as long as I in no way, either expressly or implicitly, represented the verses in the seven binders MIJ sent me as my own work.

"What if other poems seemingly written by Mary Irene Jones were to turn up? Is there a protocol for that?"

Lisle dismissed my question. "There are no other poems, I can assure you of that. Mary Irene and I went to great lengths to detail what the literary estate would include. Sister Marlene can verify that enumeration, if you like, though the FBI pulled a copy of the will during the early part of the investigation into Mary Irene's disappearance. I'm sure Detective Quinn can supply you with whatever information is to be found in it. So helpful to have close police contacts, isn't it?"

I let his snide remark and the smirk that accompanied it slide, but confirmed for him that he was certainly correct about close police contacts being an asset.

"Mary Irene's personal papers—the ones listed in the police inventory compiled during the search you requested of her home—were not included in the estate auction. I checked the catalog against the inventory and was surprised to see they had been omitted. I'm sure they would have been highly sought after, as I discussed with Sister Marlene the day of the auction preview."

He sneered an "Of course you did" sneer in my direction. "No additional, heretofore unknown poetry was discovered in any of Mary Irene's papers. True, Sister Marlene has been very protective of those, but I don't dispute anything she's said with regard to them. Nor was there anything found in either house owned by UJJ LLC. Sister Marlene and I searched every corner and crawlspace together, very thoroughly."

Together might have been an exaggeration, but prompting Lisle to reflect further on anything at this point seemed ill-advised.

"Just wondering, Mr. Lisle, since you know Mary Irene so well: Do you envision her writing again if she's still alive, as the police here and in South Carolina think she might be?"

Lisle stared at me as if I were nuts. "Would you go to the lengths Mary Irene Jones apparently has to disappear, only to turn up again and say, 'Hey, never mind, I'm back?'"

No, but I wouldn't have gone to those lengths in the first place. I had no reason to doubt that Lisle was telling me what he believed to be the truth— a rare occurrence in our brief, often contentious acquaintance. So I thanked him for his time and got up to leave.

"By the way," I added, "Sister Marlene indicated there would be no charge to me or the college for this consultation. She said you two had an arrangement."

I flashed my sweetest smile and walked out before he could react.

Next stop: the nearest post office. In my car was a package addressed to Conor Tilden at his new home in South Carolina. Accompanying the package was a letter.

Conor,

Enclosed is the eighth binder your mother originally intended to send me via the U.S. Postal Service, the binder that was not in the box of unpublished manuscripts I eventually received. I found this one by accident, after I purchased her bookcase at the estate auction at her home in Philadelphia.

Knowing your mother, that bit of serendipity could have been part of her plan all along. It doesn't matter, because you can count me out of any 'Amazing New Work! Undiscovered Manuscripts by Mary Irene Jones!' adventures yet to come.

The poems in this binder are magnificent, Mary Irene's best work, in my opinion, and I hope the world gets to read them someday.
Mimi Jones

When I pulled into the post office parking lot, however, I couldn't follow through with *my* plan. Instead, I ripped open the package, tore the letter to shreds, and didn't even get out of the car. On the way home, I filled the gas tank and rustled up a pet sitter. Two hours later, I had packed enough clothes for several days and was headed for the ramp to I-95 South.

"Welcome to Virginia" signs lit up the roadside by the time my terse, pre-scheduled message hit email inboxes at the Philadelphia Police Department and the Chestnut Hill office of a busy East Coast real estate company.

"Going to the beach for a few days," I wrote. "Barrett and Yeats in good hands."

Quinn and Trish might not even see the email until I stopped for food and a few hours' rest at the closest motel I could find to the interstate, my phone turned off.

Trish would be curious but unconcerned. I was the big sister, after all.

My maybe-boyfriend, the police detective? He would probably figure out which beach I had in mind.

Chapter Thirty

On my third pass by Chamomile, a little before 6:30 a.m., I noticed that there were lights on at the tea shop's front windows, and that the sign on the door finally had been turned to "Open." A right turn at the intersection, and I could also see signs of activity behind the lace curtains that dressed the downstairs windows toward the rear, likely the kitchen. I parked in a municipal lot about two blocks away and walked toward a latte, some breakfast, and what I hoped would be a productive encounter with the establishment's owner.

In a floral-print tote bag that looked appropriate for Myrtle Beach rested pages bearing some of the loveliest verse I had read in a decade. Much as I wanted to spend hours studying their simple structure and subtle styling, keeping the poems for myself was not an option.

Black metal bistro tables and chairs beckoned between Chamomile's entrance and the street corner. At this hour, I bargained on privacy there, hoping that others seeking caffeine and sugar would primarily be takeout customers, the working folks who catered to tourists at the nearby businesses. I made myself and the poetry comfortable and waited for the server. After giving her my order, I asked to speak to Sarah.

"This early in the morning, we're always busy. Might be a little bit of a wait," the server said. If she recognized me from my previous visit, she didn't let on.

"I'm on vacation," I fibbed, and opened a cozy mystery I had purchased at a rest area somewhere in Maryland. "I have my book, and as long as you have the coffee and pastries, I have the time."

"You're welcome to hang out—unless I need the table," she replied. I gave her a thumbs-up, then glanced down at the back cover's plot teaser. *"Death is `snow' joke in this mountain village…"* I opted to amuse myself with my phone instead.

No texts, or return emails for that matter, but it wasn't even 7 o'clock. The *New York Times* offered updates on federal budget tangles in Congress and mounting Middle East tensions. After scanning the headlines, I was tempted to switch to YouTube, but the door opened and the object of my quest emerged.

The chair across from mine scraped the sidewalk as she struggled to place my face. I wasn't nearly the fixture on search engines that she was, despite my recent short burst of fame. Nor had we ever been in the same spot at the same time before, let alone met. As I watched, Mary Irene Jones put two and two together. She sighed deeply, as if resigned to the inevitability of the moment.

"Long way to come for a coffee and a scone, given the fine bakeries in Philadelphia. To what do I owe this dubious pleasure, Mimi Jones?"

Up close, the woman I had idolized most of my life looked all too human, and younger than I expected. Gray streaks segued attractively into the short, dark red layers that framed her face, precisely as her hair stylist must have commanded them. Alert green eyes challenged me, hers likely more used to a predawn rise-and-shine routine than mine were. It seemed as if this new life was agreeing with MIJ, known hereabouts as Sarah Tilden.

I raised the tote bag to table level. "You left a few things behind in your bookcase, which I bought at auction. Doesn't matter whether you forgot them, which I doubt, or hid them there hoping someone—maybe even me—would find them, as I suspect. I don't want them, and I won't release them out into the world for you. You're on your own, Mary Irene."

"Hush," she hissed an inch from my face, "that name is not to be uttered here. Forget about her. That person is gone."

Not quite. Not yet.

"If you had truly wanted to be gone, you would have left a suicide note and abandoned your car on a bridge instead of dumping it into a puddle in Delaware before bopping down here. But that would have meant a legal mess, right? And where's the fun if you can't watch your puppets dance for you? The thing about puppets, Mary Irene: Some of them just can't follow a tune. Some inconveniently summon the press. Others go rogue, maybe intimidating people in libraries, or deciding to ram a car on the highway. Or here's another example, me showing up to call you out in person on your latest bit of intrigue."

She sat back heavily on the chair, clearly several degrees of ticked off. I set the bag down and pushed it toward her with my foot. "Burn these pages if you want, or—here's a crazy thought—give them to your son. To preserve that sense of mystery you love so much, you could hide them in a piece of furniture with a false bottom. Or, you could just mail them. That's what I originally planned to do. Your choices have cost Conor so much already. What his life includes and doesn't should be his decision at last, don't you think? A mother who's a tea shop proprietor? A mother who's a famous poet? All of the above, or none? These poems are his legacy, and Liam's. Offer them to him."

She pushed the bag back.

"No, thank you. Finders keepers, have at it."

Had she given any thought to what that could mean?

"If I reveal the existence of these poems, you will *never* be able to disappear. Interest in the great Mary Irene Jones will spike again in the news pages and the poetry journals, and controversy will rage. Some people will argue that I'm passing your wonderful work off as my own. Others will say I'm passing my less acclaimed work off as yours. Either way, I'll be accused of trying to profit from them, financially or to enhance my reputation, and I'll have to explain myself. I may not be able to shield you from the glare of that spotlight. It might eventually reach Sarah Tilden and her family."

"The only person who's bothered to look very hard for me is you. Take your own suggestion and burn the pages, Mimi. I don't care if they see the light of day. If I did, I wouldn't have hidden them, now would I?"

How could anyone be so self-absorbed and so unaware at the same time?

"What about that? Explain to me why you changed your mind about sending this binder to me with the other unpublished manuscripts. That postal slip's notation about there being eight binders wasn't a mistake, was it? It was you having second thoughts about the fate of some of your best work."

Her scowl and her silence were chilling. A frosty stillness prevailed for several minutes. But words were my weapon of choice, and her reticence to use them was not going to stop me.

"You're like a gambler obsessed with the jackpot, yet you can't stop yourself from risking it all by playing one more card. First, you tucked these remarkable, moving verses into that batch of whatnot you mailed me when you first became the Invisible Woman. Then you pulled them back at the last minute and hid them, wagering that at some point someone might notice the fake shelf in your bookcase. Poems found, maybe you win big. Poems go undiscovered, maybe you still win. Deal me out either way, Mary Irene."

"This is my life, my future, how dare you call it a game! But I can twist the image too, isn't that what we poets do? Conjure treasure from a few simple syllables? Tease great truths from mere metaphor?"

She got to her feet, her eyes boring into mine as she rose.

"Cards on the table, Mimi. You liked the first hand I dealt quite well, didn't you? You walked away a winner. Stumbled into this hand and don't like it as much? Then fold and quit."

Two couples took seats at the tables on the other side of Chamomile's front door. "I have paying customers to serve," she hissed *soto voce*. "Your breakfast is on the house. And take that bag with you when you go."

She turned her back on me and greeted the new arrivals. If she thought the matter between us was settled, she was very much mistaken.

I returned to my car and drove to the same motel I'd stayed at during my last visit to Myrtle Beach. The check-in desk clerk booked me into the same room, in fact. I dumped the contents of the tote bag onto the bed. That lingering urge to treat with kid gloves these words the author regarded so lightly? Gone.

Such glorious words they were, though. Spilling forth as I sat on the bedspread and the binder opened near my knee was the short poem Mary Irene had titled "Off-spring."

> *Tiniest tributary,*
> *bubbling, rising as if drawn up by the very air.*
> *Slowly sensing the rains that will nourish you,*
> *opening to the waters that will grow you*
> *fuller and stronger.*
> *Reaching for me, then past me*
> *to a place beyond, farther than any can see today, or tomorrow.*
> *Without barrier.*
> *To hold you is to hold you back. You are only as mine*
> *as I allow you to be,*
> *as you allow yourself to be.*
> *Until you no longer flow alongside me*
> *but away, of your own accord.*
> *To hold you is to hold you back. You are only as mine*
> *as I allow you to be,*
> *as you allow yourself to be.*
> *Until you no longer flow alongside me*
> *but away, of your own accord.*

I opened my laptop and consulted my notes. Then I got into my car and drove to the location Quinn and I had staked out not so long ago.

The one Conor Tilden now called his home.

He was a tech dude, a systems engineer. Doubtful Conor did the cubicle drill, though I was prepared to wait as long as necessary if I found the house empty. If Jen answered the door and chose to block access to her husband, I'd find a way to talk to him. I could be as stubborn as his mother, that other Mary Irene Jones, regardless of what his birth certificate said.

A single vehicle was parked in the driveway. That wasn't a guarantee someone was home, but this whole trip was a roll of the dice, wasn't it? Mary Irene wasn't the only gambler in town. I parked behind the car, got out, and rang the doorbell, whose camera would steal away any surprise my appearance might create. Brazenness would triumph, I hoped.

I waited a minute or two, then rang again. A lock disengaged. Conor appeared, partially shielded by the door's painted white wood.

"This is unexpected."

"Forgive me if I doubt that's true, Conor. I'm sure your mother informed you between customers at Chamomile that I was here in Myrtle Beach. Are you going to invite me in, or do you want anyone who happens to walk by hear me talking to you about Mary Irene Jones and the contents of this bag?"

Confusion flashed across his face. Maybe genuine surprise.

Conor opened the door wider. "Come in, Mimi. It's always good to see you," he said, dabbling in fiction. We both knew I was the last person he wanted to see.

I took a seat on the sofa and took the binder out of my bag. "I found this hidden under a fake shelf in the bookcase I purchased at the auction of the contents of Mary Irene's household. It's identical to the seven binders she sent to me months ago via U.S. mail. In fact, the slip she filled out indicated that she was sending eight binders in all. Pretty sure this is Number Eight."

Standing there, staring down at the black folder on his coffee table, Conor looked younger than his twenty-four years. More like a lost little boy.

"What's in it?" he asked.

"Another cache of original, never-published works by the internationally renowned poet who happens to also be your mother. You didn't know they existed?"

"I wouldn't have asked if I did. She doesn't consult me when she designs her games. I'm tired of playing them, too."

Hard to tell sometimes. Twisting the truth was a family trait, based on my past experience. But I didn't need to trust Conor. I needed him to believe me.

"The dozen poems in this binder are beautiful, and heart-warming, and heart-wrenching, and the world should get the chance to read them. At the very least, you should read them, then decide for yourself."

I handed him the thin typewritten sheet bearing the thirteen lines that comprised "Off-spring." After several minutes, he brushed tears away and set the page down.

"Dear God, Mom, what do you want from me? What do *you* want, Mimi?"

To hand the poems off, wasn't that the short answer? To get rid of them and stop being the conduit through which MIJ's work flowed into the larger world?

It seemed unfair to dump these poems on Conor the way MIJ had dumped the others on me. Mary Irene had known I would benefit from her manipulation. Could I say that my actions would have the same effect on her son? Absolutely not, but this was the right thing to do, I was certain.

"What do I want? For you to determine the poems' fate. Publish them and put their proceeds into a college fund for Liam. Or publish them and endow the poetry festival your mother founded. You can do either anonymously through Sister Marlene Flaherty and let her handle the details. She has the legal authority, and for a change she may be willing to wield it on her own, without Mary Irene's covert approval."

No rebuttal was raised, so I continued to argue my case.

"If you ask me, Conor, your mother has demonstrated that she's no longer worthy of the friend who has kept her secrets for decades now. Sister Marlene is still trying to keep you a secret from me, even though she knows I've figured out the big mystery."

He sat, finally. "I don't want this responsibility. And what if these aren't the only poems hidden away?"

"That's a possibility—"

"All I want is for her to settle down and for us to be close as a family. For Liam to get to know his grandmother, and for me to get to know my mother better under something like normal circumstances. My father chooses not to acknowledge me publicly, for reasons that are no longer especially relevant, but I resigned myself to that years ago."

My bewilderment must have shown on my face.

"You know about the rumors, Mimi. Everyone who's ever given two thoughts to Mary Irene Jones knows about them. The biographers always mention the child she refuses to talk about and speculate about the identity of the father."

It was true. A chapter about that part of her life was opened in every MIJ biography and closed after a few unsatisfactory pages. Was it the famously happily married rock star or the highly placed British politician? Surely not the Irish Republican activist believed to be smitten with her. That love story might have been apocryphal, some of the people who chronicled Mary Irene's life concluded. Still others asked: What it if wasn't?

"Things must have been very confusing for you growing up," I said. "Complicated too."

Conor shook his head. "Quite simple really. I was inconvenient for both of them, though much more so for my father than my mother. A scandal would have been damaging. So my parents made a pact: Neither would acknowledge me publicly, but each would hold me as close as possible. My half-siblings came to know me as a cousin of sorts who accompanied them on long vacations every year. My Aunt Annie, my mother's sister, raised me as her own, and when I figured out the truth, she always talked me out of my rebellious threats to expose the secret. She was a saint, my aunt. I adored her. It wasn't until Jen and I learned that Liam was on the way that I understood my parents' choice, even if I certainly didn't agree with it. Liam is why my mother is here in South Carolina—why we are all here in South Carolina."

"But was it Mary Irene's choice yet again?"

His expression said it all, and I sympathized. Yet I also understood that I couldn't let it sway me.

"If you do nothing with these poems, Conor, fine. But you deserve the opportunity to make this choice."

He returned "Off-spring" to the binder and returned the binder to my tote bag. "Give them back to my mother."

"Tried that already. She doesn't want them, and she doesn't seem to care what happens to them. You, on the other hand, have options you can explore. So I'm leaving the poems here and taking myself and my empty bag back to Philadelphia. Say hello to Jen and Liam for me. Happy days at the beach are what I want most for all of you."

I showed myself out and drove to the motel. In another hour or so, I'd be back on the interstate, carrying only slightly less baggage, emotional and literary, on the return trip.

What would be, would be for all of us.

Chapter Thirty-one
2024

My first academic year as a full-time professor zipped by, between teaching several courses each semester and completing my dissertation. In February, I had delivered what I thought were final edits on my book about the manuscripts, but the Ph.D. committee at NYU intervened, seeking what seemed like citations for my citations, footnotes for my footnotes. To address those issues, I spent long hours at work, then more at my desk at home. As the months passed, I monitored multiple online sites for any potentially disruptive news that the poems Mary Irene hid in that eighth binder had been revealed, maybe published somewhere. Thus far, they had not.

I spent a lot of time on the road, traveling to speaking engagements those wonderful poems also might have disrupted, but didn't. I restricted myself to East Coast presentations, so I wouldn't be absent from too many classes or have to leave Barrett and Yeats too often. If I hadn't heard otherwise from the pet sitters I hired, I wouldn't have believed those two missed me at all. The furry conspirators typically snubbed me for at least an hour when I returned home—proof that Yeats was part cat and obviously meant to be mine all along.

The other male in my life continued to pop in unannounced with post-workout pizza and beer on random weeknights. We also went out like a real couple from time to time, when one of our jobs didn't get in the way. We had exchanged Christmas presents; he even met my family. My mother adored Mike Quinn. My sister and brother-in-law and their kids adored Mike Quinn. I adored Mike Quinn—and I had seen him at his most irritating. Then again, he could say the same of me.

On our unofficial first anniversary in April—unofficial because it was hard to say exactly which day we became more than just cop and person of interest—I gave him a vintage 1950s Swiss watch and a key to my house, which he accepted with a devilish smile. He gave me a silver chain with a beautiful pendant—a blue-green stone he said matched my eyes—and a very thick envelope.

"A payoff, Detective? I believe the police department frowns on financial transactions with sources."

He dropped tiny kisses along my neck. "If the department were smart, it would hire you as an investigator. Until then, just open the envelope, Mimi."

Inside was an invitation to a wedding. "Colleen Quinn Haggerty? And who is she?"

Quinn looked at me sheepishly. "My twin sister?"

I wanted to shout, *"You're just telling me now you have a twin sister!"* But my better, more mature side restrained me—sort of. Sarcasm could be hard to rein in.

"Do tell me more about this heretofore undisclosed twin to whose nuptials I apparently have been invited. Some details seem in order, don't you agree, Detective?"

He just loved it when I lapsed into my professor's voice, which was not unlike the voice I used when laying down the law to animals and young children of my acquaintance.

"My twin sister is getting remarried," he began. "She's four minutes older than I am—a bit bossy like you are, now that I think of it—and she has told me that under no circumstances will I be admitted to the celebration unless the woman I've been talking about for the last year is on my arm. The fact that I am one of the groomsmen won't deter her, I assure you. I wouldn't put it past Colleen to lock me out of the reception hall."

"At least she knew I existed. Go on."

"I should add that my mother also is itching to meet you, and your mother as well. Fortunately, I was able to talk Mom into delaying an introductory visit with Cass until after you survived the wedding. Too many Quinns might put you off, I warned her, and then where would we be?"

"Cute, Mike, but I see through your little ploy. You're afraid our mothers will start hatching plots for our future. I can't say that I blame you—you've seen Cass in action."

He put his hands up in surrender. "You're a smart one, Mimi Jones. Nothing gets past you."

I looked at the invitation more closely. His sister's wedding was, fortunately, set for July. No poetry festivals to help plan. No papers to grade. No additional dissertation defenses required. I noted the time and locale and the tiny lettering at the bottom of the invitation: black-tie formal.

"Who is your sister marrying?" The groom's name sounded slightly familiar.

"A congressman from Maryland. They met in college, married other people, divorced, and reconnected last year about the same time we met. Seems nice enough."

I'd have plenty of time for a lecture from Cass on how to style my hair and what to wear. One trip to a dress shop should do it—my mother was very decisive and usually made great selections without much input from me. She cared about how I looked more than I did, though for this occasion I'd likely pay a little more attention.

"Okay, put me down as your plus one."

"You're my only one. Have been for a very long time. I called it love at first search with a police forensics team. Just needed to convince you of it."

For a non-writer, Quinn definitely had a way with words. He could be even more persuasive when he wasn't speaking at all.

Chapter Thirty-two

The festivities in Maryland commenced on a Friday morning, with bride and groom taking their vows before a state Supreme Court judge Saturday afternoon and the party ultimately breaking up after breakfast on Sunday. The final tally: too many wardrobe changes, much too much food, untold cases of champagne, and dozens of Quinn relatives whose names were mentioned, repeated, then immediately forgotten by me.

The cost of the dress Cass selected for the formal occasion left me wondering whether I would need to pick up a few summertime pet-sitting gigs. It was beautiful, though, and Quinn's reaction at the sight of me in it was priceless. No photos documented that moment, or at least none that I knew of. But his new brother-in-law was a member of Congress up for reelection, so there might be some, somewhere.

We landed back at my house about 1:30 in the afternoon. Barrett and Yeats ran up from their doghouse fortress in the basement to greet him and ignore me. Quinn disappointed them, however, and planted my suitcase and dress bag next to me.

"Hate to leave, guys, but I did agree to work a shift tonight in exchange for the full day off I took on Friday. I want to grab a shower before I head in." A quick kiss and a few head pats, and he was off.

I was all smiled out, my feet ached, and I needed to do laundry and hang up the very fancy formal dress. Afterward, I took Yeats to the dog park for an evening run—for me, more like an evening stumble along behind him. When we passed through the foyer, I walked right by packages Trish and the kids must have brought in over the weekend. I found them when Yeats and I returned.

Two parcels awaited me on the table: one, a padded mailing envelope from an online book seller; the other, a box wrapped in kraft paper and marked "Fragile."

The envelope contained a slim anthology published by a small press in Georgia. The foreword mentioned that relationships were the tissue that connected these twenty-five poems. The table of contents listed only their titles, so I couldn't immediately tell whether I knew any of the writers.

I paged through a half-dozen poems before realizing the anthology was organized in alphabetical order by the writers' last names. I opened the book from the back, hoping for an index, but there was none.

The anthology's final poem was titled, "Friend Without End, Amen."

My guest does not know what prompts this particular invitation,
more like a summons, as usual; like a subpoena.
Yet she accepts, as always.
Enough for her is its potential for delight.
The moment will be sweet, she imagines,
a reunion replete with small cakes, sugared fruits, icy treats, chocolates,
surely too much for just we two, for just one day.
She picks roses from her garden, as a gift.
She brings memories.
She arrives, sits demurely, awaits her hostess, who does not quite disappoint
but does not precisely deliver.
I withhold grace and companionship,
behave as if her presence is my due.
Still my guest returns each time an invitation comes,
again and again,
determined that what she offers me,
her loyalty, will suffice one day.
She does not know it already does,
and that it is I who am cruel to demand
what I am unwilling to give:
Only what she asks of me,
Myself.

– S. Tilden

It was not one of the dozen unforgettable pieces MIJ had tucked into that eighth binder and hidden more than a year ago. Since I turned them over to Conor, those poems still had been neither publicized nor published in this country or anywhere else, based on the absence of news alerts to date.

The editors of this anthology had included scant biographical information for any of the contributors. Unless you knew differently, "Friend Without End, Amen" appeared to be a worthy effort by a heretofore unknown writer, a talented one whose style might seem familiar, but also might not. Twenty-two lines didn't offer a lot for any reader to analyze.

Was the poem intended as an apology for being careless of a devoted friend's feelings and dismissive of her fidelity? I hoped Sister Marlene, the woman who had inspired this work, also received a copy of it. For her sake, I could only hope the writer's regret was genuine and enduring this time. I doubted either party would choose to confide in me one way or the other.

The other package was postmarked Myrtle Beach, S.C. Within its brown paper wrapping was a pale green envelope that contained a note, unsigned but handwritten in penmanship I recognized and in a distinctive dark green ink.

Mimi,

Sometimes, it takes a while to find the piece that fits. None is just right, though perfection is not the point. What is? For the search to be so sincere that it redeems both the flaw and the finder.

I hope this helps to complete a tea set.

In a nest of bubble wrap sat a white ceramic cream pitcher. It had no maker's mark on the bottom. Thin cracks, ever so slight, marred its lip.

Definitely not perfect, but nothing—and no one—ever was. That's what made it beautiful.

I picked up the phone to call Quinn, then remembered he was on duty. "Relax. Put your feet up," I told myself. I texted him a kiss emoji instead. If he was busy, he'd probably ignore it, but that would be fine. There was no urgency to my news. I could tell him tomorrow.

I looked forward to tomorrow after tomorrow with Michael Quinn. After more than a year's worth of yesterdays and todays, I was sure I loved him and sure he loved me. Like the cream pitcher, we weren't perfect, we had a few cracks, but we fit.

People wrote poetry about such revelations. I had a bookcase full of verse to prove it, yet none of it written by someone named Jones.

I'd have to work on that.

Joanne McLaughlin
Bio

Joanne McLaughlin began telling stories in second grade, creating superhero fan fiction in the Philadelphia rowhouse where she grew up. Since then, Joanne has worked in public media and at newspapers in Philadelphia, upstate New York, and northeastern Ohio, involved in award-winning coverage of topics ranging from politics and public health to fashion and financial markets, as well as Pulitzer Prize-finalist architecture criticism and a Peabody Award-nominated podcast. For several years, she also served as vice president of a firm that managed and booked blues musicians.

Her novels include *Chasing Ashes*, a crime thriller, and *Never Before Noon, Never Until Now,* and *Never More Human,* a darkly romantic vampire trilogy. Her latest short fiction appears in *Ruth and Ann's Guide to Time Travel, Volume 1*; the short stories *Peppina's Sweetheart* and *Grass and Granite* are available as ebooks on Amazon.

Joanne lives in Philadelphia, where she indulges her love of design and walking from a yet another rowhouse, this one on the other side of the city. joannemclaughlin.net

Other Novels by Joanne McLaughlin

CHASING ASHES (Published by Celestial Echo Press)

In 1992, shortly before a tragic fire on their college campus, Laura Cunningham saw her best friend, Kate McDonald, for the last time. The fire's 20th anniversary elicits Laura's guilt and ignites her passion to learn what actually happened to Kate. Now a journalist, Laura teams up with her hot detective ex-husband to pursue cold leads in hopes of sparking interest in the decades-old mystery of what happened that day.

Vampires of the Court of Cruelty Trilogy

Never Before Noon (Book One):
Chloe Hart is lured back home by her legendary rock star parents, only to learn they are vampires. What does that make her?

Never Until Now (Book Two):
As the daughter of rock-and-roll legends, Chloe Hart can't escape their legacy. Nor can she ignore the horror her vampire father has unleashed.

Never More Human (Book Three)
Where does duty to family end? When her vampire mother stirs up an emotional storm, how much more can Chloe Hart take?

Other publications from Celestial Echo Press

RUTH AND ANN'S GUIDE TO TIME TRAVEL, VOLUME II

We received so many great submissions, that we decided to publish two volumes of time travel stories. This anthology has 30 stories, written by incredibly creative authors.

RUTH AND ANN'S GUIDE TO TIME TRAVEL, VOLUME I

The anthology that started it all! 21 incredible stories written by 21 amazing authors. Including an exclusive Joe Ledger story by Jonathan Maberry.

CHASING ASHES (Written by Joanne McLaughlin)
In 1992, shortly before a tragic fire on their college campus, Laura Cunningham saw her best friend, Kate McDonald, for the last time. The fire's 20th anniversary elicits Laura's guilt and ignites her passion to learn what actually happened to Kate. Now a journalist, Laura teams up with her hot detective ex-husband to pursue cold leads in hopes of sparking interest in the decades-old mystery of what happened that day.

DRACULAND

A New York City real estate developer decides to buy Dracula's Castle in Romania and turn it into a theme park. Not her best idea.

TIME BLINKED

Just like Dorothy in the Wizard of Oz, college athlete Bobby spends his days with those he loves and stays close to home. But unlike Dorothy, when Bobby's "tornado" bushwhacks his world, it doesn't move him into a fantastical realm of color and delightful beasts. He is propelled into a complicated past, where his dreams come true through a somewhat mystifying, somewhat terrifying wrinkle.

THE TRENCH COAT CHRONICLES

This murder mystery anthology is dedicated to Sam Spade, Hercule Poirot, and Dick Tracy, as well as to all the writers of hard-boiled detective stories of years past, many of whom formed the basis for the crime mysteries we read today. Enjoy this wide variety of storylines, each of which includes criminals, victims – and trench coats.

THE TWOFER COMPENDIUM

"Twins are said to share special bonds, understand each other's unspoken communication, speak their own languages, even possess powers of ESP. Their double-ness continues to fascinate the rest of us. Adored or abhorred, sheltered or shunned, twins have universally and perpetually aroused attention and curiosity. It was that

fascination that inspired this collection of twin-themed stories. In them, you'll find all matter of twins: the good, the bad, the fantastic, the fearsome, the magical, the envious, the secretive, the devious, and more. Being a twin. Fun, right? Think about it. *What could go wrong?"*
    --Merry Jones, from the Foreword

All Celestial Echo Press publications are available at Barnes & Noble and other fine bookshops, and online at Amazon.com.

Joanne McLaughlin

Joanne McLaughlin